ACCLAIM FOR

"Explosive, thrilling, action-packed – meet Alex Rider." **Guardian**

"Horowitz is pure class, stylish but action-packed ... being James Bond in miniature is way cooler than being a wizard." **Daily Mirror**

"Horowitz will grip you with suspense, daring and cheek – and that's just the first page! ... Prepare for action scenes as fast as a movie." **The Times**

"Anthony Horowitz is the lion of children's literature." **Michael Morpurgo**

"Fast and furious." **Telegraph**

"The perfect hero ... genuine 21st century stuff." **Daily Telegraph**

"Brings new meaning to the phrase 'action-packed'." **Sunday Times**

"Every bored schoolboy's fantasy, only a thousand times funnier, slicker and more exciting ... genius." **Independent on Sunday**

Titles by Anthony Horowitz

The Alex Rider series:
Stormbreaker
Point Blanc
Skeleton Key
Eagle Strike
Scorpia
Ark Angel
Snakehead
Crocodile Tears
Scorpia Rising
Russian Roulette

The Power of Five (Book One): *Raven's Gate*
The Power of Five (Book Two): *Evil Star*
The Power of Five (Book Three): *Nightrise*
The Power of Five (Book Four): *Necropolis*
The Power of Five (Book Five): *Oblivion*

The Devil and his Boy
Granny
Groosham Grange
Return to Groosham Grange
The Switch
More Bloody Horowitz

The Diamond Brothers books:
The Falcon's Malteser
Public Enemy Number Two
South by South East
The French Confection
The Greek Who Stole Christmas
The Blurred Man
I Know What You Did Last Wednesday

ALEX RIDER

ACTION
ADRENALINE
ADVENTURE

SCORPIA

ANTHONY HOROWITZ

WALKER
BOOKS

For MN

First published 2004 by Walker Books Ltd
87 Vauxhall Walk, London SE11 5HJ

This edition published 2015

4 6 8 10 9 7 5 3

Text © 2004 Stormbreaker Productions Ltd
Cover illustration © 2015 Walker Books Ltd
Trademarks Alex Rider™; Boy with Torch Logo™
© 2010 Stormbreaker Productions Ltd

The right of Anthony Horowitz to be identified as author
of this work has been asserted by him in accordance with
the Copyright, Designs and Patents Act 1988

This book has been typeset in Officina Sans

Printed and bound by CPI Group (UK) Ltd, Croydon, CR0 4YY

British Library Cataloguing in Publication Data:
a catalogue record for this book
is available from the British Library

ISBN 978-1-4063-6488-0

www.walker.co.uk

CONTENTS

EXTRA WORK

For the two thieves on the 200cc Vespa scooter, it was a case of the wrong victim, in the wrong place, on the wrong Sunday morning in September.

It seemed that all life had gathered in the Piazza Esmeralda, a few miles outside Venice. Church had just finished and families were strolling together in the brilliant sunlight: grandmothers in black, boys and girls in their best suits and communion dresses. The coffee bars and ice-cream shops were open, their customers spilling onto the pavements and out into the street. A huge fountain – all naked gods and serpents – gushed jets of ice-cold water. And there was a market. Stalls had been set up selling kites, dried flowers, old postcards, clockwork birds and sacks of seed for the hundreds of pigeons that strutted around.

In the middle of all this were a dozen English schoolchildren. It was bad luck for the two thieves that one of them was Alex Rider.

It was the beginning of September. Less than a month had passed since Alex's final confrontation with Damian Cray on Air Force One – the American presidential plane. It had been the end of an adventure that had taken him to Paris and Amsterdam, and finally to the main runway at Heathrow Airport even as twenty-five nuclear missiles had been fired at targets all around the world. Alex had managed to destroy these missiles. He had been there when Cray died. And at last he had gone home with the usual collection of bruises and scratches only to find a grim-faced and determined Jack Starbright waiting for him. Jack was his housekeeper but she was also his friend, and, as always, she was worried about him.

"You can't keep this up, Alex," she said. "You're never at school. You missed half the summer term when you were at Skeleton Key and loads of the spring term when you were in Cornwall and then at that awful academy Point Blanc. If you keep this up, you'll flunk all your exams and then what will you do?"

"It's not my fault—" Alex began.

"I know it's not your fault. But it's my job to do something about it, and I've decided to hire a tutor for what's left of the summer."

"You're not serious!"

"I am serious. You've still got quite a bit of holiday left. And you can start right now."

"I don't want a tutor—" Alex started to protest.

"I'm not giving you any choice, Alex. I don't care what gadgets you've got or what smart moves you might try – this time there's no escape!"

Alex wanted to argue with her but in his heart he knew she was right. MI6 always provided him with a doctor's note to explain his long absences from school, but the teachers were more or less giving up on him. His last report had said it all:

Alex continues to spend more time out of school than in it, and if this carries on, he might as well forget his GCSEs. Although he cannot be blamed for what seems to be a catalogue of medical problems, if he falls any further behind, I fear he may disappear altogether.

So that was it. Alex had stopped an insane, multi-millionaire pop singer from destroying half the world – and what had he got for it? Extra work!

He started with ill grace – particularly when he discovered that the tutor Jack had found actually taught at Brookland, his own school. Alex wasn't in his class, but even so it was an embarrassment and he hoped nobody would find out. However, he had to admit that Mr Grey was good at his job. Charlie Grey was young and easy-going, arriving on a bicycle with a saddlebag crammed with books. He taught humanities but seemed to know his way round the entire syllabus.

"We've only got a few weeks," he announced. "That may not seem very much, but you'd be surprised how much you can achieve one to one. I'm going to work you seven hours a day, and on top of that I'm going to leave you with homework. By the end of the holidays you'll probably hate me. But at least you'll start the new school year on a more or less even keel."

Alex didn't hate Charlie Grey. They worked quietly and quickly, moving through the day from maths to history to science and so on. Every weekend, the teacher left behind exam papers, and gradually Alex saw his percentages improve. And then Mr Grey sprang his surprise.

"You've done really well, Alex. I wasn't going to mention this to you, but how would you like to come with me on the school trip?"

"Where are you going?"

"Well, last year it was Paris; the year before that it was Rome. We look at museums, churches, palaces ... that sort of thing. This year we're going to Venice. Do you want to come?"

Venice.

It had been in Alex's mind all along – the final minutes on the plane after Damian Cray had died. Yassen Gregorovich had been there, the Russian assassin who had cast a shadow over so much of Alex's life. Yassen had been dying, a bullet lodged in his chest. But just before the end he'd managed to blurt out a secret that had been buried for fourteen years.

Alex's parents had been killed shortly after he was born and he had been brought up by his father's brother, Ian Rider. Earlier this year, Ian Rider had died too, supposedly in a car accident. It had been the shock of Alex's life to discover that his uncle was actually a spy and had been killed on a mission in Cornwall. That was when MI6 had made their appearance. Somehow they had succeeded in sucking Alex into their world, and he had been working for them ever since.

Alex knew very little about his mother and father, John and Helen Rider. In his bedroom he had a photo of them: a watchful, handsome man with close-cut hair standing with his arm round a pretty, half-smiling woman. He had been in the army and still looked like a soldier. She had been a nurse, working in radiology. But they were strangers to him; he couldn't remember anything about them. They had died while he was still a baby. In a plane crash. That was what he had been told.

Now he knew otherwise.

The plane crash had been as much a lie as his uncle's car accident. Yassen Gregorovich had told him the truth on Air Force One. Alex's father had been an assassin – just like Yassen. The two of them had even worked together; John Rider had once saved Yassen's life. But then his father had been killed by MI6 – the very same people who had forced Alex to work for them three times, lying to him, manipulating him and finally dumping him when he was no longer needed. It was almost impossible to believe, but Yassen had offered him a way to find proof.

Go to Venice. Find Scorpia. And you will find your destiny...

Alex had to know what had happened fourteen years ago. Discovering the truth about John Rider would be the same as finding out about himself. Because, if his father really had killed people for money, what did that make him? Alex was angry, unhappy ... and confused. He had to find Scorpia, whatever it was. Scorpia would tell him what he needed to know.

A school trip to Venice couldn't have come at a better time. And Jack didn't stop him from going. In fact, she encouraged him.

"It's exactly what you need, Alex. A chance to hang out with your friends and just be an ordinary schoolboy. I'm sure you'll have a great time."

Alex said nothing. He hated having to lie to her, but there was no way he could tell her the truth. Jack had never met his father; this wasn't her affair.

So he let her help him pack, knowing that, for him, the trip would have little to do with churches and museums. He would use it to explore the city and see what he unearthed. Five days wasn't a long time. But it would be a start. Five days in

Venice. Five days to find Scorpia.

And now here he was. In an Italian square. Three days of the trip had already gone by and he had found nothing.

"Alex – you fancy an ice cream?"

"No. I'm all right."

"I'm hot. I'm going to get one of those things you told me about. What did you call it? A *granada* or something..."

Alex was standing beside another fourteen-year-old boy who happened to be his closest friend at Brookland. He had been surprised to hear that Tom Harris was going to be on the trip, as Tom wasn't exactly interested in art or history. Tom wasn't interested in any school subjects and was regularly bottom in everything. But the best thing about him was that he didn't care. He was always cheerful, and even the teachers had to admit that he was fun to be with. And what Tom lacked in the classroom, he made up for on the sports field. He was captain of the school football team and Alex's main rival on sports day, beating him at hurdles, four hundred metres and the pole vault. Tom was small for his age, with spiky black hair and bright blue eyes. He wouldn't have been found dead in a museum, so why was he here? Alex soon found out. Tom's parents were going through a messy divorce, and they had packed him off to get him out of the way.

"It's a *granita*," Alex said. It was what he always

ordered when he was in Italy: crushed ice with fresh lemon juice squeezed over it. It was halfway between an ice cream and a drink and there was nothing in the world more refreshing.

"Come on. You can order it for me. When I ask anyone for anything in Italian they just stare at me like I'm mad."

In fact, Alex only spoke a few phrases himself. Italian was one language Ian Rider hadn't taught him. Even so, he went with Tom and ordered two ices from a shop near the market stalls, one for Tom and one – Tom insisted – for himself. Tom had plenty of money. His parents had showered him with euros before he left.

"Are you going to be at school this term?" he asked.

Alex shrugged. "Of course."

"You were hardly there last term – or the term before."

"I was ill."

Tom nodded. He was wearing Diesel light-sensitive sunglasses that he had bought at Heathrow duty-free. They were too big for his face and kept slipping down his nose. "You do realize that no one believes that," he commented.

"Why not?"

"Because nobody's that ill. It's just not possible." Tom lowered his voice. "There's a rumour you're a thief," he confided.

"What?"

"That's why you're away so much. You're in trouble with the police."

"Is that what you think?"

"No. But Miss Bedfordshire asked me about you. She knows we're mates. She said you got into trouble once for nicking a crane or something. She heard about that from someone and she thinks you're in therapy."

"Therapy?" Alex was staggered.

"Yeah. She's quite sorry for you. She thinks that's why you have to go away so much. You know, to see a shrink."

Jane Bedfordshire was the school secretary, an attractive woman in her twenties. She had come on the trip too, as she did every year. Alex could see her now on the other side of the square, talking to Mr Grey. A lot of people said there was something going on between them, but Alex guessed the rumour was probably as accurate as the one about him.

A clock chimed twelve. In half an hour they would have lunch at the hotel where they were staying. Brookland School was an ordinary west London comprehensive and they'd decided to keep costs down by staying outside Venice. Mr Grey had chosen a hotel in the little town of San Lorenzo, just ten minutes away by train. Every morning they'd arrive at the station and take the water bus into the heart of the city. But not today. This was Sunday and they had the morning off.

"So are you—" Tom began. He broke off. It had happened very quickly but both boys had seen it.

On the opposite side of the square a motorbike had surged forward. It was a 200cc Vespa Granturismo, almost brand new, with two men riding it. They were both dressed in jeans and loose, long-sleeved shirts. The passenger had on a visored helmet, as much to hide his identity as to protect him if they crashed. The driver – wearing sunglasses – steered towards Miss Bedfordshire, as if he intended to run her over. But, a split second before contact, he veered away. At the same time, the man riding pillion reached out and snatched her handbag. It was done so neatly that Alex knew the two men were professionals – *scippatori* as they were known in Italy. Bag snatchers.

Some of the other pupils had seen it too. One or two were shouting and pointing, but there was nothing they could do. The bike was already accelerating away. The driver was crouched low over the handlebars; his partner was cradling the leather bag in his lap. They were speeding diagonally across the square, heading towards Alex and Tom. A few moments before, there had been people everywhere, but suddenly the centre of the square was empty and there was nothing to prevent their escape.

"Alex!" Tom shouted.

"Stay back," Alex warned. He briefly considered blocking the Vespa's path. But it was hopeless.

The driver would easily be able to swerve round him – and if he chose not to, Alex really would spend the following term in hospital. The bike was already doing about twenty miles an hour, its single-cylinder four-stroke engine carrying the two thieves effortlessly towards him. Alex certainly wasn't going to stand in its way.

He looked around him, wondering if there was something he could throw. A net? A bucket of water? But there was no net and the fountain was too far away, although there were buckets...

The bike was less than twenty metres away, accelerating all the time. Alex sprinted and snatched a bucket from the flower stall, emptied it, scattering dried flowers across the pavement, and filled it with bird seed from the stall next door. Both stall owners were shouting something at him but he ignored them. Without stopping, he swung round and hurled the seed at the Vespa just as it was about to flash past him. Tom watched – first in amazement, then with disappointment. If Alex had thought the great shower of seed would knock the two men off the bike, he'd been mistaken. They were continuing regardless.

But that hadn't been his plan.

There must have been two or three hundred pigeons in the square and all of them had seen the seed spraying out of the bucket. The two riders were covered in it. Seed had lodged in the folds of their clothes, under their collars and in the sides of their shoes. There was a small pile of it caught in the driver's crotch. Some had fallen into Miss Bedfordshire's bag; some had become trapped in the driver's hair.

For the pigeons, the bag thieves had suddenly become a meal on wheels. With a soft explosion of grey feathers, they came swooping down, diving on the two men from all directions. Suddenly the driver had a bird clinging to the side of his face, its beak hammering at his head, ripping the seed out of his hair. There was another pigeon at his throat, and a third between his legs, pecking at the most sensitive area of all. His passenger had two on his neck, another hanging off his shirt, and another half buried in the stolen bag. And more were joining in. There must have been at least twenty pigeons, flapping and batting around them, a swirling cloud of feathers, claws and – triggered by greed and excitement – flying splatters of white bird droppings.

The driver was blinded. One hand clutched the handlebars, the other tore at his face. As Alex watched, the bike performed a hundred and eighty degree turn so that now it was coming back, heading straight towards them, moving faster than ever. For a moment he stood poised, waiting to hurl himself aside. It looked as if he was going to be run over. But then the bike swerved a second time and now it was heading for the fountain, the two men barely visible in a cloud of beating wings. The front wheel hit the fountain's edge and the bike crumpled. Both men were thrown off. The birds scattered. In the brief pause before he hit the water, the man riding pillion yelled and let go of the handbag. Almost in slow motion, the bag arced through the air. Alex took two steps and caught it.

And then it was all over. The two thieves were a tangled heap, half submerged in cold water. The Vespa was lying, buckled and broken, on the ground. Two policemen, who had arrived when it was almost too late, were hurrying towards them. The stall owners were laughing and applauding. Tom was staring. Alex went over to Miss Bedfordshire and gave her the bag.

"I think this is yours," he said.

"Alex..." Miss Bedfordshire was lost for words. "How...?"

"It was just something I picked up in therapy," Alex said.

He turned and walked back to his friend.

THE WIDOW'S PALACE

"Now, this building is called the Palazzo Contarini del Bovolo," Mr Grey announced. "*Bovolo* is the Venetian word for snail shell and, as you can see, this wonderful staircase is shaped a bit like a shell."

Tom Harris stifled a yawn. "If I see one more palace, one more museum or one more canal," he muttered, "I'm going to throw myself under a bus."

"There aren't any buses in Venice," Alex reminded him.

"A water bus, then. If it doesn't hit me, maybe I'll get lucky and drown." Tom sighed. "You know the trouble with this place? It's like a museum. A bloody great museum. I feel like I've been here half my life."

"We're leaving tomorrow."

"Not a day too soon, Alex."

Alex couldn't bring himself to agree. He had never been anywhere quite like Venice – but then there was nowhere in the world remotely like it, with its narrow streets and dark canals twisting around each other in an intricate, amazing knot. Every building seemed to compete with its neighbour to be more ornate and more spectacular. A short walk could take you across four centuries and every corner seemed to lead to another surprise. It might be a canalside market with great slabs of meat laid out on the tables and fish dripping blood onto the paving stones. Or a church, seemingly floating, surrounded by water on all four sides. A grand hotel or a tiny restaurant. Even the shops were works of art, their windows framing exotic masks, brilliantly coloured glass vases, dried pasta and antiques. It was a museum, maybe, yet one that was truly alive.

But Alex understood what Tom was feeling. After four days, even he was beginning to think he'd had enough. Enough statues, enough churches, enough mosaics. And enough tourists all crammed together beneath a sweltering September sun. Like Tom, he was beginning to feel overcooked.

And what about Scorpia?

The trouble was, he had absolutely no idea what Yassen Gregorovich had meant by his last words. Scorpia could be a person. Alex had looked in the phone book and found no fewer than fourteen people with that name living in and around Venice. It could be a business. Or it could be a single build-ing. *Scuole* were homes set up for poor people. La Scala was an opera house in Milan. But Scorpia didn't seem to be anything. No signs pointed to it; no streets were named after it.

It was only now he was here, nearing the end of the trip, that Alex began to see it had been hopeless from the start. If Yassen had told him the truth, the two men – he and John Rider – had been hired killers. Had they worked for Scorpia? If so, Scorpia would be very carefully concealed ... per-haps inside one of these old palaces. Alex looked again at the staircase that Mr Grey was describing. How was he to know that these steps didn't lead to Scorpia? Scorpia could be anywhere. It could be everywhere. And after four days in Venice, Alex was nowhere.

"We're going to walk back down the Frezzeria towards the main square," Mr Grey announced. "We can eat our sandwiches there and after lunch we'll visit St Mark's Basilica."

"Oh great!" Tom exclaimed. "Another church!"

They set off, a dozen English schoolchildren, with Mr Grey and Miss Bedfordshire in front, talking animatedly together. Alex and Tom trailed at the back, both of them gloomy. There was one day left, and, as Tom had made clear, that was one day too many. He was, as he put it, all cultured out. But he wasn't returning to London with the rest of the group. He had an older brother living in Naples and he was going to spend the last few days of the summer holidays with him. For Alex the end of the visit would mean failure. He would go home, the autumn term would begin, and...

And that was when he saw it, a flash of silver as the sun reflected off something at the edge of his vision. He turned his head. There was nothing. A canal leading away. Another canal crossing it. A single motor cruiser sliding beneath a bridge. The usual facade of ancient brown walls dotted with wooden shutters. A church dome rising above the red roof tiles. He had imagined it.

But then the cruiser began to turn, and that was when he spotted it a second time and knew it was really there: a silver scorpion decorating the side of the boat, pinned to the wooden bow. Alex stared as it swung into the second canal. It wasn't a gondola or a chugging public vaporetto, but a sleek, private launch – all polished teak, curtained windows and leather seats. There were two crew members in immaculate white jackets and shorts, one at the wheel, the other serving a drink to the only passenger. This was a woman, sitting bolt upright, looking straight ahead. Alex only had time to glimpse black hair, an upturned nose, a face with no expression. Then the motor launch completed its turn and disappeared from sight.

A scorpion decorating a motor launch.
Scorpia.
It was the most slender of connections but

suddenly Alex was determined to find out where the boat was going. It was almost as if the silver scorpion had been sent to guide him to whatever it was he was meant to find.

And there was something else. The stillness of the woman. How was it possible to be carried through this amazing city without registering some emotion, without at least moving your head from left to right? Alex thought of Yassen Gregorovich. He would have been the same. He and this woman were two of a kind.

Alex turned to Tom. "Cover for me," he said urgently.

"What now?" Tom asked.

"Tell them I wasn't feeling well. Say I've gone back to the hotel."

"Where are you going?"

"I'll tell you later."

With that Alex was gone, ducking between an antiques shop and a café up the narrowest of alleyways, trying to follow the direction of the boat.

But almost at once, he saw that he had a problem. The city of Venice had been built on over a hundred islands. Mr Grey had explained this on their first day. In the Middle Ages the area had been little more than a swamp. That was why there were no roads – just waterways and oddly shaped bits of land connected by bridges. The woman was on the water; Alex was on the land. Following her would be like trying to find his way through an impossible maze in which their paths would never meet.

Already he had lost her. The alleyway he had taken should have continued straight ahead. Instead it suddenly veered off at an angle, obstructed by a tall block of flats. He ran round the corner, watched by two Italian women in black dresses, sitting outside on wooden stools. There was a canal ahead of him, but it was empty. A flight of heavy stone steps led down to the murky water but there was no way forward ... unless he wanted to swim.

He peered to the left and was rewarded with a glimpse of wood and water churned up by the propellers of the motor launch as it passed a fleet of gondolas roped together beside a rotting jetty. There was the woman, still sitting in the stern, now sipping a glass of wine. The boat continued under a bridge so tiny there was barely room to pass.

There was only one thing he could do. He swivelled round and retraced his steps, running as fast as he could. The two women noticed him again and shook their heads disapprovingly. He hadn't realized how hot it was. The sun seemed to be trapped in the narrow streets, and even in the shadows the heat lingered. Already sweating, he burst back out onto the street where he had begun. Fortunately there was no sign of Mr Grey or the rest of the school party.

Which way?

Suddenly every street and every corner looked the same. Relying on his sense of direction, Alex chose left and sprinted past a fruit shop, a candle shop and an open-air restaurant where the waiters were already laying the tables for lunch. He came to a bend and there was the bridge – so short he could cross it in five steps. He stopped in the middle and leant over the edge, gazing down the canal. The smell of stagnant water pricked his nostrils. There was nothing. The launch had gone.

But he knew which way it had been heading. It still wasn't too late – if he could keep moving. He darted on. A Japanese tourist was just about to take a photo of his wife and daughter. Alex heard the camera shutter click as he ran between them. When they got back to Tokyo, they would have a picture of a slim, athletic boy with fair hair hanging over his forehead, dressed in shorts and a Superdry T-shirt, with sweat pouring down his face and determination in his eyes. Something to remember him by.

A crowd of tourists. A busker playing the guitar. Another café. Waiters with silver trays. Alex ploughed through them all, ignoring the shouts of protest hurled after him. Now there was no sign of water anywhere; the street seemed to go on for ever. But he knew there must be a canal somewhere ahead.

He found it. The road fell away. Grey water flowed past. He had reached the Grand Canal, the largest waterway in Venice. And there was the motor launch with the silver scorpion now fully visible. It was at least thirty metres away, surrounded by other vessels, and moving further into the distance with every second that passed.

Alex knew that if he lost it now he wouldn't find it again. There were too many channels opening up on both sides that it could take. It could slip into the private mooring of one of the palaces or stop at any of the smart hotels. He noticed a wooden platform floating on the water just ahead of him and realized it was one of the landing stages for the Venice water buses. There was a kiosk selling tickets, and a mass of people milling about. A yellow sign gave the name of this point on the canal: SANTA MARIA DEL GIGLIO. A large, crowded boat was just pulling out. A number one bus. His school party had taken an identical boat from the main railway station the day they had arrived, and Alex knew that it travelled the full length of the canal. It was moving quickly. Already a couple of metres separated it from the landing stage.

Alex glanced back. There was no chance he would be able to find his way through the labyrinth of streets in pursuit of the motor launch. The vaporetto was his only hope. But it was too far away. He had missed it and there might not be another one for at least ten minutes. A gondola drew past, the gondolier singing in Italian to the grinning family of tourists he was carrying. For a second Alex thought about hijacking the gondola. Then he had a better idea.

He reached out and grabbed hold of the oar, snatching it out of the gondolier's hands. Taken by surprise, the gondolier shouted out, twisted round and lost his balance. The family looked on in alarm as he plunged backwards into the water. Meanwhile Alex had tested the oar. It was about five metres long, and heavy. The gondolier had been holding it vertically, using the splayed paddle end to guide his craft through the water. Alex ran. He stabbed down with the blade, thrusting it into the Grand Canal, hoping the water wouldn't be too deep.

He was lucky. The tide was low and the bottom of the canal was littered with everything from old washing machines to bicycles and wheelbarrows, cheerfully thrown in by the Venetian residents with no thought of pollution. The bottom of the oar hit something solid and Alex was able to use the length of wood to propel himself forward. It was exactly the same technique he had used pole-vaulting at Brookland sports day. For a moment he was in the air, leaning backwards, suspended over the Grand Canal. Then he swung down, sweeping through the open entrance of the water bus and landing on the deck. He dropped the oar behind him and looked around. The other passengers were staring at him in amazement. But he was on board.

There were very few ticket collectors on the water buses in Venice, which was why there was nobody to challenge Alex about his unorthodox method of arrival or demand a fare. He leant over the edge, grateful for the breeze sweeping across the water. And he hadn't lost the motor launch. It was still ahead of him, travelling away from the main lagoon and back into the heart of the city. A slender wooden bridge stretched out over the canal and Alex recognized it at once as the Bridge of the Academy, leading to the biggest art gallery in the city. He had spent a whole morning there, gazing at works by Tintoretto and Lorenzo Lotto and numerous other artists whose names all seemed to end in o. Briefly he wondered what he was doing. He had abandoned the school trip. Mr Grey and Miss Bedfordshire would probably already be on the phone to the hotel, if not the police. And why? What did he have to go on? A silver scorpion adorning a private boat. He must be out of his mind.

The vaporetto began to slow down. It was approaching the next landing stage. Alex tensed. He knew that if he waited for one load of passengers to get off and another to get on, he would never see the motor launch again. He was on the other side of the canal now. The streets were a little less crowded here. Alex caught his breath. He wondered how much longer he could run.

And then he saw, with a surge of relief, that the motor launch had also arrived at its destination. It was pulling into a palace a little further up, stopping behind a series of wooden poles that slanted out of the water as if, like javelins, they had been thrown there by chance. As Alex watched, two uniformed servants emerged from the palace. One moored the boat; the other held out a white-gloved hand. The woman grasped the hand and stepped ashore. She was wearing a tight-fitting cream dress with a jacket cut short above the waist. A handbag swung from her arm. She could have been a model striding off the cover of a glossy magazine. She didn't hesitate. While the servants busied themselves unloading her suitcases, she climbed the steps and disappeared behind a stone column.

The water bus was about to leave again. Quickly Alex climbed out onto the landing stage. Once again he had to work his way round the buildings that crowded onto the Grand Canal. But this time he knew what he was looking for. A few minutes later, he found it.

It was a typical Venetian palace, pink and white, its narrow windows built into a fantastic embroidery of pillars, arches and balustrades, like something out of *Romeo and Juliet*. But what made the place so unforgettable was its position. It didn't just face the Grand Canal. It sank right into it, the water lapping against the brickwork. The woman from the boat had gone through some sort of portcullis, as if entering a castle. But it was a castle that was float-ing. Or sinking. It was impossible to say where the water ended and the palace began.

The palace did at least have one side that could be reached by land. It backed onto a wide square with trees and bushes planted in ornamental tubs. There were men – servants – everywhere, setting up rope barriers, positioning oil-burning torches and unrolling a red carpet. Carpenters were at work, constructing what looked like a small bandstand. More men were carrying a variety of crates and boxes into the palace. Alex saw champagne bottles, fireworks, different sorts of food. They were obviously preparing for a serious party.

Alex stopped one of them. "Excuse me," he said. "Can you tell me who lives here?"

The man spoke no English. He didn't even try to be friendly. Alex asked a second man, but with exactly the same result. He recognized the type: he had met men like them before. The guards at Point Blanc Academy. The technicians at Cray Software Technology. These were people who worked for someone who made them nervous. They were paid to do a job and they never stepped out of line. Were they people with something to hide? Perhaps.

Alex left the square and walked round the side of the palace. A second canal ran the full length of the building and this time he was luckier. There was an elderly woman in a black dress with a white apron sweeping the towpath. He went up to her.

"Do you speak English?" he asked. "Can you help me?"

"*Si, con piacere, mio piccolo amico.*" The woman nodded. She put the broom down. "I spend many year in London. I speak good English. Who can I do?"

Alex pointed at the building. "What is this place?"

"It is the Ca' Vedova." She tried to explain. "*Ca'* ... you know ... in Venice we say *casa*. It means palace. And *vedova*?" She searched for the word. "It is the Palace of the Widow. Ca' Vedova."

"What's going on?"

"There is a big party tonight. For a birthday. Masks and costumes. Many important people come."

"Whose birthday?"

The woman hesitated. Alex was asking too many questions and he could see that she was becoming suspicious. But once again age was on his side. He was only fourteen. What did it matter if he was curious? "Signora Rothman. She is very rich lady. The owner of the house."

"Rothman? Like the cigarette?"

But the woman's mouth had suddenly closed and there was fear in her eyes. Alex looked round and saw one of the men from the square standing at the corner, watching him. He realized he had outstayed his welcome – and no one had been that pleased to see him in the first place.

He decided to have one last try. "I'm looking for Scorpia," he said.

The old woman stared at him as if she had been slapped in the face. She picked up the broom and her eyes darted over to the man watching them. It was lucky he hadn't heard the exchange. He had sensed something was wrong, but he hadn't moved. Even so, Alex knew it was time to go.

"It doesn't matter," he said. "Thank you for your help."

He made his way quickly up the canal. Yet another bridge loomed ahead of him and he crossed it. Although he didn't know exactly why, he was grateful to leave the Widow's Palace behind him.

As soon as he was out of sight, he stopped and considered what he had learnt. A boat with a silver scorpion had led him to a palace, which was owned by a beautiful and wealthy woman who didn't smile. The palace was protected by a number of mean-looking men, and the moment he had mentioned the name Scorpia to a cleaning lady, he had suddenly become as welcome as the plague.

It wasn't much to go on, but it was enough. There was going to be a masked ball tonight, a birthday party. Important people had been invited. Alex wasn't one of them, but already he had decided. He planned to be there all the same.

INVISIBLE SWORD

The full name of the woman who had entered the *palazzo* was Julia Charlotte Glenys Rothman. This was her home – or one of them, anyway. She also had a flat in New York, a mews house in London and a villa overlooking the Caribbean Sea and the white sands of Turtle Bay on the island of Tobago.

She walked along a softly lit corridor that ran the full length of the building from the jetty at one end to a private lift at the other, her high heels clicking on the terracotta tiles. There was not one servant in sight. She reached out and pressed the lift button, the white silk of her glove briefly touching silver, and the door opened. It was a small lift, barely big enough for one person. But she lived alone. The servants used the stairs.

The lift took her to the third floor and opened directly onto a modern conference room with no carpet, no pictures on the walls, no ornamentation of any sort. Stranger still, although it should have offered some of the most beautiful views in the world, the room had been built without a single window. But if no one could look out, nor could anyone look in. It was safer that way. The lighting came from halogen lamps built into the walls, and the only furniture in the room was a long glass table surrounded by leather chairs. There was a door opposite the lift but it was locked. Two guards were standing on the other side, armed and ready to kill anyone who so much as approached in the next half-hour.

There were eight men waiting for her around the table. One was in his seventies, bald and wheezy with sore eyes, wearing a crumpled grey suit. The man sitting next to him was Chinese, while the man opposite, fair-haired, wearing an open-necked shirt, was from Australia. It was clear that the people congregated in this place came from many different parts of the world, but they had one thing in common: a stillness, a coldness even, that made the room as cheerful as a morgue. Not one of them greeted Mrs Rothman as she took her seat at the head of the table. Nor did they bother looking at the time. If she had arrived, it must be exactly one o'clock. That was when the meeting was meant to begin.

"Good afternoon," Mrs Rothman said.

A few heads nodded but nobody spoke. Greetings were a waste of words.

The nine people sitting around the table on the third floor of the Widow's Palace made up the executive board of one of the most ruthless and successful criminal organizations in the world. The old man's name was Max Grendel; the Chinese man was Dr Three. The Australian had no name at all. They had come to this room without windows to go over the final details of an operation that would, in just a few weeks, make them richer by the sum of one hundred million pounds.

The organization was called Scorpia.

It was a fanciful name, they all knew it, invented by someone who had probably read too much James Bond. But they had to call themselves something, and in the end they had chosen a name drawn from their four main fields of activity.

Sabotage. Corruption. Intelligence. Assassination.

Scorpia. A name which worked in a surprising number of languages and which rolled off the tongue of anyone who might wish to employ them. Scorpia. Seven letters that were now on the database of every police force and security agency in the world.

The organization was formed in the early eighties, during the so-called Cold War, the secret war that had been fought for decades between the Soviet Union, China, America and Europe. Every government in the world had its own army of spies and assassins, all of them prepared to kill or to die for their country. What they weren't prepared for, though, was to find themselves out of work; and twelve of them, seeing that the Cold War would soon be over, realized that was exactly what they would be. They wouldn't be needed any more. It was time to go into business for themselves.

They came together one Sunday morning in Paris. Their first meeting took place at the Maison Berthillon, a famous ice-cream parlour on the Ile St-Louis, not far from Notre-Dame. They were all acquainted: they had tried to kill each other often enough. But now, in the pretty, wood-panelled room with its antique mirrors and lace curtains, and over twelve dishes of Berthillon's famous wild strawberry ice cream, they discussed how they might work together and make themselves rich. At this meeting, Scorpia was born.

Since then it had flourished. Scorpia was all over the world. It had brought down two governments and arranged for a third to be unfairly elected. It had destroyed dozens of businesses, corrupted politicians and civil servants, engineered several major ecological disasters, and killed anyone who got in its way. It was now responsible for a tenth of the world's terrorism, which it undertook on a contract basis. Scorpia liked to think of itself as the Microsoft of crime – but in fact, compared to Scorpia, Microsoft was strictly small-time.

Of the original twelve, only nine were left. One had died of cancer; two had been murdered. But that wasn't a bad record after twenty years of violent crime. There had never been a single leader of Scorpia. All nine were equal partners but one executive was always assigned to each new project, working in alphabetical order.

The project they were discussing this afternoon had been given a code name: Invisible Sword. Julia Rothman was in command.

"I would like to report to the board that everything is progressing on schedule," she announced.

There was a trace of a Welsh accent in her voice. She had been born in Aberystwyth. Her parents had been Welsh nationalists, burning down the cottages of English holidaymakers who had bought them as second homes. Unfortunately they had torched one of these cottages with the English family still inside it, and when Julia was six she found herself in an institution while her parents began a life sentence in jail. This was, in a way, the start of her own criminal career.

"It is now three months," she went on, "since we were approached by our client, a gentleman in the Middle East. To call him rich would be an understatement. He is a multi-billionaire. This man has looked at the world, at the balance of power, and he has decided that something has gone seriously wrong. He has asked us to remedy it.

"In a nutshell, our client believes that the West has become too powerful. He looks at Great Britain and America. It was the friendship between them that won the Second World War. And it is this same friendship that now allows the West to invade any country that it pleases and to take anything it wants. Our client has asked us to end the British–American alliance once and for all.

"What can I tell you about our client?" Mrs Rothman smiled sweetly. "Perhaps he is a visionary, interested only in world peace; perhaps he is completely insane. Either way, it makes no difference to us. He has offered us an enormous sum of money – one hundred million pounds to be exact – to do what he wants. To humble Britain and America and to ensure they cease to work together as a world power. And I am happy to be able to tell you that twenty million pounds, the first instalment of that money, arrived in our Swiss bank account yesterday. We are now ready to move into phase two."

There was silence in the room. As the men waited for Mrs Rothman to speak again, the faint hum of an air conditioner could be heard. But no sound came from outside.

"Phase two – the final phase – will take place in under three weeks from now. I can promise you that very soon the British and the Americans will be at one another's throats. More than that: by the end of the month both countries will be on their knees. America will be hated throughout the entire world; the British will have witnessed a horror beyond anything they could ever have imagined. We will all be a great deal richer. And our friend from the Middle East will consider his money well spent."

"Excuse me, Mrs Rothman. I have a question..."

Dr Three bowed his head politely. His face seemed to be made of wax and his hair – jet black – looked twenty years younger than the rest of him. It had to be dyed. He was very small and might have been a retired teacher. He might have been many things, but he was, in fact, the world expert on torture and pain. He had written several books on the subject.

"How many people do you intend to kill?" he asked.

Julia Rothman considered. "It's still difficult to be precise, Dr Three," she replied. "But it will certainly be thousands. Many thousands."

"And they will all be children?"

"Yes. They will mainly be twelve and thirteen years old." She sighed. "It is, it goes without saying, very unfortunate. I adore children, even though I'm glad I never had any of my own. But that's the plan. And I have to say, the psychological effect of so many young people dying will, I think, be useful. Does it concern you?"

"Not at all, Mrs Rothman." Dr Three shook his head.

"Does anyone have any objections?"

Nobody spoke, but out of the corner of her eye,

Mrs Rothman noticed Max Grendel shift uncomfortably on his chair at the far end of the table. At seventy-three, he was the oldest man there, with sagging skin and liver spots on his forehead. He suffered from an eye disease that made him weep constantly. He was dabbing at his eyes now with a tissue. It was hard to believe that he had been a commander in the German secret police and had once personally strangled a foreign spy during a performance of Beethoven's Fifth.

"Are preparations complete in London?" the Australian asked.

"Construction in the church finished a week ago. The platform, the gas cylinders and the rest of the machinery will be delivered later today."

"Will Invisible Sword work?"

It was typical of Levi Kroll to be blunt and to the point. He had joined Scorpia from Mossad, the Israeli secret service, and still thought of himself as a soldier. For twenty years he had slept with an FN 9mm pistol under his pillow. Then, one night, it had gone off. He was a large man with a beard that covered most of his face, concealing the worst of his injuries. An eyepatch hid the empty socket where his left eye had once been.

"Of course it will work," Mrs Rothman snapped.

"It's been tested?"

"We're testing it right now. But I have to tell you that Dr Liebermann is something of a genius. A boring man if you have to spend time with him – and heaven knows I've had to do plenty of that. But he's created a brand-new weapon and the beauty of it is, all the experts in the world won't know what it is or how it operates. Of course, they'll work it out in the end, and I've made plans for that eventuality. But by then it will be too late. The streets of London will be littered with corpses. It'll be the worst thing to happen to children in a city since the Pied Piper."

"And what about Liebermann?" Dr Three asked.

"I haven't decided yet. We'll probably have to kill him too. He invented Invisible Sword but he has no idea how we plan to use it. I expect he'll object. So he'll have to go."

Mrs Rothman looked around. "Is there anything else?" she asked.

"Yes." Max Grendel spread his hands across the surface of the table. Mrs Rothman wasn't surprised that he had something to say. He was a father and a grandfather. Worse than that, in his old age he had become sentimental.

"I have been with Scorpia from the very beginning," he said. "I still remember our first meeting in Paris. I have earned many millions working with you and I've enjoyed everything we've done. But this project ... Invisible Sword. Are we really going to kill so many children? How will we be able to live with ourselves?"

"Rather more comfortably than before," Julia Rothman muttered.

"No, no, Julia." Grendel shook his head. A single tear trickled from one of his diseased eyes. "This will come as no surprise to you. We spoke of this the last time we met. But I have decided that enough is enough. I'm an old man. I want to retire to my castle in Vienna. Invisible Sword will be your greatest achievement, I am sure. But I no longer have the heart for it. It is time for me to step down. You must go ahead without me."

"You can't retire!" Levi Kroll protested sharply.

"Why did you not tell us about this earlier?" another of the men asked angrily. He was black but with Japanese eyes. There was a diamond the size of a pea embedded in one of his front teeth.

"I told Mrs Rothman," Max Grendel said reasonably. "She's the project leader. I felt there was no need to inform the entire board."

"We really don't need to argue about this, Mr Mikato," Julia Rothman said smoothly. "Max has been talking about retiring for a long time now and I think we should respect his wishes. It's certainly a shame. But, as my late husband used to say, all good things come to an end."

Mrs Rothman's multimillionaire husband had fallen to his death from a seventeenth-storey window. It had happened just two days after their marriage.

"It's very sad, Max," she continued. "But I'm sure you're doing the right thing. It's time for you to go."

*   *   *

She went with him down to the jetty. The motor launch had left but there was a gondola waiting to take him back down the canal. They walked slowly arm in arm.

"I'll miss you," she said.

"Thank you, Julia." Max Grendel patted her arm. "I'll miss you too."

"I don't know how we'll manage without you."

"Invisible Sword cannot fail. Not with you at the helm."

She stopped suddenly. "I almost forgot," she exclaimed. "I have something for you." She snapped her fingers and a servant ran forward carrying a large box wrapped in pink and blue paper, tied with a silver bow. "It's a present for you," she said.

"A retirement present?"

"Something to remember us by."

Max Grendel had stopped beside the gondola. It was bobbing up and down on the choppy surface. A gondolier dressed in a traditional striped jersey stood in the back, leaning on his oar. "Thank you, my dear," he said. "And good luck."

"Enjoy yourself, Max. Keep in touch."

She kissed him, her lips lightly touching his withered cheek. Then she helped him into the gondola. He sat down awkwardly, placing the brightly coloured box on his knees. At once the gondolier pulled away. Mrs Rothman raised a hand. The little boat cut swiftly through the grey water.

Mrs Rothman turned and went back into the Widow's Palace.

Max Grendel watched her sadly. He knew that life wouldn't be the same without Scorpia. For two decades he had devoted all his energies to the organization. It had kept him young, kept him alive. But now there were his grandchildren to consider. He thought of the twins, little Hans and Rudi. They were twelve years old. The same age as Scorpia's targets in London. He couldn't be part of it. He had made the right decision.

He had almost forgotten the package resting on his knees. That was typical of Julia. Perhaps it was because she was the only woman on the executive board, but she had always been the one who was most emotional. He wondered what she had bought him. The parcel was heavy. On an impulse, he untied the ribbon, then ripped off the paper.

It was an executive briefcase, obviously expensive. He could tell from the quality of the leather, the hand-stitching ... and there was the label. It had been made by Gucci. His initials – MUG – had been engraved in gold just under the handle. With a smile he opened it.

And screamed as the contents spilled over him.

Scorpions. Dozens of them. They were at least ten centimetres long, dark brown with tiny pincers and fat, swollen bodies. As they poured into his lap and began to swarm up his shirt, he recognized what they were: hairy thick-tailed scorpions from the *Parabuthus* species, one of the most deadly in the world.

Max Grendel fell backwards, shrieking, his eyes bulging, arms and legs flailing as the hideous creatures found the gaps in his clothes and crawled inside his shirt and down under the waistband of his trousers. The first one stung him on the side of his neck. Then he was being stung over and over again, jerking helplessly, the screams dying in his throat.

His heart gave out long before the neurotoxins killed him. As the gondola floated gently on, being steered now towards the island cemetery of Venice, tourists might have noticed an old man lying still with his hands spread wide, gazing with sightless eyes at the bright Venetian sky.

BY INVITATION ONLY

That night, the Widow's Palace slipped back three hundred years in time.

It was an extraordinary sight. The oil-burning torches had been lit and the flames cast flickering shadows across the square. The servants had changed into eighteenth-century costumes with wigs, tightly fitting stockings, pointed shoes and waistcoats. A string quartet played beneath the night sky, sitting on the bandstand that Alex had seen being constructed that afternoon. The stars were out in their thousands and there was even a full moon. It was as if whoever had organized the party had managed to control the weather too.

Guests were arriving by water and on foot. They too were in costume, wearing elaborate hats and richly coloured velvet cloaks that swept the ground. Some carried ebony walking sticks; others had swords and daggers. But not a single face could be seen among the crowd making its way to the front door. Features were concealed behind white masks and gold masks, masks encrusted with jewels and masks surrounded by huge plumes of feathers. It was impossible to know who had been invited to Mrs Rothman's party – but not just anyone could walk in. The Grand Canal entrance to the palace was closed and everyone was being directed to the main door that Alex had seen earlier that day. Four security guards wearing the bright red tunics of Venetian courtiers were positioned there, checking each invitation.

Alex watched all this from the other side of the square. He was crouched behind one of the miniature trees with Tom, the two of them outside the pool of light thrown by the torches. It hadn't been easy to persuade Tom to come. Alex's disappearance before lunch had been noticed almost immediately, and Tom had been left to make up an unconvincing story about a stomach ache in front of an angry Mr Grey. Alex should have been in serious trouble when he finally met up with the group back at the hotel, and if it hadn't been for Miss Bedfordshire – who was still grateful to him for recovering her handbag – he would have been grounded for the night. Anyway, this was Alex. Everyone knew they could rely on him to act oddly.

But to disappear again! It was the last evening of the trip and the group had been given two hours' free time which they were meant to spend in San Lorenzo, in the cafés or the square. Alex had other plans. He had found everything he needed in Venice that afternoon before he went back to the hotel. But he knew he couldn't do this alone. Tom had to come too.

"Alex, I can't believe you're doing this," Tom whispered now. "Why is this party such a big deal anyway?"

"I can't explain."

"Why not? I don't understand you sometimes. We're meant to be friends but you never tell me anything."

Alex sighed. He was used to this. When he thought of all the things that had happened to him in the last six months, the way he had been dragged into the world of espionage, a web of secrecy and lies, this was the worst part. MI6 had turned him into a spy. And at the same time they had made it impossible for him to be what he wanted – an ordinary schoolboy. He had been juggling two lives, one day saving the world from a nuclear holocaust, the next struggling with his chemistry homework. Two lives, but he had ended up trapped between them. He didn't know where he belonged any more. There was Tom, there was Jack Starbright and there was Sabina Pleasure – although she had now moved to America. Apart from them, he had no real friends. It wasn't his choice, but somehow he had ended up alone.

Alex made up his mind. "All right," he said. "If you'll help me, I'll tell you everything. But not yet."

"When?"

"Tomorrow."

"I'm going to Naples tomorrow to stay with my brother."

"Before you go."

Tom considered. "I'll help you anyway, Alex," he said. "Because that's what friends are for. And if you really do want to tell me, you can save it until we're back at school. OK?"

Alex nodded and smiled. "Thanks."

He reached behind him for the sports bag he had brought with him from the hotel. Inside it were the various items he had bought that afternoon. Quickly he stripped off his shorts and T-shirt, then pulled on a pair of loose-fitting silk trousers and a velvet waistcoat that left his arms and chest bare. Next he took out a tub of what looked like jelly, except that it was coloured gold. Body paint. He scooped some out and rubbed it between his palms, then smeared it over his arms, neck and face. He signalled to Tom, who grimaced and then finished his shoulders. All his visible skin was now gold.

Finally he brought out gold sandals, a white turban with a single mauve feather, and a plain half-mask, just big enough to cover his eyes. He had asked the costume shop to supply him with everything he would need to become a Turkish slave. He hoped the overall effect didn't make him look as ridiculous as he felt.

"Are you ready?" he asked.

Tom nodded, wiping his hands on his trousers. "You know, you do look a bit sad," he muttered.

"I don't care ... so long as it works."

"I think you're completely mad."

Alex watched as more people arrived at the palace. If his plan was going to work, he had to choose the right moment. He also had to wait for the right guests. They were still coming thick and fast, milling around the main entrance while the guards checked their invitations. He glanced over at the canal. A water taxi had just pulled in and a couple were climbing out, a man in a frock coat and a woman in a black cloak that trailed behind her. Both were masked. They were perfect.

He nodded to Tom. "Now."

"Good luck, Alex." Tom took something out of the sports bag and darted forward, making no attempt to avoid being seen. Seconds later Alex stole round the edge of the square, keeping to the shadows.

There was a snarl-up at the entrance. A guard was holding an invitation and questioning one of the guests. That was helpful too. Alex needed as much confusion as possible. Tom must have seen that this was the right moment, because suddenly there was a loud bang and all heads turned to see a boy capering in the square, laughing and shouting. He had just let off a firework and, with everyone watching, he lit another.

"Come stai?" he shouted. *How are you?* "*Quanto tempo ci vuole per andare a Roma?*" *How long does it take to get to Rome?* Alex had picked the phrases out of a guidebook. They were the only Italian Tom had been able to learn.

Tom threw the second firework and there was another bang. At the same time, Alex hurried down to the canal just as the two guests climbed the steps to the square. His sandals flapped on the paving stones as he ran, but nobody noticed him. They were all staring at Tom, who was singing "You'll Never Walk Alone" at the top of his voice. Alex bent down and picked up the train of the woman's cloak. As she headed towards the main entrance he walked behind her, holding the material off the ground.

It worked exactly as he had hoped. The crowd quickly tired of the mad English boy who was making a fool of himself. One of the guards had already been sent to deal with him. Out of the corner of his eye, Alex saw Tom turn and run away. The couple reached the door and the man in the frock coat handed over their invitation. A guard glanced at the new arrivals and ushered them through. He had assumed that Alex was with the guests; they had brought a Turkish boy with them as part of their disguise. Meanwhile, the guests had assumed that Alex worked in the palace and had been sent to escort them in. Why else would he have appeared?

The three of them passed through the door and into a grand reception hall with a domed, mosaic-covered ceiling, white columns and a marble floor. A pair of double-height glass doors opened onto a courtyard with a fountain surrounded by ornamental shrubs and flowers. At least a hundred guests were gathered there, chatting, laughing and drinking champagne from crystal glasses. It was obvious they were all pleased to be there. Servants, dressed identically to the ones outside, circulated with silver trays of food. A man sitting at a harpsichord played Mozart and Vivaldi. In keeping with the atmosphere, all the electric lights had been turned off, but there were beacons mounted on the walls as well as dozens of oil lamps, their flames bowing and dancing in the evening breeze.

Alex had followed his lord and lady into the courtyard but now he dropped the cloak and slipped away to one side. He looked up. The palace rose three floors above him, connected by a spiralling staircase like the one he had seen at the Palazzo Contarini del Bovolo. The first floor opened onto a gallery with yet more arches and columns, and some of the guests had made their way up there and were strolling slowly together, gazing down on the crowds below. Looking around him, Alex found it hard to believe that it really was the twenty-first century. A perfect illusion had been created within the palace walls.

Now that he was here, he was unsure what to do. Had he really found Scorpia? How could he be sure? It occurred to him that if Yassen Gregorovich had been telling the truth and his father had once worked for these people, they might be happy to meet him. He would ask them what had happened, how his father had died, and they would tell him. He had no need to creep around in disguise.

But suppose he was wrong? He remembered the look of fear on the old woman's face when he had mentioned the name Scorpia. And then there were the hard-eyed men working outside the palace. They spoke no English and Alex doubted he would be able to explain what he was doing if they caught him. By the time someone had laid their hands on an English dictionary, he might find himself floating face down in the canal.

No. He had to find out more before he made his move. Who was this woman – Mrs Rothman? What was she doing here? It seemed incredible to Alex that a grand masked ball in a Venetian palace could in any way be connected to a murder that had taken place fourteen years ago.

The notes of the harpsichord rang out. The conversation was getting louder as more and more people arrived. Most of them had removed their masks – it was impossible otherwise to eat or drink – and Alex saw that this was truly an international gathering. The guests were mainly speaking in Italian but there were many black and Asian faces among the crowd. He caught sight of a short Chinese man deep in discussion with another man who had a diamond set into one of his front teeth. A woman he thought he knew crossed the court-yard in front of him, and with a start he recognized her as one of the most famous film actresses in the world. Now that he looked around he saw that the place was packed with Hollywood stars. Why had they been invited? Then he remembered. This was the beginning of September, the time of the Venice International Film Festival. Well, that told him something about Mrs Rothman if she had the clout to invite celebrities like these.

Alex knew he mustn't linger too long. He was the only teenager in the palace and it would only be a matter of time before someone noticed him. He was horribly exposed. His arms and shoulders were bare. The silk trousers were so thin he could hardly feel them on him. The Turkish disguise might have enabled him to get in, but it was awkward and unhelpful now that he was actually here. He decided to make a move. There was no sign of Mrs Rothman on the ground floor. She was the person he most wanted to see. Perhaps he would find her somewhere upstairs.

He made his way through the party-goers and climbed the spiral staircase. He reached the gallery and saw a series of doors leading off into the palace itself. It was less crowded here and a few people glanced curiously at him as he proceeded. Alex knew that the important thing was not to hesitate. If he allowed himself to be challenged, he would soon be thrown out. He went through a door and found himself in an area that was a cross between a very wide corridor and a room in its own right. A gold-framed mirror hung on one wall above an ornate antique table, on which was a large vase of flowers. A huge wardrobe stood opposite. Apart from this, the area was empty.

There was a door at the far end and Alex was about to continue towards it, when he heard muffled voices approaching. He looked around for somewhere to hide. There was only the wardrobe. He didn't have time to slip inside, but he slid against the wall next to it. Like the courtyard, this floor was lit by oil lamps. He hoped the bulk of the wardrobe would cast a large enough shadow to conceal him.

The door opened. Two people came out, talking in English: one a man, the other a woman.

"We have received the release certificates and the batch will be on its way the day after tomorrow." The man was speaking. "As I explained to you, Mrs Rothman, timing is everything."

"The cold chain."

"Exactly. The cold chain cannot be broken. The boxes will be flown to England. After that..."

"Thank you, Dr Liebermann. You have done very well."

The two of them had stopped, just out of sight from where Alex was hiding. However, leaning forward slightly, he could see their reflections in the mirror.

Mrs Rothman was stunning. There was no other way for Alex to describe her. She was more like a film star than any of the actresses he had seen downstairs, her long black hair falling in waves to her shoulders. She had a mask, but it was in her hand, on the end of a wooden rod, so he was able to see her face: the brilliant dark eyes, the bloodred lips, the perfect teeth. She was wearing a fantastic dress made of ivory-coloured lace, and somehow Alex knew that it wasn't a costume but a real antique. A gold necklace set with dark blue sapphires circled her throat.

Her companion was also wearing fancy dress – a long, fur-lined cloak, a wide-brimmed hat and leather gloves. He too was holding a mask but it was an ugly thing with small eyes and a long beak. He had come as a traditional plague doctor and, Alex thought, he hardly needed the disguise. His face was pale and lifeless, his lips flecked with saliva. He was very tall, towering over Mrs Rothman. Yet still, somehow, she dwarfed him. Alex wondered why he had been invited.

"You do promise me, Mrs Rothman," Dr Liebermann said, taking off a pair of heavy glasses and wiping them nervously. "Nobody is going to get hurt."

"Does it really matter?" she replied. "You're being paid five million euros. A small fortune. Think about it, Dr Liebermann. You're set up for life."

Alex risked another glance and saw the woman standing side-on, waiting for the man to speak. Dr Liebermann was frozen. Caught between greed and fear.

"I don't know," he rasped. "Perhaps if you were paying me more..."

"Then maybe we'll have to think about doing just that!" Mrs Rothman sounded completely relaxed. "But let's not spoil the party by talking about business. I'm coming down to Amalfi myself in two days' time. I want to be there when the batch leaves, and we can talk about money then." She smiled. "Right now, let's go and have a glass of champagne and I can introduce you to some of my famous friends."

They had started walking again and as they talked they went past Alex. For a moment he was tempted to show himself. This was the woman he had come to find. He should approach her before she disappeared into the crowd. But at the same time he was intrigued. Release certificates and cold chains. He wondered what they had been talking about. Once again he decided it would be better to find out a little more before he revealed himself.

He stepped out into the corridor and went down to the door through which Mrs Rothman and her companion had come. He opened it and found himself in a huge room – and one that could truly be called palatial. It must have been at least thirty metres long, with a row of floor-to-ceiling windows that gave wonderful views over the Grand Canal. The floor was polished wood but almost everything else was white. There was a massive fireplace made of white marble with a pale tiger-skin rug (Alex winced; he could think of nothing more disgusting) spread out in front of it. White bookshelves lined the far wall, filled with leather-bound books, and, next to a second door, Alex saw a white antique table on which lay what looked like a remote control for a TV. In the centre of the room stood a solid walnut desk. Mrs Rothman's? Alex went over to it.

The surface was bare apart from a white leather blotting pad and a tray with two silver fountain pens. Alex imagined Mrs Rothman sitting here. It was the sort of desk a judge or a company chairman would have, a desk designed to impress. He looked around quickly, checking there were no security cameras, then tried one of the drawers. It was unlocked but it contained only writing paper and envelopes. He tried the next drawer down. Surprisingly, that one opened too and this time he found himself looking at some sort of brochure with a yellow cover and a name printed in black:

CONSANTO ENTERPRISES

He opened the brochure. On the first page was a picture of a building. It was obviously high-tech, long and angular with walls made entirely of reflective glass. There was an address at the bottom: Via Nuova, Amalfi.

Amalfi. That was the place Mrs Rothman had mentioned a few moments earlier.

He flicked over to another page. There were photos of various men and women in suits and white coats. The staff of Consanto, perhaps? One of them – in the middle of the top row – was Harold Liebermann. His name was printed underneath but the text was in Italian. Alex wouldn't be able to learn anything from it. He closed the brochure and tried another drawer.

Something moved.

Alex had been sure he was alone. He had been surprised that there was no sign of any security in the room, particularly if this was Mrs Rothman's study. But he was suddenly aware that something had changed. It took him a few seconds to realize what it was, and at once he felt the hairs on the back of his neck bristle.

What he had taken to be a tiger-skin rug had just stood up.

It was a tiger, alive and angry.

A Siberian tiger. How did he know it was Siberian? The colour, of course. The stripes were more white and gold than orange and black, and there weren't so many as usual. As the creature turned its gaze on him, weighing him up, Alex tried to remember what he knew about this rarest of species. There were fewer than five hundred Siberian tigers left in the wild, with only slightly more in captivity. It was the largest living cat in the world. And ... yes! It had retractable claws. That was a very useful piece of information to consider as the animal prepared to tear him apart.

Because Alex had no doubt that that was exactly what was about to happen. The tiger seemed to have awoken from a deep sleep but its yellow eyes were now fixed on him and he could almost hear the messages being sent to the brain. Food. That was another thing, he remembered now. A Siberian tiger could eat one hundred pounds of meat in a single sitting. By the time this one finished with him, there wouldn't be a great deal left.

Alex's mind was in a whirl. What exactly had he stumbled on in the Widow's Palace? What sort of woman didn't bother with locks and security cameras but kept a live tiger by her desk? The creature stretched. Alex saw the perfect muscles rippling beneath the thick fur. He tried to move but found that he couldn't. He wondered what had happened to him, then realized. He was terrified. Rooted to the spot. He was just steps away from a predator that had, for centuries, inspired dread across the world. It was almost beyond belief that this animal should have found itself imprisoned in a Venetian palace. But it was here. That was all that mattered.

And whatever the surroundings, the carnage would be the same.

The tiger growled. It was a low, rumbling noise, more terrible than anything Alex had ever heard. He tried to find the strength to move, to put a barrier between them. But there was nothing.

The tiger took a stride forward. It was preparing to spring. Its eyes had darkened. Its jaw hung open, revealing two lines of white, dagger-sharp teeth. It growled a second time, louder and more continuous.

Then it leapt.

FLOOD TIDE

Alex did the only thing he could. Faced with five hundred pounds of snarling tiger hurtling towards him, he fell to his knees, slid along the wooden floor and disappeared under the desk. The tiger landed above him. He could sense its bulk, separated from him only by the surface of the desk – and he could hear its claws gouging into the wood. Two things went through his mind. The first was the sheer improbability of coming face to face with a live tiger. The second was the knowledge that, if he didn't find a way out of the room fast, this might be the last thought he would ever have.

He had a choice of two doors. The one he had come in through was the closest. The tiger was half on the floor, half on the desk, momentarily confused. In the forest it would have found him at once, but this world was alien to it. Alex seized his chance and scrambled forward. It was only when he was out in the open, away from the scant protection of the desk, that he realized he wasn't going to make it.

The tiger was watching him. Alex had twisted round, his hands behind him, his legs bent sideways, in the act of standing up. The tiger's front paws were resting on the desk. Neither of them moved. Alex knew that the door was too far away. There was nowhere else to hide. A surge of anger flooded through him. He should never have come in here. He should have been more careful.

The tiger roared. A deep, rattling blast of air that made every nerve tingle. It was, quite simply, the sound of terror.

And then the second door opened and a man came in.

All Alex's attention was fixed on the tiger, but he noticed that the man wasn't wearing a costume. He was dressed in a polo-neck jersey, jeans and trainers; the clothes looked quietly, confidently expensive. And from the way they clung to the muscles in his arms and chest, Alex could see that he was extremely fit. He was young, in his mid-twenties. And he was black.

But there was something wrong.

The man turned his head and Alex saw that one side of his face was covered in strange white blotches, as if he had been involved in some sort of chemical accident or perhaps a fire. Then Alex noticed his hands. They too were different colours. The man should have been handsome. But in fact he was just a mess.

The man took in the scene instantly. He saw that the tiger was about to pounce. Without a second thought he reached out and picked up the remote control that Alex had noticed on the table. He pointed it vaguely in the direction of the tiger and pressed a button.

And then the impossible happened. The tiger climbed off the desk. Alex saw its eyes begin to dim, and it slumped down on the floor. Alex stared. The tiger had been transformed, in seconds, from a dreadful monster to nothing more than an over-sized pussy cat. And then it was asleep, its chest rising and falling, its eyes closed.

How had it worked?

Alex looked back at the man who had just come in. He was still holding the device, whatever it was, in his hand. For a moment Alex wondered if the animal was even real. Could it possibly be some sort of robot that could be switched on and off by remote control? No. That was ridiculous. He had been close enough to the tiger to notice every detail. He had smelt its breath. He could see it now, twitching, as it returned to the forests it had come from ... in its dreams. It was a living thing. But somehow it had been turned off as quickly and as easily as a light bulb. Alex had never felt more out of his depth. He had followed a boat with a silver scorpion, and it had led him into some sort of Italian wonderland.

"Chi sei? Cosa fai qui?"

The man was talking to him. Alex didn't understand the words but he got the gist. *Who are you? What are you doing here?* He stood up, wishing that he had been able to change out of his costume. He felt half naked and horribly vulnerable. He wondered if Tom was still waiting for him outside. No. He had told him to go back to the hotel.

The man spoke to him a second time. Alex had no choice.

"I don't speak Italian," he said.

"You're English?" The man switched effortlessly into Alex's language.

"Yes."

"What are you doing in Mrs Rothman's study?"

"My name is Alex Rider—"

"And my name is Nile. But that's not what I asked you."

"I'm looking for Scorpia."

The man – Nile – smiled, showing perfect teeth. With the tiger neutralized, Alex was able to examine him more closely. Without the skin problem, he would be classically handsome. He was clean-shaven, elegant, in perfect physical shape. His hair was cut close to his skull, with a pattern of curving lines shaved around his ears. Although he looked relaxed, Alex knew that he was already in a combat stance, poised on the balls of his feet. This was a dangerous man; he radiated self-confidence and control. He wasn't alarmed to find a teenager here in the study. Instead he seemed to be amused.

"What do you know about Scorpia?" the man asked. His voice was soft and very precise.

Alex said nothing.

"It's a name you overheard downstairs," Nile said. "Or perhaps you found it in the desk. Were you searching the desk? Is that why you're here? Are you a thief?"

"No."

Alex had already decided he'd had enough. Any minute now, someone else would arrive. It was time to go. He turned away and began to move towards the door he had first come in.

"If you take one more step, I'm afraid I'll have to kill you," Nile warned.

Alex didn't pause.

He heard the light footfall on the wooden floor behind him and timed it exactly right. At the last moment, he stopped and swivelled round, lashing out with his heel in a back kick that should have driven into the man's abdomen, winding him at the very least, and possibly knocking him out. But with a sense of shock Alex felt his foot meet only empty air. Nile had either anticipated what he was about to do or twisted away with unbelievable speed.

Alex turned full circle, trying to follow through with a front jab – the *kizami-zuki* – he had learnt in karate. But it was too late. Nile had dodged again and there was a blur of movement as the edge of his hand scythed down. It was like being hit by a block of wood. Alex was almost thrown off his feet. The whole room shuddered and went dark. Desperately he tried to adopt a defensive position, crossing his arms, keeping his head low. Nile had been expecting it. Alex felt an arm close around his throat. A hand pressed against his head. With a single twist, Nile could now break his neck.

"You shouldn't have done that," Nile said, talking as if to a little child. "I did warn you and you didn't listen. So now you're dead."

There was a moment of blinding pain, a flash of white light. Then nothing.

Alex came round with the feeling that his head had been wrenched off. Even after he had opened his eyes it took a few seconds for his vision to return. He tried to move a hand and was relieved to see his fingers curl inwards. So his neck wasn't broken. He tried to play back what had happened. Nile must have let go of his head at the last moment and used an elbow strike. Alex had been knocked out before but he had never woken up in as much pain as this. Had Nile meant to kill him? Somehow he doubted it. Even from their short encounter, Alex knew that he had met a master of unarmed combat, someone who knew exactly what he was doing and didn't make mistakes.

Nile had knocked Alex out and dragged him here. Where was he? With his head still pounding, Alex gazed around him. He didn't like the look of what he saw. He was in a small chamber, somewhere underneath the palace, he guessed. The walls were made of mottled plaster and the way they sloped reminded him of a cellar. The floor had recently been flooded. He was standing on a sort of trellis-work of damp and rotting wooden planks. The room was lit by a single bulb behind a dirty glass covering. There were no windows. Alex shivered. It was cold in here, despite the earlier heat of the September evening. And there was something else. He ran a finger along one of the walls and felt a coating of slime. He had thought the cellar was painted a dirty shade of green, but now he realized that the flooding had risen further than the floor. It had continued all the way up to the ceiling. Even the light bulb had at some stage been underwater.

As his senses slowly returned, Alex became aware of the smell of water in the air and recognized the stench of the rotting vegetables, mud and salt of the Venice canal system. He could even hear water. It was lapping not on the other side of the wall but somewhere beneath him. He knelt down and examined the floor. One of the boards was loose and he was able to swivel it enough to make a narrow opening. He stretched a hand through and touched water. There was no way out. He turned round. A short flight of wooden steps led up to a solid-looking door. He went up to it and pressed his weight against it. The door was covered in slime too. There was no give in it at all.

What now?

Alex was still dressed in the silk trousers and waistcoat that had been his costume. There was nothing to protect him against the dank chill. He thought briefly about Tom, and that gave him a little comfort. If he hadn't returned to the hotel by the morning, Tom would surely raise the alarm. Daybreak couldn't be far away. Alex had no idea how long he'd been unconscious, and he had taken off his watch when he put on his disguise, something he was now regretting. There was no sound on the other side of the door. It seemed he had no choice but to wait.

He crouched in a corner, wrapping his arms around himself. Most of the gold paint had come off, and he felt ragged and dirty. He wondered what Scorpia would do with him. Surely someone – Nile or Mrs Rothman – would come down, if only to find out why he had bothered to break in.

Incredibly, he managed to fall asleep. The next thing he knew, he had jerked awake with a crick in his neck. A cold numbness had spread through his body. Some sort of siren had woken him. He could hear it howling – not inside the building but far away. At the same time, he was aware that something in the room had changed. He glanced down and saw water spreading across the floor.

For a second he was puzzled. Had a pipe burst? Where was the water coming from? Then his thoughts came together and he understood his fate. Scorpia wasn't interested in him. Nile had told him he was going to die and he had meant what he said.

The siren was warning that there was going to be a flood. Venice has an alarm system in place all year round. The city stands at sea level and because of the wind and the atmospheric pressure, there are frequent storm surges. These cause water from the Adriatic to pour into the Venice lagoon, with the result that the canals break their banks and whole streets and squares simply disappear for several hours. Cold black water was bubbling up into the room even now. How high would it go? Alex didn't need to ask. The stains on the walls went all the way up to the ceiling. The water would rise over him and he would struggle helplessly, unable to save himself, until he drowned. Eventually the level would fall again and they would clear out his body, perhaps dumping it in the lagoon.

He leapt to his feet and ran to the door, slamming his hands against it. He was shouting too, although he knew it was hopeless. Nobody came. Nobody cared. He surely wasn't the first to end up locked in here. Ask too many questions, go into rooms where you had no right to be, and this was the result.

The water was rising steadily. It must have been five centimetres deep already. The floor had disappeared. There were no windows, and the door was rock solid. There was only one possible way out of here and Alex was almost too afraid to try it. But one of the planks was loose. Maybe there was some sort of well or large pipe underneath. After all, he reasoned, there had to be some way for the water to come in.

And it was gushing in now, more quickly than ever. Alex hurried back down the stairs. The water level was well over his ankles, almost reaching his knees. He made a quick calculation. At this rate, the room would be completely submerged in about three minutes. He ripped off the waistcoat and threw it aside. He wouldn't need that now. He waded forward, searching with his feet for the loose plank. He remembered that it was somewhere in the middle and soon found it, stubbing his toe against one side of the opening. He knelt down, the water now circling his waist. He wasn't even sure he could squeeze through. And if he did, what would he find on the other side?

He tried to feel with his hands. There was an upsurge of water right beneath him. This was the source of the inflow. The water was coming directly up from some sort of opening. So this had to be the way out. The only question was – could he do it? He would have to force himself, head first, through the tiny gap, find the opening and swim into it. If he got stuck he would drown upside down. If the passage was blocked he would never make it back again. He was kneeling in front of the worst death imaginable. And the water was creeping up his spine, pitiless and cold.

Bitter anger shivered through him. Was this the destiny that Yassen Gregorovich had promised him? Had he come to Venice simply for this? The sirens were still howling. The water had covered the first two steps and was already lapping at the third. Alex cursed, then took several deep breaths, hyperventilating. When he had forced as much air into his lungs as he thought they could take, he toppled over and plunged head first through the hole.

The gap was barely big enough. He felt the edge of the wooden floorboards bite into his shoulders, but then he was able to use his hands to propel himself onward. He was utterly blind. Even if he had opened his eyes, the water would have been black. He could feel it pressing against his nostrils and lips. It was ice cold and stinking. God! What a way to die. His stomach had passed through the opening but his hips were stuck. Alex twisted like a snake and the lower part of his body came free.

He was already running out of air. He wanted to turn and go back, but now fresh panic gripped him as he realized that he was trapped inside some sort of tube with no room to go any way except down. His shoulders banged against solid brick. He kicked out with one leg and was rewarded with a stab of pain as his foot hit the wall that enclosed him. He felt the current swirling round his face and neck – ropes of water that wanted to bind him for ever in this black death. He became aware of the full horror of his situation now that there was no escape from it. No adult would have been able to get this far. It was only because he was smaller that he had been able to make his way into this well shaft or whatever it was. But there was no room for manoeuvre. The walls were already touching him on every side. If the tube became any narrower, he would be stuck fast.

He forced himself on. Forward and down, his hands groping ahead of him, dreading the metal bars that would tell him Nile had been laughing at him from the start. His lungs were straining; the pressure was hammering at his chest. He tried not to panic, knowing it would only use up his air more quickly, but already his brain was screaming at him to stop, to breathe in, to give up and accept his fate. Forward and down. He could hold his breath for two minutes. And it couldn't have been more than a minute since he had taken the plunge. Don't give in! Just keep moving...

By now he must be ten or fifteen metres under the cellar floor. He reached out and whimpered as his knuckles struck brick. A few precious bubbles of air escaped between his lips and chased up his body, past his flailing legs. At first he thought he had come to a dead end. He opened his eyes for a split second. It made no difference at all. Open or closed, there was nothing to see: he was in pitch darkness. His heart seemed to stop beating. In that moment, Alex experienced what it would be like to die.

But then his other hand felt the curve of the wall and he realized that at last the well shaft was bending. He had reached the bottom of an elongated J and somehow he had to get round he turn. Perhaps this was where it finally joined the canal. As it twisted, it tightened. As if the swirling water wasn't enough, Alex felt the brick-work close in on him, scratching his legs and chest. He knew he had very little air left. His lungs were straining and there was a giddy emptiness in his head. He was about to slide into unconscious-ness. Well, that would come as a blessing. Maybe he would never feel the water rushing into his mouth and down his throat. Maybe he would be asleep before the end.

He turned the corner. His hands hit some-thing – bars of some sort – and he was able to pull his legs round. Only then did he discover that his worst fears had been realized. He had come to the end of the well shaft but there was a metal barrier, a circular gate. He was holding it. There was no way out.

Perhaps it was the sense of having come so far, of being cheated at the end, that gave him strength. Alex pushed and the metal hinges, weakened by the rust of three hundred years, shattered. The gate opened. Alex swam through. His shoulders came clear and he knew that there was nothing above him except water. He kicked out and felt the broken edge of the gate cut into his thigh. But there was no pain. Just a surge of desperation, a need for this to be over.

He was facing up. He could see nothing but he trusted to his natural buoyancy to take him the right way. He felt bubbles tickling his cheeks and eyelids and knew that, without wanting to, he was releasing the last of his breath. How far down had he gone? Did he have enough air left to reach the surface? He kicked as hard as he could, scrabbling with his hands – doing the crawl, only vertically. Once again he opened his eyes, hoping to see light ... moonlight, lanterns ... anything. And maybe there was a glimmer, a white ribbon flickering across his vision.

Alex screamed. Bubbles exploded from his lips. And then the scream itself erupted as he broke through the surface into the dawn light. For a moment his arms and shoulders were clear of the water and he took a huge gulp of air, then fell back. Water splashed all around him. Lying on his back, cushioned by the water, he breathed again. Rivulets of water streamed down his face. Alex knew they were mixed with tears.

He looked around him.

He guessed it was about six o'clock in the morning. The siren was still sounding but there was nobody about. And that was just as well. Alex was floating in the middle of the Grand Canal. He could see the Bridge of the Academy, a vague shape in the half-light. The moon was still in the sky, but the sun was already stealing up behind the silent churches and palaces, casting a faint light across the lagoon.

Alex was so cold that he could no longer feel anything. He was aware only of the deathly grip of the canal, trying to drag him down. With the last of his strength he swam across to a flight of uneven stone steps on the far side of the Grand Canal, away from the Widow's Palace. Whatever happened, he never wanted to go near that place again.

He was naked from the waist up. He had lost his sandals and his trousers were in tatters. Blood was running down one leg, mingling with the filthy canal water. He was soaked. He had no money and his hotel was a train ride away, outside Venice. But Alex didn't care. He was alive.

He took one look back. There was the palace, dark and silent. The party had long ago come to an end.

Slowly he limped away.

THOUGHTS ON A TRAIN

Tom Harris sat back in the second-class carriage of the *pendolino* – the fast train from Venice to Naples – and looked out of the window as the buildings and fields slipped by. He was thinking about Alex Rider.

Alex's absence had, of course, been noticed the night before. Mr Grey had assumed he was late getting back to the hotel, but when his bed was still empty at half past ten, the alarm buttons had been pressed. Mr Grey had alerted the police and then telephoned Alex's guardian – an American woman called Jack Starbright – in London. Everyone at Brookland knew that Alex had no parents; it was one of the many things that made him different. It was Jack who had calmed the situation down.

"You know what Alex is like. Sometimes he lets his curiosity get the better of him. I'm glad you called, but I'm sure he'll show up. You really don't need to worry."

But Tom *was* worried. He had seen Alex swallowed up by the crowd at the Widow's Palace and knew it was something more than curiosity that had led his friend there. He didn't know what to do. Part of him wanted to tell Mr Grey what the two of them had done. Alex might still be in the palace. He might need help. But another part of him was afraid of getting into trouble ... and perhaps getting Alex into even more trouble than he was in already. In the end he decided to keep silent. They were leaving the hotel at half past ten the next morning. If by that time there was still no news from Alex, he would come forward and tell them where he was.

In fact, Alex rang the hotel at half past seven. He was, he said, on his way to England. He had got homesick and had decided to leave early. Mr Grey took the call.

"Alex," he said. "I can't believe you've done this. I'm meant to be responsible for you. When I brought you on this trip, I trusted you. You've completely let me down."

"I'm sorry, sir." Alex sounded wretched and that was how he felt.

"That's not good enough. Because of you, I may not be allowed to take other kids on future trips. You're spoiling it for everyone."

"I didn't mean this to happen," Alex said. "There are things you don't understand. When I see you next term, I'll try to explain it to you ... as much as I can. I really am sorry, sir. And I'm grateful to you for the way you've helped me this summer. But you don't have to worry about me. I'll be all right."

There were a lot of things Mr Grey wanted to say but he stopped himself. He had got to know Alex well in all their hours together and liked him. He also knew that Alex was like no other boy he'd ever met. He didn't believe for a minute that Alex was homesick. Nor did he think he was on his way back to England. But sometimes, just occasionally, it was better not to ask.

"Good luck, Alex," he said. "Look after yourself."

"Thank you, sir."

The rest of the school party had been told that Alex had already left. Miss Bedfordshire had packed his bags for him, and everyone else had been too busy sorting out their own things to think about him any more. Only Tom knew that Alex was lying. They had been sharing a room in the hotel, and Alex's passport was still on the bedside table. Acting on impulse, Tom had taken it with him. He had given Alex his brother's address in Naples. There was still a chance he might show up there.

The scenery flashed past, as uninteresting as scenery nearly always becomes when seen through the grimy window of a train. Tom had parted company with the school party outside the hotel. They were flying back to England. He had a ticket to Naples, where his brother would be waiting to meet him. He had about six hours to kill. There was a Nintendo DS in his backpack and a book – *Northern Lights*. Tom didn't much like reading but everyone in his class had been told they had to get through at least one novel during the summer holidays. There were just a few days left until the start of term and he was only on page seven.

He wondered what had happened to Alex. And why had Alex been so determined to break into the Widow's Palace in the first place? As the train rattled on, leaving the outskirts of Venice behind, Tom thought about his friend. They had met two years ago. Tom – who was about half the size of anyone else in his year – had just been beaten up. This was something that seemed to happen to him quite often. In this case it was a bunch of sixteen-year-olds led by a boy called Michael Cook who had suggested he should use his lunch money to buy them cigarettes. Tom had politely refused and a short while later Alex had come across him sitting on the pavement, picking up his tattered books and wiping blood from his nose.

"You OK?"

"Yeah. I've got a broken nose. I've lost my lunch money. And they've told me they're going to do it all again tomorrow. But otherwise I'm fine."

"Mike Cook?"

"Yeah."

"Maybe I should have a word with him."

"What makes you think he'll listen to you?"

"I've got a way with words."

Alex had met the bully and two of his friends behind the bike shed the following day. It was a short meeting but Michael Cook never bothered anyone else again. It was also noticed that, for the following week, he limped and spoke in a strangely high-pitched voice.

That was the start of a close friendship. Tom and Alex lived near each other and often cycled home together. They were in lots of teams together – despite his size, Tom was extremely quick on his feet. When Tom's parents started talking about divorce, Alex was the only person he told.

In return, Tom probably knew more about Alex than anyone at Brookland. He had visited his house a few times and had met Jack, the cheerful, red-haired American girl who wasn't exactly his nanny or housekeeper but seemed to be looking after him. Alex had no parents. Everyone knew that Alex had lived with his uncle – who must have been rich, judging from the house. But then he had died in a car accident. It had been announced in school assembly and Tom had gone round to the house a couple of times, hoping to find Alex, but he had never been in.

After that, Alex had changed. It had started with his first long absence from school in the spring term, and everyone assumed that he must have been knocked off balance by his uncle's death. But then he had disappeared again in the summer term. There was no explanation. Nobody seemed to have any idea where he went. When the two of them had finally met again, Tom had been surprised how much his friend had changed. He had been hurt. Tom had seen some of the scars. But Alex also seemed to have got a lot older. There was something in his eyes that hadn't been there before, as if he had seen things he would never be able to forget.

And now this business in Venice! Maybe Miss Bedfordshire was right after all, and Alex really did need to see a shrink. Tom reached for his Nintendo DS, hoping to put the whole thing out of his mind. He knew he ought to continue with the book, and he promised himself he would go back to it in two or three hundred miles' time ... after they had gone through Rome.

He became aware that someone was standing over him, and automatically fumbled for his ticket. He looked up and gaped. It was Alex.

He was dressed in old-fashioned jeans and a baggy jersey, both one size too big. He was dirty; his hair was matted and untidy. Tom glanced down and saw that he was barefoot. He looked worn out.

"Alex?" Tom was almost too shocked to speak.

"Hi." Alex gestured to an empty seat. "Do you mind if I join you?"

"No. Sit down..." Tom had a whole table to himself – which was just as well. The other passengers were staring at Alex in horror. "How did you get here? What happened? Where did you get those clothes?" Suddenly the questions were tumbling out.

"I'm afraid I stole the clothes," Alex confessed. "I nicked them off a washing line. I couldn't get any shoes, though."

"What happened to you last night? I saw you go into the palace. Did they find you?" Tom wrinkled his nose. "Did you fall in a canal or something?"

Alex was too tired to answer any of his questions. "I've got a favour to ask you, Tom," he said.

"Do you want me to hide you from the police?"

"I need to borrow some money. I couldn't buy a ticket. And I'm going to have to get some new clothes."

"That's OK. I've got plenty of money."

"And I need to stay with you – with your brother – for a while. Is that going to be all right?"

"Sure. Jerry won't mind. Alex..."

But Alex had slumped forward, his head cradled in his hands. He was sound asleep.

The train picked up speed, curving round the Gulf of Venice and continuing its journey south.

* * *

When Alex woke up, the train was still travelling through the Italian countryside. He slowly uncurled himself. Already he was feeling better. The train hadn't just left Venice behind, it had carried him away from his experiences of the night before. He sat up and saw Tom staring at him. A sandwich, a bag of crisps and a Coke sat on the table between them.

"I thought you'd be hungry," Tom said.

"I'm starving. Thanks." Alex opened the can of Coke. It was lukewarm, but he didn't mind. "Where are we?" he asked.

"We went through Rome about an hour ago. I think we'll be there quite soon." Tom waited while Alex drank. He put his book down. "You look terrible," he commented. "Are you going to tell me what happened last night?"

"Sure." Alex had decided before he even got on the train that he was going to have to tell Tom everything. It wasn't just that he needed Tom's help. He was tired of lying. "But I'm not sure you're going to believe it," he added.

"Well, I've been reading my book for the last two and a half hours," Tom said, "and I'm only on page nineteen. So I think I'd prefer listening to you, whatever you've got to say."

"All right..."

Alex had only ever told one other person the truth about himself, and that had been his friend Sabina Pleasure. She hadn't believed him – not until she'd found herself knocked out and tied up in the basement of the country mansion owned by the insane multimillionaire Damian Cray. Now Alex told Tom everything he had told her, starting with the truth behind the death of his uncle and continuing all the way up to his escape from the flooded chamber the night before. The strange thing was that he enjoyed telling his story. He wasn't boasting about being a spy and working for secret intelligence. Quite the opposite. For too long he had been a servant of MI6, forced by them to keep quiet about everything he had done. They had even made him sign the Official Secrets Act. By telling the truth, he was doing exactly what they didn't want him to do and it came as a relief, a great weight off his shoulders. It made him feel that he was the one in control.

"...I couldn't go back to the hotel. Not without money. Not without shoes. But I knew you were taking the train to Naples, so I walked up to the station and waited for you. I followed you onto the train. And here I am."

Alex finished and waited nervously for Tom's response. Tom had said nothing for the last twenty minutes. Would he, like Sabina, walk out on him?

Tom nodded slowly. "Well, that makes sense," he said at last.

Alex stared. "You believe me?"

"I can't think of any other reason to explain

everything that's happened. Missing so much school. And all those injuries. I mean, I thought your housekeeper might be beating you up, but that didn't seem likely. So, yes. You must be a spy. But that's pretty heavy, Alex. I'm glad it's you, not me."

Alex couldn't help smiling. "Tom, you really are my best mate."

"I'm happy to help. But there's one thing you haven't told me. Why were you interested in Scorpia in the first place? And what are you doing now, coming to Naples?"

Alex hadn't mentioned his father. That was the one area that still troubled him. It was too private to share with anyone. "I've got to find Scorpia," he began. He paused, then continued carefully. "I think my dad may have had some sort of involvement with them. I never knew him. He died shortly after I was born."

"Did they kill him?"

"No. It's difficult to explain. I just want to find out about him. I've never met anyone who knew him. Even my uncle never talked much about him. I just have to know who he was."

"And Naples?"

"I heard Mrs Rothman talking about a company in Amalfi. That's not too far from Naples. I think it's called Consanto. I saw the name in a sort of brochure in her desk, and the person she was talking to had his photograph inside. She said she'd be there in two days. That's tomorrow. I'd be interested to know why."

"But, Alex..." Tom frowned. "You met this black guy, Nile..."

"Actually, he wasn't exactly black. He was more sort of ... black and white."

"Well, the moment you mentioned Scorpia, he locked you in a cellar and tried to drown you. Why go back? I mean, it sounds to me like they're not that keen to meet you."

"I know." Alex couldn't deny that Tom was right. And he had learnt very little about Mrs Rothman. He couldn't even be certain that she was connected to Scorpia. The one thing he did know was that she – or the people who worked for her – was utterly ruthless. But he couldn't leave it. Not yet. Yassen Gregorovich had shown him a path. He had to follow it to the end. "I just want to take a look, that's all."

Tom shrugged. "Well, I suppose you can't be in any worse trouble than you are with Mr Grey. When you get back to school, I think he's going to murder you."

"Yeah. I know. He didn't sound too happy on the phone."

There was a brief silence. The train rushed through a station, a blur of neon and concrete, without stopping.

"It must mean a lot to you," Tom said. "Finding out about your dad."

"Yes. It does."

"My mum and dad have been shouting at each other for ages. All they ever do is fight. Now they're splitting up and they're fighting about that. I don't care about either of them any more. I don't think I even like them." For a brief moment Tom looked sadder than Alex had ever seen him. "So I think I understand what you're saying, and I hope you find out something good about your dad, because right now I can't think of anything good about mine."

Jerry Harris, Tom's elder brother, met them at the station and took them by taxi to his flat. He was twenty-two years old and had come to Italy on his gap year but had somehow forgotten to return. Alex liked him immediately. Jerry was totally laid-back, thin to the point of scrawny, with bleached hair and a lopsided smile. It made no difference to him that Alex had turned up uninvited, and he didn't comment on Alex's appearance or the fact that he seemed to have made the journey from Venice without shoes.

He lived in the Spanish Quarter of the city. It was a typical Naples street: narrow, with buildings five or six storeys high on both sides and washing lines strung out between them. Looking up, Alex saw a fantastic patchwork of crumbling plaster, wooden shutters, ornate railings, window boxes and terraces with Italian women leaning out to chat with their neighbours. Jerry was renting a top-floor flat. There was no lift. The three of them climbed a twisting staircase with a different smell and sound on each floor: disinfectant and a baby crying on the first, pasta and a violin playing on the second...

"This is it," Jerry announced, unlocking a door. "Make yourselves at home."

Home was an open-plan space with hardly any furniture, white painted walls, a wooden floor and views over the city. There was a kitchen in the corner, every surface piled high with dirty plates, and a door leading to a small bedroom and bathroom. Somehow, someone had dragged a battered leather three-seater sofa all the way up. It sat in the middle of the room surrounded by a tangle of sports equipment, only some of which Alex recognized. There were two skateboards, ropes and pitons, an oversized kite, a mono-ski and what looked like a parachute. Tom had already told Alex that his brother was into extreme sports. He was teaching English as a foreign language in Naples, but only to pay for his trips mountaineering, surfing or whatever.

"You two hungry?" Jerry asked.

"Yeah." Tom slumped down on the sofa. "We've been on a train for, like, six hours. You got any food?"

"You've got to be kidding! No. We'll go out and get a pizza or something. How's things, Tom?

How are Mum and Dad?"

"The same."

"As bad as that?" Jerry turned to Alex. "Our parents are complete crap. I'm sure my brother's told you. I mean, calling him Tom and me Jerry. How crap can you get?" He shrugged. "What are you doing down here, Alex? You want to visit the coast?"

On the train Alex had impressed on Tom the importance of not repeating anything he'd said. Now he winced as Tom announced, "Alex is a spy."

"Is he?"

"Yeah. He works for MI6."

"Wow. That's awesome."

"Thanks." Alex wasn't sure what to say.

"So what are you doing in Naples, Alex?"

Tom answered for him. "He wants to find out about a company. Constanza."

"Consanto," Alex said.

"Consanto Enterprises?" Jerry opened the fridge and took out a beer. Alex noticed that, apart from beer, there was nothing else in the fridge. "I know about them. I used to have one of their people learning English. He was a research chemist or something. I hope he was a better chemist than he was a linguist, because his English was awful."

"Who are Consanto?" Alex asked.

"They're one of these big pharmaceutical companies. They make drugs and biological stuff. They've got a plant near Amalfi."

94

"Can you get me in?" Alex was hopeful.

"You've got to be kidding. I doubt the pope could get in. I drove past once and it's this really high-tech sort of place. It looks like something out of a sci-fi film. And it's got all these fences and security cameras and stuff."

"They must have something to hide," Tom said.

"Of course they've got something to hide, you dimwit," Jerry muttered. "All these drugs companies are coming up with new patents and they're worth a fortune. I mean, like, if someone discovers a cure for Aids or something, it would be worth billions. That's why you can't get in. The guy I was teaching never said anything about his work. He wasn't allowed to."

"Like Alex."

"What?"

"Being a spy. He's not allowed to say anything about that either."

"Right." Jerry nodded.

Alex looked from one to the other. Despite the fact that there were eight years between them, the two brothers were obviously close. He wished he could spend more time with them. He felt more relaxed now than he had in a long time. But that wasn't why he was here. "Can you take me to Amalfi?" he asked.

"Sure." Jerry shrugged and finished his beer. "I haven't got any lessons tomorrow. Would that be OK?"

"It would be great."

"It's not that far from Naples. I can borrow my girlfriend's car and drive you down there. You can see Consanto for yourself. But I'm telling you now, Alex, there's definitely no way in."

CONSANTO

Standing beside the car, in the full heat of the mid-morning sun, Alex had to admit that Jerry Harris was right. Consanto had certainly done everything it possibly could to protect whatever it was hiding.

There was a single main building, rectangular in shape and at least fifty metres long. Alex had seen the picture in the brochure and he was struck by how much the actual building resembled it – as if the photograph had been blown up a thousand times, cut out, and somehow made to stand up. It wasn't quite real. Alex was looking at a wall of reflective glass. Even the sunlight couldn't seem to find a way in. It was a huge silver block with a single sign – CONSANTO – cut out of solid steel.

Jerry was standing next to him, dressed in knee-length shorts and a sleeveless T-shirt. He had brought along a pair of binoculars and Alex examined the wide concrete steps that led up to the main entrance. There were a few outlying buildings, warehouses and ventilation plants, and a car park with about a hundred cars. He trained the binoculars on the roof of the main complex. He could see two water tanks, a row of solar panels and, next to them, a brick tower with a single, open door. A fire escape? If he could reach it, he might just find a way in.

But it was obvious that he could get nowhere near. The entire site was surrounded by a fence more than six metres high and topped with razor wire. A single track led to a checkpoint, with a second one right behind it. Every car that went in and out was searched. And, just to be sure, cameras mounted on steel poles swivelled and rotated, the lenses sweeping over every centimetre of ground. Even a fly trying to get in would have been noticed. And swatted, Alex thought gloomily.

Consanto Enterprises had chosen this position carefully. Amalfi, the busy, densely populated Mediterranean port, was a few miles to the south, and there were a few isolated villages to the north. The complex was in a sort of hole, a flat and rocky stretch of landscape with few trees or buildings – nowhere to hide. Alex was standing with the sea about half a mile behind him. There were sailing boats dotted about and a single ferry ploughed through the water on its way to the island of Capri. His overwhelming impression was that it would be impossible to approach Consanto from any direction without being spotted. He was probably being filmed even now.

"You see what I mean?" Jerry said.

Tom had his back to the buildings; he was looking at the sea. "Anyone fancy a swim?" he asked.

"Yeah." Jerry nodded slowly. "You bring any trunks?"

"No."

"It doesn't matter. We can swim in our boxers."

"I'm not wearing boxers."

Jerry glanced at his brother. "You are so gross!"

Alex watched as a supply van made its way past the first control post. It really did look impossible. Even if he managed to sneak into a car or a truck, he would be found when it was searched. There was no point waiting until nightfall. There were dozens of arc lamps arranged around the perimeter and they would flick on the minute it grew dark. He could see uniformed guards patrolling the grounds with German shepherd dogs on leashes. They would probably be there all night too.

He was about to give up. He couldn't get in from the front or the sides; he couldn't climb the fence. He looked past the complex. It had been set against a sheer cliff. The rock face rose at least three hundred metres and he noticed a cluster of buildings, far away, at the summit.

He pointed. "What's that?" he asked.

Jerry followed the direction of Alex's finger. "I

don't know." He thought for a moment. "It's probably Ravello. It's a hilltop village."

"Can we go there?"

"Yeah. Sure."

Alex put it all together in an instant. The flat roof with the fire escape, seemingly open. The village perched high up on the cliff. The equipment he had seen in Jerry's flat in Naples. Suddenly it was very simple.

Consanto Enterprises might look impregnable. But Alex had found a way in.

The faded eighteenth-century villa stood some distance away from Ravello, reached by a path that twisted along the side of the mountain, high above the pine trees. It was a wonderful place to escape to, lost in its own world, far away from the crowds on the beaches and in the streets below. A cool evening breeze drifted in from the sea and the light had turned from a blue to a mauve to a deep red as the sun slowly set. There was an ornamental garden with a long avenue running down the centre and, at the far end, a terrace that appeared unexpectedly with white marble heads mounted on the parapet. Beyond the terrace, there was nothing. The garden simply came to an abrupt end with a sheer drop straight down to the coastal road, the Consanto complex and the rocky flatlands three-hundred-odd metres below.

The tourists had long ago left for the evening.

The villa was about to close. Alex stood on his own, thinking about what he had to do. His mouth was dry and there was an unpleasant churning in his stomach. This was madness. There had to be another solution. No. He had examined all the possibilities. This was the only way.

He knew that BASE jumping was one of the most dangerous of all extreme sports, and that every BASE jumper would know someone who had been injured or killed. BASE stands for Building, Antenna, Span and Earth. It means, essentially, parachuting without the use of an aircraft. BASE jumpers will throw themselves off skyscrapers, dams, rock faces and bridges. The jumps themselves aren't against the law, but they're usually done without permission, often in the middle of the night. Trespassing, being outside the system, is all part of the fun.

They had driven all the way back to Naples to get the equipment which Jerry Harris had agreed to lend to Alex. Jerry had used the long journey to give Alex as much information about the techniques and the potential dangers as he could. A crash course, Tom had muttered gloomily. Just what Alex didn't need.

"The first and most important rule is the one that beginners find hardest," Jerry said. "When you jump, you've got to wait as long as possible before you release the canopy. The longer you wait, the further you travel away from the side of the cliff.

And you must keep your shoulders level. The last thing you need is a one eighty onto a hard-core object."

"What's that in English?" Alex asked.

"It's what occurs when you get an off-heading opening. Basically, it means you go the wrong way and hit the cliff."

"And what happens then?"

"Yeah. Well ... you die."

Alex was wearing a helmet, knee pads and elbow pads. Jerry had also lent him a pair of sturdy hiking boots. But that was all. He would need to react instantly as he fell through the sky, and too much protective gear would only slow him down. Besides, as Jerry had pointed out, nobody had ever made a BASE jump without basic training. If something went wrong, all the protective clothes in the world wouldn't do him one bit of good.

And the difference between life and death?

For Alex it boiled down to two hundred and twenty square feet of F111 nylon. Skydivers need on average one square foot of parachute for every pound of their body weight and equipment. But BASE jumpers need almost half that again. Alex's chute had been designed for Jerry, who was heavier than he was. He would have plenty of material.

He was carrying a seven-cell Blackjack canopy which Jerry had bought second hand for a little under one thousand American dollars. An ordinary parachute normally contains nine cells –

nine separate pockets. The larger BASE canopy is thought to be more docile, easier to fly and land accurately. Alex's own weight would drag it out of the deployment bag as he fell, and it would inflate over his head, taking the shape of an aerofoil, the ram-air design of all modern parachutes.

Jerry stood next to him, pointing a black gadget about the size and shape of a pair of binoculars at the ground. He was taking a reading. "Three hundred and fifty-seven metres," he said. He took out a laminated card – an altitude delay planner – and quickly consulted it. "You can do a four," he said. "It'll give you approximately fifteen seconds under canopy. A six max. But that'll mean landing almost at once."

Alex understood what he was saying. He could free-fall for between four and six seconds. The less time he spent dangling underneath the parachute, the less chance he would have of being spotted from below. On the other hand, the faster he arrived, the more chance he would have of breaking most of his bones.

"And when you get down there, remember..."

"Flaring."

"Yes. If you don't want to break both your legs, you have to slow yourself down about three or four seconds before impact."

"Not three or four seconds *after* impact," Tom added helpfully. "That'll be too late."

"Thanks!"

Alex looked around. There was nobody in sight. He half wished a policeman or somebody from the villa would come along and put a stop to this before he could actually jump. But the gardens were empty. The white marble heads stared past him, not remotely interested.

"You'll go from nought to sixty miles an hour in about three seconds," Jerry went on. "I've put on a mesh slider, but you're still going to feel the opening shock. But at least that'll warn you you're about to land. That's when you get both feet and knees together. Put your chin on your chest. And try not to bite your tongue in half. I almost did on my first time."

"Yes." Single words were about all Alex could manage.

Jerry looked over the precipice. "The roof of Consanto is right beneath us and there's no wind. You won't have much time to steer but you can try pulling on the toggles." He rested a hand on Alex's shoulder. "I could do this for you, if you like," he said.

"No." Alex shook his head. "Thanks, Jerry. But it's down to me. It was my idea..."

"Good luck."

"Break a leg!" Tom exclaimed. "Or rather – don't."

Alex moved to the edge between two of the statues and looked down. He was right over the complex, although from this height it looked tiny, like a silver Lego brick. Most of the workers would have left by now but there would still be guards. He would just have to hope that nobody looked up in the few seconds it would take him to arrive. But that was what he had observed earlier, outside the gate. Consanto faced the sea. The main road and the entrance were on the same side. That was where all their attention was focused, and if Alex was lucky, he would be able to drop in – quite literally – unnoticed.

His stomach heaved. There was no feeling in his legs. He felt as if he were floating. He tried to take a deep breath but the air didn't seem to want to rise above his chest. Did it really matter to him so much, penetrating Consanto, finding out how it might be involved with Scorpia? What would Tom and his brother say if he changed his mind, even at this last minute?

To hell with it, he thought. Lots of teenagers did BASE jumps. Jerry himself had recently jumped off the New River Gorge Bridge in West Virginia. It had been Bridge Day, the one day in the year when the jump was legal in America, and he had said there'd been dozens of kids waiting in line. It was a sport. People did it for fun. If he hesitated for one more second, he would never do it. It was time to get it over with.

In a single movement he climbed onto the parapet, checked the line from the pilot chute, took one last look at the target and jumped.

It was like committing suicide.

It was like nothing he had ever experienced.

Everything was a blur. There was the sky, the edge of the cliff and (unless he imagined it) Tom's staring face. Then it all tilted. The blue rushed into the grey with the white of the roof punching up. The wind hammered into his face. His eyes were being sucked into the backs of their sockets with the sudden acceleration. He had to deploy. No. Jerry had warned him about this. How many seconds?

Now!

He threw out the pilot chute, hoping it would find the clean airflow that was meant to surround him. Had it worked? The chute had already disappeared, dragging with it the bridle line which would in turn suck the Blackjack canopy out of its pack. God! He'd left it too late. He was falling too fast. A long, silent scream with the wind in his ears, skin crawling. Where was the bloody chute? Where was up? Where was down? Falling...

And then there was a sudden wrenching, braking sensation. He thought he was being torn in half. He could see something, ropes and billowing material, just at the edge of his vision. The canopy! But that didn't matter. Where was he going? He looked down and saw his own feet, dangling in space. A white rectangle was racing up to meet them. The roof of the complex – but it was too far away. He was going to miss. Quick. Pull the toggles. That's better. The roof tilted back towards him. What had he forgotten?

Flaring! He pulled down on both brakes, dropping the tail of the canopy so that – like a plane landing – he came in at an upward angle. But had he left it too late?

All he could see was the surface of the roof. Then he hit it. He felt the shock travel through his ankles, his knees and up into his thighs. He ran forward. The canopy was dragging him. Jerry had warned him about this. There might be a stronger breeze lower down and if he wasn't careful he would be pulled off the roof. He could see the edge racing towards him. He dug in his heels, reaching behind him for the risers. He caught hold of them and pulled them in. Stop running! With just centimetres to spare, he managed to get a grip with the balls of his feet. He leant back, tugging the canopy towards him. He sat down hard.

He had arrived.

For a few seconds he did nothing. He was experiencing the massive high that all BASE jumpers know and which makes the sport so addictive. His body was releasing a flood of adrenalin and it was coursing through his entire system. His heart was pumping at double speed. He could feel every hair on his skin standing up. He looked back up at the cliff. There was no sign of Tom or his brother. Even if they had been standing there, they would have been too small to see. Alex couldn't believe how far he'd travelled, or how quickly he'd arrived. And as far as he could tell, the guards had kept their heads down, their eyes on the ground, not the air. So much for Consanto's security!

Alex waited until his heart and pulse rate had returned to normal, then pulled off the helmet and protective pads. He quickly folded the chute and packed it as best as he could inside the bag. He could taste blood in his mouth and realized that, despite Jerry's warnings, he'd still managed to bite his tongue.

Keeping low, he carried the bag with the canopy over to the door that he had seen earlier from the ground. He was going to have to leave Jerry's equipment up here on the roof until it was time to leave. He had more or less worked out how he was going to get out of Consanto. The easiest way would simply be to call the police and get himself arrested. At the very worst, he would be prosecuted for trespassing. But he was only fourteen. He doubted he would find himself in an Italian jail – more likely they would pack him off back to England.

The door was ajar. He had been right about that. A dozen cigarette butts on the roof told their own story. Despite all the security guards, the cameras and the high-tech alarms, a single smoker in need of a fag had found his way up here and blown the whole place wide open.

Well, that was fine. Alex slipped in through the door and found a flight of metal steps leading down. There was a set of more solid-looking doors – steel with small glass windows – and for a moment Alex thought his way was blocked. But there must have been some sort of sensor. They slid open as he approached, then closed again after him. Perhaps the anonymous smoker had set it up that way. Alex turned and waved a hand. The doors didn't move. A numerical keypad on the wall told him the bad news. Getting in this way was one thing. But to get out again, he would need a code. He was trapped.

There was only one way to go and that was forward. He followed a blank white corridor down to another set of doors which hissed open and shut as he passed through. He had entered the core of the complex. There was an immediate difference to the air quality. It was extremely cold and smelt metallic. He glanced up and noticed a brightly polished silver duct running the full length of the passage. There were dials and monitors everywhere. Already his head was beginning to ache. This place was just too clean.

He kept moving, wanting to see as much as possible before he was discovered. There didn't seem to be anyone around – all the workers must have gone home for the night – but it could only be a matter of time before security looked in. He heard a door open somewhere. Alex's heart flipped and he quickly searched for somewhere to hide. The corridor was bare, brightly lit by powerful neon lights behind glass panels. There wasn't so much as a shadow to give him cover. He saw a doorway and hurried over to it, but the door was locked. Alex pressed himself against the door, hoping against hope that he wouldn't be seen.

A man appeared round the corner. At first it was hard to be sure that it *was* a man. The figure was wrapped in a pale blue protective suit that covered every centimetre of his body. He had a hood over his head and a glass mask in front of his face, obscuring most of his features – but then he turned sideways and Alex caught a glimpse of glasses and a beard. The man was pushing what looked like a huge tea urn, shining chrome, mounted on wheels. The urn was as tall as he was, with a series of valves and pipes on the lid. To Alex's relief the man turned off down a second corridor.

Alex looked at the door which had provided him with minimal cover. It had a thick glass window – like the front of a washing machine – and there was a large room on the other side, still lit but empty. Alex supposed it must be a laboratory but it looked more like a distillery, with more urns, some of them suspended on chains. There was a metal staircase leading up to some sort of gantry and a whole wall lined with what looked like enormous fridge doors. All the metal looked brand new, brilliantly polished.

As Alex watched, a woman crossed the room. The complex obviously wasn't as deserted as he had thought. She was also dressed in protective clothes, with a mask over her face, and she was pushing a silver trolley. His breath frosted on the glass as he tried to peer in. It didn't make any sense, but the woman seemed to be carrying eggs ... hundreds of them, neatly lined up on trays. They were the size of ordinary chickens' eggs, every one of them pure white. Could the woman be part of the catering team? Alex doubted it. There was something almost sinister about the eggs. Perhaps it was their uniformity, the fact that they were all so obviously identical. The woman went behind some machinery and disappeared. Increasingly puzzled, Alex decided it was time to move on.

He went down the second corridor, following the direction of the man with the urn. Now he could hear machinery, a soft, rhythmic clattering. He came to a glass panel set in the wall and looked through it into a darkened room, where a second woman sat in front of a bizarre, complicated machine that seemed to be sorting hundreds of test tubes, rotating them, counting them, labelling them and finally delivering them into her hands.

What was being made at Consanto Enterprises? Chemical weapons, perhaps? And how the hell was he going to get out again? Alex glanced down and noticed his hands, still grubby from his BASE jump. He was dirty and sweaty and he was surprised he hadn't set off every single alarm in the building. Surrounded by these white panelled walls with the air being sucked in and sterilized, he had become the equivalent of an enormous germ and the monitors should have screamed the moment he came near.

He arrived at another set of doors and was relieved when these slid open to allow him through. Perhaps he might be able to find his way out after all. But these doors led only to another corridor, a little wider than the one he had just left, but equally unpromising. It occurred to him that he was still on the top floor. He had entered from the roof. He needed to find a lift or staircase that would take him down.

Suddenly a door about ten metres away opened and a man appeared, staring at Alex in disbelief.

"Who the hell are you, and what are you doing here?" he demanded.

Alex registered that the man was talking in English. At the same time, he recognized him: the bald head, the hooked nose and the thick black glasses. He was wearing a white laboratory coat hanging loose over a jacket and tie but the last time Alex had seen him he had been in fancy dress. This was Dr Liebermann, the guest he had seen talking to Mrs Rothman at the party in Venice.

"I..." Alex wasn't sure what to say. "I'm lost," he muttered helplessly.

"You can't come in here! This is a secure area. Who are you?"

"My name's Tom. My dad works here."

"What is his name? What is his department?" Dr

Liebermann wasn't going to buy the little boy lost routine. "How did you get here?" he asked.

"My dad brought me. But if you'd like to show me the way out, that's fine by me."

"No! I'm calling security. You can come with me!"

Dr Liebermann took a step back towards the room from which he'd come. Alex wasn't sure what to do. Should he try to run? Once the alarm went off, it would only be a matter of minutes before he was caught. And what then? He had assumed that Consanto would simply hand him over to the police. But if they were hiding something here, if he had seen something secret, maybe he wouldn't be that fortunate.

Dr Liebermann was reaching out for something and Alex saw an alarm button next to the door.

"It's all right, Harold. I'll deal with this."

The voice came from behind Alex.

Alex spun round and felt his heart sink. It was like a bad dream. Nile, the man who had knocked him unconscious and left him to drown, was standing behind him, a smile on his face, totally relaxed. He too was wearing a white coat. In his case, it hung over jeans and a tight-fitting T-shirt. He had a grey attaché case in one hand but, as Alex watched, he set it down on the floor beside him.

"I wasn't expecting to see you again." Harold Liebermann was puzzled.

"Mrs Rothman sent me back."

"Why?"

"Well, as you can see, Dr Liebermann, there's been a very serious breakdown in security. Before she left she asked me to deal with it."

"Do you know this boy? Who is he?"

"His name is Alex Rider."

"He said his name was Tom."

"He's lying. He's a spy."

Alex was caught in the middle of this conversation, one man on either side of him. He was trapped. He felt dazed, and he knew there was nothing he could do. Nile was too fast and too strong for him. He had already proved that.

"What are you going to do?" Dr Liebermann demanded. He sounded peeved, as if neither Alex nor Nile had any right to be there.

"I just told you, Harold. We can't have security problems. I'm going to deal with it."

Nile reached under his coat and produced one of the most lethal-looking weapons Alex had ever seen. It was a samurai sword, very slightly curving, with an ivory hilt and a flat, razor-sharp blade. But it was half sized – somewhere between a sword and a dagger. Nile held it for a moment in his hand, obviously enjoying the fine balance, then raised it to the height of his shoulder. Now he could throw it or slash with it. Either way, Alex knew instantly, he was facing a master. He had perhaps seconds to live.

"You can't kill him here!" Dr Liebermann exclaimed in exasperation. "You'll get blood everywhere!"

"Don't worry, Harold," Nile replied. "This is going through the neck and into the brain. There'll be very little blood."

Alex crouched down, preparing to dodge, knowing that he wouldn't have a chance. Nile was still smiling, obviously enjoying himself.

He threw the sword.

There was a single movement. Alex hadn't even seen Nile take aim but the blade was already a blur, flashing down the length of the passageway. It passed over Alex's shoulder. Had Nile missed? No. That was impossible. He suddenly realized that Nile hadn't been aiming at him.

Alex turned and saw Dr Liebermann already dead, still standing, a look of surprise on his face. He had managed to bring one hand up so that it was lightly holding the blade of the sword now sticking out of his neck. He pitched forward and lay motionless.

"Straight into the brain," Nile muttered. "Just like I said."

As Alex watched, stunned, Nile walked past him and crouched down beside Dr Liebermann. He pulled the sword free, used the dead man's tie to wipe it clean, and returned it to its sheath, which hung from his waist beneath his lab coat. He looked up.

"Hello, Alex," he said cheerfully. "You're the last person I expected to see here. Mrs Rothman will be pleased."

"You don't want to kill me?" Alex murmured. He still couldn't believe what had just happened.

"Not at all."

Nile stood up and went back to the attaché case and opened it. Alex was finding it very difficult to keep up with what was happening. Inside the case, he saw a keyboard, a small computer screen, two square packets and a series of wires. Nile knelt down and tapped rapidly on the keyboard. A series of codes appeared on the screen: black and white like the fingers that were typing them. He continued talking as he typed.

"I hope you'll forgive me, Alex. I have to say, I'm terribly sorry for what happened at the Widow's Palace. I didn't realize who you were – John Rider's son. I think it's brilliant how you managed to escape, by the way. I'd never have forgiven myself if I'd had to go in and fish you out with a boat-hook." He finished typing, pressed ENTER, then closed the lid of the case. "But we can't talk now. Mrs Rothman is just along the coast, in Positano. She's dying to meet you. So let's go."

"Why did you kill Dr Liebermann?" Alex asked.

"Because Mrs Rothman ordered me to." Nile straightened up. "Look, I'm sure you've got a lot of questions, but I can't answer them right now. I've just set a bomb to blow this place to smithereens in" – he glanced at his watch – "ninety-two seconds. So I don't think we have time for a chat."

He slid the case near Dr Liebermann's head,

checked the dead man one last time, then walked away. Alex followed him. What else could he do? Nile came to a set of doors and tapped in a code. The doors opened and they went through. They were moving quickly. Nile had the athlete's ability to cover a lot of ground with no apparent effort at all. Here was the staircase that Alex had been looking for. They went down three floors and came to another door. Nile punched in a number and suddenly they were in the open air. There was a car – a two-seater Alfa Romeo Spider – waiting outside with the roof down.

"Hop in!" Nile said. From the way he was talking, he and Alex could have just come from the cinema and been on their way home.

Alex got in and they drove off. How much time had passed since Nile had set the bomb? It was now completely dark outside. The sun had finally disappeared. They followed a tarmac drive to the main checkpoint. Nile smiled at the guard.

"Grazie. E'stato bello verdervi..."

Thank you. It was good to see you. Alex already knew from their first meeting that Nile spoke Italian. The guard nodded and raised the barrier.

Nile gunned the accelerator and the car shot off smoothly. Alex twisted round in his seat. A few seconds later there was an enormous explosion. It was as if a fist of orange flame had decided to punch its way out of the main complex. Windows shattered. Smoke and fire rushed out. Thousands of pieces of glass and steel, a deadly rainfall, showered down. Alarms – shrill and deafening – erupted. A huge bite had been taken out of the side and the roof of the building. Alex had seen the size of the bomb. It was hard to believe that it could have caused so much damage.

Nile glanced in the mirror, examining his handiwork. He tutted.

"These industrial accidents," he murmured. "You can never tell when one is going to happen next."

He steered the Alfa Spider along the coastal road, already doing eighty miles an hour. Behind him Consanto Enterprises burned, the flames leaping up and reflecting in the dark and silent sea.

DESIGNER LABELS

Alex stood on the balcony and gazed at the sweeping view of the town of Positano and the black water of the Mediterranean beyond. Two hours had passed since sunset but the warmth lingered in the air. He was dressed in a towelling robe, his hair still wet from the power shower with its jets of steaming hot water blasting him from all directions. There was a glass of fresh lime juice and ice on the table next to him. From the moment he had met Nile for the second time, he had thought he was in a dream. Now that dream seemed to have taken him in a new and very strange direction.

The hotel, first. It was called The Sirenuse and, as Nile had been eager to tell him, it was one of the most luxurious in the whole of southern Italy. Alex's room was huge and didn't look like a hotel room at all – more like a guest suite in an Italian palace. The bed was king-sized with pure white

Egyptian cotton sheets. He had his own desk, a thirty-six inch TV with Bose Bluetooth speakers, a sprawling leather sofa and, on the other side of the huge windows, his own private terrace. And the bathroom! As well as the power shower, there was a bath big enough for a football team, together with a spa bath. Everything was marble, and decorated with hand-crafted tiles. The million-aire suite. Alex shuddered to think how much it must cost a night.

Nile had driven him down here from what was left of Consanto Enterprises. Neither of them had spoken on the short journey. There were a hundred things Alex wanted to ask Nile, but the rush of wind and the roar of the Alfa Spider's 162kW quad camshaft V6 engine made conversation impossible. Anyway, Alex got the impression that Nile wasn't the one with the answers. It had only taken them twenty minutes, following the coastline, and suddenly they were there, parked in front of a hotel that was deceptively small and ordinary – from the outside.

While Alex signed in, Nile made a quick call on his mobile.

"Mrs Rothman is absolutely thrilled you're here," he said. "She's going to have dinner with you at nine thirty. She's asked me to send up some clothes." He weighed Alex up. "I've got a good eye for size. Do you have any particular likes or dislikes when it comes to style?"

Alex shrugged. "Whatever you want."

"Good. The bellboy will take you up to your room. I'm so glad I ran into you, Alex. I know you and I are going to be friends. Enjoy your dinner. The food here is world class."

He went back to the car and drove away.

I know you and I are going to be friends. Alex shook his head in disbelief. Just two nights ago the same man had knocked him unconscious and left him in a subterranean cell to drown.

He was shaken out of these thoughts by the arrival of an elderly man in a uniform, who gestured and then led Alex up to his room on the second floor, taking him along corridors filled with antiques and fine art. At last he was left on his own. He checked at once. The door was unlocked. The two phones on the desk had dialling tones. He could presumably call anyone, anywhere in the world ... and that included the police. He had, after all, just witnessed the destruction of a large part of Consanto Enterprises and the murder of Harold Liebermann. But Nile obviously trusted him to stay silent, at least until he had met Mrs Rothman. He could also walk out if he wanted to. Simply disappear. But again, they assumed he would want to stay. It was all very puzzling.

Alex sipped his drink and considered the view.

It was a beautiful night, the sky stretching to eternity with thousands of brilliant stars. He could hear the waves rolling in, far below. The town of

Positano was built on a steep hillside, shops, restaurants, houses and flats all piled up on top of one another, with a series of interlocking alleyways and a single, narrow street zigzagging all the way down to the horseshoe bay below. There were lights everywhere. The holiday season was drawing to a close but the place was still crowded with people determined to enjoy the summer right to the end.

There was a knock at the door. Alex went back into the room and walked across the shining marble floor. A waiter in a white jacket and a black bow tie had appeared. "Your clothes, sir," he said. He handed Alex a case. "Mr Nile suggested the suit for tonight," he added as he turned to leave.

Alex opened the case. It was full of clothes, all of them expensive, all of them brand new. The suit was on the top. He took it out and laid it on the bed. It was charcoal grey, silk, with a Miu Miu label. There was a white shirt to go with it: Armani. Underneath, he found a slim leather box. He opened it and gasped. They had even provided him with a new watch, a Baume & Mercier with a polished steel bracelet. He lifted it out and weighed it in his hand. It must have cost thousands of pounds. First the room, now all this! He was certainly having money thrown at him – and like the water in the power shower, it was coming from all directions.

He thought for a moment. He wasn't sure what

he was letting himself in for but he might as well play along with it for the time being. It was almost nine thirty and he was ravenous. He got dressed and examined himself in the mirror. The suit was in the classic mod style, with small lapels that barely came down to his chest, and tightly fitted trousers. The tie was dark blue, narrow and straight. Mrs Rothman had also provided him with black suede shoes from D&G. It was quite an outfit. Alex barely recognized himself.

At exactly nine thirty he entered the restaurant on the lower ground floor. The hotel, he now realized, was built on the side of the hill, so it was much bigger than it seemed, with much of it on levels below the entrance and reception. He found himself in a long arched room with tables spilling out onto another long terrace. It was lit by hundreds of tiny candles in glass chandeliers. The place was crowded. Waiters were hurrying from table to table and the room was filled with the clatter of knives against plates and the low murmur of conversation.

Mrs Rothman had the best table, in the middle of the terrace, with views over Positano and out to sea. She was sitting on her own with a glass of champagne, waiting for him. She wore a low-cut black dress set off by a simple diamond necklace. She saw him, smiled and waved. Alex walked over to her, feeling suddenly self-conscious in the suit. Most of the other diners seemed to be casually dressed. He wished now that he hadn't put on the tie.

"Alex, you look wonderful." She ran her dark eyes over him. "The suit fits you perfectly. It's Miu Miu, isn't it? I love the style. Please, sit down."

Alex took his place at the table. He wondered what anyone watching might think. A mother and her son out for the evening? He felt like an extra in a film – and he was beginning to wish someone would show him the script.

"It's been a while since I ate dinner with my own toy boy. Will you have some champagne?"

"No, thank you."

"What then?"

A waiter had appeared out of nowhere and was hovering by Alex, ready to take his order.

"I'll have an orange juice, please. Freshly squeezed. With ice."

The waiter bowed and went to fetch it. Alex waited for Mrs Rothman to speak. He was playing the game her way, and she was the one with the rules.

"The food here is absolutely wonderful," she informed him. "Some of the best cooking in Italy – and, of course, Italian is the best food in the world. I hope you don't mind, but I've already ordered for you. If there's anything you don't like, you can send it back."

"That's fine."

Mrs Rothman lifted her glass. Alex could see

the tiny bubbles rising to the surface in the honey-coloured liquid. "I shall drink to your health," she announced. "But first you have to say you've forgiven me. What happened to you at the Widow's Palace was monstrous. I feel totally embarrassed."

"You mean, trying to kill me," Alex said.

"My dear Alex! You came to my party without an invitation. You crept round the house and sneaked into my study. You mentioned a name which should have got you killed instantly, and you're really very lucky that Nile decided to drown you rather than break your neck. So although what happened was very unfortunate, you can hardly say it was unprovoked. Of course, it would all have been different if we'd known who you were."

"I told Nile my name."

"It obviously didn't register with him, and he didn't mention it to me until the morning afterwards. I was so shocked when I heard. I couldn't believe it. Alex Rider, the son of John Rider, in my house – and he'd been locked in that place and left to..." She shuddered and briefly closed her eyes. "We had to wait for the water to go down before we could open the door. I was sick with worry. I thought we were going to be too late. And then... We looked inside and there was nobody there. You'd done a Houdini and disappeared. I assume you swam down the old well?"

Alex nodded.

"I'm amazed it was big enough. Anyway, I was furious with Nile. He wasn't thinking. The very fact that you were called Rider should have been enough. And for him to run into you a second time at Consanto! What were you doing there, by the way?"

"I was looking for you."

She paused, thinking. "You must have seen the brochure in my desk. And did you overhear me talking to Harold Liebermann?" She didn't wait for an answer. "There's one thing I absolutely have to know. How did you get into the complex?"

"I jumped off the terrace at Ravello."

"With a parachute?"

"Of course."

Mrs Rothman threw back her head and laughed loudly. At that moment, she looked more like a film star than anyone Alex had ever met. Not just beautiful, but supremely confident. "That's wonderful," she declared. "That's really quite wonderful."

"It was a borrowed parachute," Alex added. "It belonged to the brother of a friend of mine. I've lost all his equipment. And they'll be wondering where I am."

Mrs Rothman was sympathetic. "You'd better call them and let them know you survived. And tomorrow I'll make sure your friend gets his money back for the equipment. It's the least I can do after everything that's happened."

The waiter arrived with Alex's orange juice and

the first course: two plates of ravioli. The little white parcels were wonderfully fresh, filled with wild mushrooms and served with a salad of rocket and Parmesan. Alex tasted one. He had to admit that the food was as delicious as Mrs Rothman had promised.

"What's wrong with Nile?" he asked.

"He can be exceptionally stupid. Act first, ask questions later. He never stops to think."

"I meant his skin."

"Oh that! He suffers from vitiligo. I'm sure you've heard of it. It's a skin disorder. His skin is lacking pigment cells or something like that. Poor Nile! He was born black but he'll be white by the time he dies. But let's not talk about him. There are so many other things we need to discuss."

"You knew my father."

"I knew him very well, Alex. He was an extremely good friend of mine. And I have to say, you're his spitting image. I can't tell you how strange it is to be sitting here with you. Here I am, fifteen years older. But you..." She looked deep into his eyes. Alex saw that she was examining him but at the same time he felt as if she were sucking something out of him. "It's almost as if he's come back," she said.

"I want to know about him."

"What can I tell you that you don't know already?"

"I don't know anything, except what Yassen

Gregorovich told me." Alex paused. This was the moment he had been dreading. This was the reason he was here. "Was he an assassin?" he asked.

But Mrs Rothman didn't answer. Her gaze had drifted away. "You met Yassen Gregorovich," she said. "Was it he who led you to me?"

"I was there when he died."

"I was sorry about Yassen. I heard he'd been killed."

"I want to know about my father," Alex insisted. "He worked for an organization called Scorpia. He was a killer. Is that right?"

"Your father was my friend."

"You're not answering my question," he said, trying not to get angry. Mrs Rothman seemed friendly enough but he already knew that she was very rich and very ruthless. He suspected that he would regret it if he got on the wrong side of her.

Mrs Rothman herself was perfectly calm. "I don't want to talk about him," she said. "Not yet. Not until I've had a chance to talk about you."

"What do you want to know about me?"

"I know a great deal about you already, Alex. You have an amazing reputation. That's the reason why we're sitting here tonight. I have an offer to make, something that may startle you. But I want you to understand, right from the start, that you're completely free. You can walk away any time. I don't want to hurt you. Quite the opposite. All I'm asking is that you consider what I have to say and then tell me what you think."

"And then you'll tell me about my dad?"

"Everything you want to know."

"All right."

Mrs Rothman had finished her champagne. She gestured with one hand and immediately a waiter appeared to refill her glass. "I love champagne," she said. "Are you sure you won't change your mind?"

"I don't drink alcohol."

"That's probably wise." Suddenly she was serious. "From what I understand, you've worked for MI6 four times," she began. "There was that business with the Stormbreaker computers. Then the school they sent you to in the French Alps. Then you were in Cuba. And finally you crossed paths with Damian Cray. What I want to know is, why did you do it? What did you get out of it?"

"What do you mean?"

"Were you paid?"

Alex shook his head. "No."

Mrs Rothman considered for a moment. "Then … are you a patriot?"

Alex shrugged. "I like Britain," he said. "And I suppose I'd fight for it if there was a war. But I wouldn't call myself a patriot. No."

"Then you need to answer my question. What are you doing risking your life and getting injured for MI6? You're not going to tell me it's because you're fond of Alan Blunt and Mrs Jones. I've met both of them and I can't say they did anything for me! You've put your life on the line for them, Alex. You've been hurt – nearly killed. Why?"

Alex was confused. "What are you getting at?" he demanded. "Why are you asking me all this?"

"Because, as I said, I want to make you an offer."

"What offer?"

Mrs Rothman ate some of her ravioli. She used only a fork, cutting each pasta envelope in half, then spearing it with the prongs. She ate very delicately, and Alex could see the pleasure in her eyes. It wasn't just food for her. It was a work of art.

"How would you like to work for me?" she asked.

"For Scorpia?"

"Yes."

"Like my father?"

She nodded.

"You're asking me to become a killer?"

"Perhaps." She smiled. "You have a great many skills, Alex. For a fourteen-year-old you're quite remarkable – and, of course, being so young, you could be very useful to us in all sorts of different ways. I imagine that's why Mr Blunt has been so keen to hang on to you. You can do things and go places that an adult can't."

"What is Scorpia?" Alex demanded. "What were you doing at Consanto? What *is* Consanto? What were they making in that complex? And why did you have to kill Dr Liebermann?"

Mrs Rothman finished eating her first course and

laid down her fork. Alex found himself hypnotized by the diamonds around her neck. They were reflecting the light from the candles, each jewel multiplying and magnifying the yellow flames.

"What a lot of questions!" she remarked. She shrugged. "Consanto Enterprises is a perfectly ordinary biomedical company. If you want to know about them, you can look them up on the internet. They have offices all over Italy. As to what we were doing there, I can't tell you. At the moment we're involved in an operation called Invisible Sword, but there's no reason for you to know anything about it. Not yet. I will, however, tell you why we had to kill Dr Liebermann. It's really very simple. It was because he was unreliable. We paid him a great deal to help us in a certain matter. He was worried about what he was doing and at the same time he wanted more money. A man like that can be a danger to us all. It was safer to get rid of him.

"But let's go back to your first question. You want to know about Scorpia. That's why you were in Venice and that's why you've followed me here. Very well. I'll tell you."

She sipped her champagne, then set the glass down. Alex suddenly realized that their table had been positioned so that they could talk without being overheard. Even so, Mrs Rothman moved a little closer before she spoke.

"As you guessed, Alex, Scorpia is a criminal

organization," she began. "The S stands for sabotage. The CORP comes from corruption. The I is intelligence – in other words, spying. And the A is for assassination. These are our main areas of expertise, though there are others. We are successful and that has made us powerful. We can be found all over the world. The secret services can't do anything about us. We're too big and they've left it too late. Anyway, occasionally some of them make use of us. They pay us to do their dirty work for them. We've learnt to live side by side!"

"And you want me to join you?" Alex put down his knife and fork, although he hadn't finished eating. "I'm not like you. I'm not like that at all."

"How strange. Your father was."

That hurt. She was talking about a man he had never had a chance to know. But her words cut straight to the heart of who and what he was.

"Alex, you have to grow up a little bit and stop seeing things in black and white. You work for MI6. Do you think of them as the good guys, the ones in white hats? I suppose that makes me the bad guy. Maybe I should be sitting here in a wheelchair with a bald head and a scar down my face, stroking a cat." She laughed at the thought. "Unfortunately it's not as simple as that any more. Not in the twenty-first century. Think about Alan Blunt for a minute. Quite apart from the number of people he's had killed around the world, look at the way he's used *you*, for heaven's sake! Did he ask nicely before he pulled you out of school and turned you into a spy? I don't think so! You've been exploited, Alex, and you know it."

"I'm not a killer," Alex protested. "I never could be."

"It's very strange that you should say that. I mean, I don't notice Damian Cray at the next table. I wonder what happened to him? Or how about that nice Dr Grief? I understand he didn't survive his last meeting with you."

"They were accidents."

"You seem to have had an awful lot of accidents in the last few months."

She paused. When she spoke again her voice was softer, like a teacher talking to a favourite pupil.

"I can see you're still upset about Dr Liebermann," she said. "Well, let me reassure you. He wasn't a nice man and I don't think anybody's going to miss him. In fact, I wouldn't be surprised if his wife didn't send us a thank-you card." She smiled as if at some private joke. "You could say his death was a shot in the arm for us all. And you have to remember, Alex. It was his choice. If he hadn't lied and cheated his company and come to work for us, he would still be alive. It wasn't all our fault."

"Of course it was your fault. You killed him!"

"Well, yes. I suppose that's true. But we're a very large international business. And sometimes it does happen that people get in our way and they end up dead. I'm sorry, but that's just how it is."

A waiter came and took away the plates. Alex finished his orange juice, hoping the ice would help clear his head.

"I still can't join Scorpia," he said.

"Why not?"

"I have to go back to school."

"I agree." Mrs Rothman leant towards him. "We have a school; I want to send you there. It's just that our school will teach you things that you might find a little more useful than logarithms and English grammar."

"What sort of things?"

"How to kill. You say you could never do it, but how can you be sure? If you go to Malagosto, you'll find out. Nile was a star student there; he's a perfect killer – or he would be. Unfortunately he has one rather irritating weakness."

"You mean his disease?"

"No. It's rather more annoying than that." She hesitated. "You could be better than him, Alex, in time. And although I know you don't like me mentioning it, your father was actually an instructor there. A brilliant one. We were all devastated when he died."

And there it was again. Everything began and ended with John Rider. Alex couldn't avoid it any longer. He had to know.

"Tell me about my father," he said. "That's the

reason I'm here. That's the only reason I came. How did he end up working for you? And how did he die?" Alex forced himself to go on. "I don't even know what his voice sounded like. I don't know anything about him at all."

"Are you sure you want to? It may hurt you."

Alex was silent.

Their waiter arrived with the main course. Mrs Rothman had chosen roast lamb; the meat was slightly pink and garlicky. A second waiter refilled her glass.

"All right," she said when they had gone. "Let's finish eating and talk about other things. You can tell me about Brookland. I want to know what music you listen to and what football team you support. Do you have a girlfriend? I'm sure a boy as handsome as you gets plenty of offers. Now I've made you blush. Have your dinner. I promise it's the best lamb you'll ever eat.

"And after we've finished, I'll take you upstairs and then I'll tell you everything you want to know."

ALBERT BRIDGE

She led him to a room at the top of the hotel. There was no bed, just two chairs and a trestle table with an Apple computer and, next to it, a few files.

"I had this flown down from Venice as soon as I knew you were here," Mrs Rothman explained. "I thought it was something you'd want to see."

Alex nodded. After the bustle of the restaurant, he felt strange being here – like an actor on stage when the scenery has been removed. The room was large with a high ceiling, and its emptiness made everything echo. He walked over to the table, suddenly nervous. At dinner he had asked certain questions. Now he was going to be given the answers. Would he like what he heard?

Mrs Rothman came and stood beside him, her high heels rapping on the marble floor. She seemed completely relaxed. "Sit down," she invited.

Alex slipped off his jacket and hung it over the

back of a chair. He loosened his tie, then sat. Mrs Rothman stood next to the table, studying him. It was a moment before she spoke.

"Alex," she began. "It's not too late to change your mind."

"I don't want to," he said.

"It's just that, if I'm going to talk to you about your father, I may say things that will upset you and I don't want to do that. Does the past really matter? Does it make any difference?"

"I think it does."

"Very well..."

She opened a file and took out a black and white photograph. It showed a handsome man in military uniform, wearing a beret. He was looking straight at the camera with his shoulders back and his hands clasped behind him. He was clean-shaven, with watchful, intelligent eyes.

"This is your father, aged twenty-five. The photograph was taken five years before you were born. Do you really know nothing about him?"

"My uncle spoke to me about him a bit. I know he was in the army."

"Well, maybe I can fill in some gaps for you. I'm sure you know that he was born in London and went to a secondary school in Westminster. From there he went to Oxford and got a first in politics and economics. But his heart had always been set on joining the army. And that's what he did. He joined the Parachute Regiment at Aldershot. That in itself was quite an achievement. The Paras are one of the toughest regiments in the British Army, second only to the SAS. And you don't just join them; you have to be invited.

"Your father spent three years with the Paras. He saw action in Northern Ireland and Gambia, and he was part of the attack on Goose Green in the Falkland Islands in May 1982. He carried a wounded soldier to safety even though he was under fire and, as a result of this, he received a medal from the Queen. He was also promoted to the rank of captain."

Alex had once seen the medal: the Military Cross. Ian Rider had always kept it in the top drawer of his desk.

"He returned to England and got married," Mrs Rothman went on. "He had met your mother at Oxford. She was studying medicine and eventually became a nurse. But I can't tell you very much about her. We never met and he never spoke about her, not to me.

"Anyway, I'm afraid it was shortly after he got married that things started to go wrong ... not, of course, that I'm blaming your mother. But just a few weeks after the wedding, your father was in a pub in London when he got involved in a fight. There were some people making remarks about the Falklands War. They were probably drunk. I don't know. There was a skirmish and he struck a man and killed him. It was a single blow to the throat

... just like he had been trained to inflict. And that, I'm afraid, was that."

Mrs Rothman took out a newspaper clipping from the file and handed it to Alex. It had to be at least fifteen years old. He could tell from the faded print and the way the paper had yellowed. He read the headline:

Jail for 'brilliant soldier' who lost his way

John Rider, described as a brilliant

There was another photo of John Rider but now he was in civilian dress, surrounded by photographers, getting out of a car. The picture was a little blurred and it had been taken long ago, but looking at it Alex could almost feel the pain of the man, the sense that the world had turned against him.

He read the article.

John Rider, described as a brilliant soldier by his commanding officer, was sentenced to four years for manslaughter following the death of Ed Savitt nine months ago in a Soho bar.

The jury heard that Rider, twenty-seven, had been drinking heavily when he became involved in a fight with Savitt, a taxi driver. Rider, who was decorated for valour in the Falklands War, killed Savitt with a single blow to the head. The jury heard that Rider was a highly trained expert in several martial arts.

Summing up, Judge Gillian Padgham said: "Captain Rider has thrown away a promising army career in a single moment of madness. I have taken his distinguished record into consideration. But he has taken a life and society demands that he pays the price…"

"I'm sorry," Mrs Rothman said softly. She had been watching Alex closely. "You didn't know."

"My uncle showed me the medal once," Alex said. He had to stop for a moment. His voice was hoarse. "But he never showed me this."

"It wasn't your father's fault. He was provoked."

"What happened next?"

"He was sent to jail. There was quite an outcry about it. He had a lot of public sympathy. But the fact was, he had killed a man and he was found guilty of manslaughter. The judge had no choice."

"And then?"

"They let him out after just a year. It was done very quietly. Your mother had stood by him; she never lost faith in him and he went back to live with her. Unfortunately his army career was over; he had received a dishonourable discharge. He was very much on his own."

"Go on." Alex's voice was cold.

"He found it difficult to get a job. It wasn't his fault; that's just the way it is. But by this time, he had come to the attention of our personnel department." Mrs Rothman paused. "Scorpia are always on the lookout for fresh talent," she explained. "It seemed quite obvious to us that your father had been unfairly treated. We thought he would be perfect for us."

"You approached him?"

"Yes. Your parents had very little money by this time. They were desperate. One of our people met your father, and two weeks later he came to us for evaluation." She smiled. "We test every new recruit, Alex. If you decide to join us, and I still hope you will, we'll take you to the same place we took your father."

"Where is that?"

"I mentioned the name to you. Malagosto. It's near Venice." Mrs Rothman wouldn't be any more precise than that. "We could see at once that your father was extremely tough and exceptionally talented," she went on. "He passed every test we threw at him with flying colours. We knew, by the way, that he had a brother – Ian Rider – working for MI6. I was always a little surprised that Ian didn't try to help him when he got into trouble, but I suppose there was nothing he could do. Anyway, it made no difference, the two of them being brothers. Your father was indeed perfect for us. And after what had happened to him, I have to say that we were certainly perfect for him."

Alex was getting tired. It was almost eleven. But he knew there was no way he was leaving this room until the whole story had been told.

"So he joined Scorpia," he said.

"Yes. Your father worked for us as an assassin. He spent four months in the field."

"How many men did he kill?"

"Five or six. He was more interested in working as an instructor in the training school where he had been evaluated. You might like to know, Alex, that Yassen Gregorovich was one of the assassins he helped train. Your father actually saved Yassen's life when they were on an assignment in the Amazon jungle."

Alex knew that Mrs Rothman was telling the truth. Yassen had said as much himself in the final seconds before he died.

"I got to know your father very well," Mrs Rothman went on. "We had dinner together many times, once even in this hotel." She threw her head back, letting her black hair trail down her neck, and for a moment her eyes were far away. "I was very attracted to him. He was an extremely good-looking man. He was also intelligent and he made me laugh. It was just unfortunate that he was married to your mother."

"Did she know what he was doing? Did she know about you?"

"I very much hope not." Suddenly Mrs Rothman

was businesslike. "I have to tell you now how your father died. I wish you hadn't asked me to do this. Are you sure you want me to carry on?"

"Yes."

"All right." She took a deep breath. "MI6 wanted him. He was one of our best operatives and he was training others to become as effective as him. And so they set about hunting him down. I won't go into the details, but they set a trap for him on the island of Malta. As it happened, Yassen Gregorovich was there too. He escaped – but your father was captured. We assumed that would be the last of him and that we would never see him again. You may think that the death penalty has been abolished in Britain, but – as they say – accidents happen. But then there was a development...

"Scorpia had kidnapped the eighteen-year-old son of a senior British civil servant, a man with considerable influence in the government – or so we thought. Again, it's a complicated story and it's late, so I won't give you all the details. But the general idea was that if the father didn't do what we wanted, we would kill the son."

"That's what you do, is it?" Alex asked.

"Corruption and assassination, Alex. It's part of what we do. Anyway, as we quickly discovered, the civil servant was unable to do what we wanted. Unfortunately this meant we would have to kill the son. You can't make a threat and then have second thoughts about it, because if you do, nobody will ever fear you again. And so we were about to kill the boy in as dramatic a way as possible. But then, out of the blue, MI6 got in touch with us and offered us a deal.

"It was a straight swap. They'd give us back John Rider in return for the son. The executive board of Scorpia met and, although it was only carried by a narrow vote, we decided to go ahead with the deal. Normally we would never have allowed an operation to become entangled in this way, but your father had been extremely valuable to us and, as I said, I was personally very close to him. So it was agreed. We would make the exchange at six o'clock in the morning – this was March. And it would take place on Albert Bridge."

"March? What year was this?"

"It was fourteen years ago, Alex: 13th March. You were two months old."

Mrs Rothman leant over the table and rested a hand beside the computer keyboard.

"Scorpia have always made a practice of recording everything that we do," she explained. "There's a good reason for this. We're a criminal organization. It automatically follows that nobody trusts us – not even our clients. They assume we lie, cheat … whatever. We film what we do to prove that we are, in our own way, honest. What you are about to see was originally shot on video tape but we've had it re-digitised. We filmed the hand-over on Albert Bridge. If the civil servant's son had been hurt in some way, we would have been able to prove that it wasn't because of us."

She hit one of the keys and the screen flickered into life, showing images that had been taken in another time, when Alex was just eight weeks old. The first shot showed Albert Bridge, stretching over a chilly River Thames with Battersea Park on one side and the lower reaches of Chelsea on the other. It was drizzling. Tiny specks of water hovered in the air.

"We had three cameras," she said. "We had to conceal them carefully or MI6 would have removed them. But as you'll see, they tell the whole tale."

The first image. Three men in suits and overcoats. With them, a young man with his hands bound in front of him. This must be the son. He looked younger than eighteen. He was shivering.

"You are looking at the southern end of the bridge," Mrs Rothman explained. "This was what had been agreed. Our agents would bring the son up from the park. MI6 and your father would be on the other bank. The two of them would walk across the bridge and the exchange would be made. As simple as that."

"There's no traffic," Alex said.

"At six o'clock in the morning? There would have been little anyway, but I suspect MI6 had probably closed the roads."

The image changed. Alex felt something twist in his stomach. The camera was concealed somewhere on the edge of the bridge, high up. It was showing him his father, the first moving image of John Rider he had ever seen. He was wearing a thick padded jacket. He was looking around him, taking everything in. Alex wished the camera would zoom in closer. He wanted to see more of his father's face.

"This is the classic method of exchange," Mrs Rothman told him. "A bridge is a neutral area. The two participants – in this case the boy and your father – are on their own. Nothing should go wrong."

She reached out a finger and touched the *pause* button.

"Alex," she warned. "Your father died on Albert Bridge. I know you never knew him; you were just a baby when this happened. But I'm still not sure it's something you should see."

"Show me," Alex ordered. His voice sounded far away.

Mrs Rothman nodded. She pressed *play*.

The image unfroze. The pictures were now being taken by a hidden camera, hand-held, out of focus. Alex caught sight of the span of the bridge, hundreds of light bulbs curving through the air. There was the river again and, captured briefly in the distance, the great chimneys of Battersea Power Station. There was a cut. Now the picture was steady, a wide angle perhaps taken from a boat.

The three men with the civil servant's son were

at one end. His father was at the other. Alex could make out three figures behind him; presumably they worked for MI6. The image quality was poor. Dawn was only just breaking and there was little light. The water had no colour. A signal must have been given because the young man began to walk forward. At the same time, John Rider left the other group, also with his hands bound in front of him.

Alex wanted to reach out and touch the screen. He was watching his father walk towards the three Scorpia men. But the figure in the picture was only a centimetre high. Alex knew it was his father. The face matched the photographs he had seen. But he was too far away. He couldn't see if John Rider was smiling or angry or nervous. Could he have had any idea of what was about to happen?

John Rider and the civil servant's son met in the middle of the bridge. They paused and seemed to speak to each other – but the only sound on the film was the soft patter of the rain and the occasional rush of an unseen speeding car. Then they began to walk again. The son was on the north side of the bridge, the side controlled by MI6. John Rider was moving south, a little faster now, heading for the waiting men.

"This is when it happened," Mrs Rothman said softly.

Alex's father was almost running. He must have sensed that something was wrong. He moved awkwardly, his hands still clasped in front of him. On

147

the north side of the bridge, one of the MI6 people took out a radio transmitter and spoke briefly. A second later, there was a single shot. John Rider seemed to stumble and Alex realized that he had been hit in the back. He took two more steps, twisted and collapsed.

"Do you want me to turn it off, Alex?"

"No."

"There's a closer shot..."

The camera angle was lower. Alex could see his father lying on his side. The three Scorpia men had produced guns. They were running, aiming at the civil servant's son. Alex wondered why. The teenager hadn't had anything to do with what had just taken place. But then he understood. MI6 had shot John Rider. They hadn't kept their side of the bargain. So the son had to die too.

But he had reacted incredibly quickly. He was already running, his head down. He seemed to know exactly what was happening. One of the Scorpia men fired and missed. Then there was a sudden explosion, a machine gun opening fire. Alex saw bullets ricocheting off the iron girders of the bridge. Light bulbs smashed. The tarmac surface seemed to leap up. The men hesitated and fell back. Meanwhile the teenager had reached the far end of the bridge. A car surged forward out of nowhere. Alex saw the door open and the son was pulled inside.

Mrs Rothman froze the image.

"It seems that MI6 wanted the son back but they weren't prepared to pay with your father's freedom," she said. "They double-crossed us and shot him in front of our eyes. You saw for yourself."

Alex said nothing. The room seemed to have got darker, shadows chasing in from the corners. He felt cold from head to toe.

"There is one last part of the film," Mrs Rothman went on. "I hate seeing you like this, Alex. I hate having to show you. But you've seen this much; you might as well see the rest."

The last section of the film replayed the final moments of John Rider's life. Once again he was on his feet, beginning to run while the civil servant's son hurried the other way.

"Look at the MI6 agent who gave the order to fire," Mrs Rothman said.

Alex gazed at the tiny figures on the bridge.

Mrs Rothman pointed. "We had the image computer enhanced."

Sure enough, the camera leapt in closer, and now Alex could see that the MI6 agent with the transmitter was in fact a woman, wearing a black raincoat.

"We can get in closer."

The camera jumped forward again.

"And closer."

The same action, repeated a third and fourth time. The woman taking out her radio transmitter. But now her face filled the screen. Alex could see her fingers holding the device in front of her mouth. There was no sound, but he saw her lips move, giving the order, and he understood perfectly what she said.

Shoot him.

"There was a sniper in an office block on the north bank of the Thames," Mrs Rothman told him. "It was really just a matter of timing. The woman you're looking at masterminded the operation. It was one of her early successes in the field, one of the reasons why she was promoted. You know who she is."

Alex had known at once. She was fourteen years younger on the screen but she hadn't changed all that much. And there could be no mistaking the black hair – cut short – the pale, businesslike face, the black eyes that could have belonged to a crow.

Mrs Jones, the deputy head of Special Operations at MI6.

Mrs Jones, who had been there when Alex was first recruited and who had pretended that she was his friend. When he had returned to London, hurt and exhausted after his ordeal with Damian Cray, she had come looking for him and tried to help him. She had said she was worried about him. And all the time she had been lying. She had sat next to him and smiled at him, knowing that she had taken his father from him just weeks after he was born.

Mrs Rothman turned off the screen.

There was a long silence.

"They told me he died in a plane crash," Alex said in a voice that wasn't his own.

"Of course. They didn't want you to know."

"So what happened to my mother?" He felt a sudden rush of hope. If they had been lying about his father, then maybe she wasn't dead. Could it be at all possible? Was his mother somewhere in England, still alive?

"I'm so sorry, Alex. There *was* a plane crash. It happened a few months later. It was a private plane, and she was on her own, travelling to France." Mrs Rothman rested a hand on his arm. "Nothing can make up for what's been done to you, for all the lies you've been told. If you want to go back to England, back to school, I'll understand. I'm sure you just want to forget the whole lot of us. But if it's any consolation, I adored your father. I still miss him. This was the last thing he sent me, just before he was taken prisoner in Malta."

She had opened a second file and taken out a postcard. It showed a strip of coastline, a setting sun. There were just a few lines, handwritten.

My dearest Julia,
A dreary time without you. Can't wait to be at the Widow's Palace with you again.
John R.

Alex recognized the handwriting although he had never seen it before, and in that instant any last, lingering doubt was swept away.

The writing was his father's.

But it was identical to his own.

"It's very late," Mrs Rothman said. "You really ought to get to bed. We can talk again tomorrow."

Alex looked at the screen as if expecting to see Mrs Jones mocking him across fourteen years, destroying his life before it had even really begun. For a long while he didn't speak. Then he stood up.

"I want to join Scorpia," he said.

"Are you sure?"

"Yes."

Go to Venice. Find Scorpia. Find your destiny, Yassen had told him. And that was what had happened. He had made up his mind. There could be no going back.

HOW TO KILL

The island was only a few miles from Venice but it had been forgotten for a hundred years. Its name was Malagosto and it was shaped roughly like a crescent moon, just half a mile long. There were six buildings on the island, surrounded by wild grasses and poplars, and they all looked condemned. The largest of them was a monastery, built around a courtyard, with a red-brick bell tower, slanting very slightly, next to it. There was a crumbling hospital and then a row of what looked like apartment blocks with shattered windows and gaping holes in the roofs. A few boats went past Malagosto but never docked there. It was forbidden. And the place had a bad reputation.

There had once been a small, thriving community on the island. But that had been long ago, in the Middle Ages. It had been ransacked in 1380, during the war with Genoa, and after that it had been used for plague victims. Sneeze in Venice, it was said, and you would end up in Malagosto. When the plague died out it became a quarantine centre, and then, in the eighteenth century, a sanctuary for the insane. Finally it had been abandoned and left to rot. But there were fishermen who claimed that, on a cold winter's night, you could still hear the screams and demented laughter of the lunatics who had been the island's last residents.

Malagosto was the perfect base for Scorpia's Training and Assessment Centre. They had bought the island on a lease from the Italian government in the mid-eighties and they had been there ever since. If anyone asked what was happening there, they were told that it was now a business centre where lawyers, bankers and office managers could come for motivation and bonding sessions. This was, of course, a lie. Scorpia sent new recruits to the school that they ran on Malagosto. It was here that they learnt how to kill.

Alex Rider sat at the front of the motor launch, watching as the island drew nearer. It was the same motor launch that had led him to the Widow's Palace and the silver scorpion on the bow glistened in the sun. Nile was sitting opposite him, totally relaxed, dressed in white trousers and a blazer.

"I spent three months in training here," he shouted over the noise of the engine. "But that was a long time after your dad."

Alex nodded but said nothing. He could see the bell tower looming up, rising crookedly over the tops of the trees. The wind chased through his hair and the spray danced in his eyes.

Julia Rothman had left Positano before them that morning, returning to Venice, where she was involved in something that required her presence. They had met briefly after breakfast and this time she had been more serious and businesslike. Alex would spend the next few days on Malagosto, she said – not for full training, but for an initial assessment that would include a medical examination, psychological testing and a general overview of his fitness and aptitude. It would also give Alex time to reflect on his decision.

Alex's mind was dead. He had made his decision and, as far as he was concerned, nothing else mattered. Only one good thing had come out of last night. He hadn't forgotten Tom Harris and his brother. They had heard nothing from him since he had broken into Consanto yesterday evening – and there was still the question of all Jerry's equipment, left behind on the roof. But Mrs Rothman had promised to deal with that, as Alex had reminded her.

"Go ahead and call them," she had said. "Apart from anything else, we don't want them worrying about you and raising the alarm. As for the parachute and all the rest of it, I already told you. I'll send your friend's brother enough money to cover the cost. Five thousand euros? That should do it." She had smiled. "You see, Alex? That's what I mean. We want to look after you."

After she had gone, Alex called Tom from his room. Tom was delighted to hear from him.

"We saw you land so we knew you hadn't got splatted," he said. "Then nothing happened for a while. And then the whole place blew up. Was that you?"

"Not exactly," Alex said.

"Where are you?"

"I'm in Positano. I'm OK. But, Tom, listen to me..."

"I know." Tom's voice was flat. "You're not coming back to school."

"Not for a bit."

"Is this MI6 again?"

"Sort of. I'll tell you one day." That was a lie. Alex knew he would never see his friend again. "Just tell Jerry that someone's going to pay for all his stuff. They're sending him the cash. And tell him thanks from me."

"What about Brookland?"

"It would be easier if you said you never saw me. As far as they're concerned, I disappeared in Venice and that was that."

"Alex ... you sound strange. Are you sure you're all right?"

"I'm fine, Tom. Goodbye."

He hung up and felt a wave of sadness. It was as

if Tom was the last link to the world he had known – and he had just severed the connection.

The boat pulled in. There was a jetty, carefully concealed in a natural fault line in the rock so that nobody could be watched arriving at or leaving the island. Nile sprang ashore. He had the ease and grace of a ballet dancer. Alex had noticed the same thing once about Yassen Gregorovich.

"This way, Alex."

Alex followed. The two of them walked up a twisting path between the trees. For a moment the buildings were hidden.

"Can I tell you something?" Nile said. He flashed Alex his friendliest smile. "I was delighted you decided to join us. It's great to have you on the winning side."

"Thank you."

"But I hope you never change your mind, Alex. I hope you never try to trick us or anything like that. I'm sure you won't. But after what happened at the Widow's Palace, I'd hate to have to murder you again."

"Yes. It wasn't much fun the last time," Alex agreed.

"It would really upset me. Mrs Rothman is expecting great things from you. I hope you don't let her down."

They had passed through the copse and there was the monastery, its great walls peeling from age and neglect. There was a heavy wooden door with a smaller door set in it, and next to it the one sign that the building might, after all, have been adapted to modern times: a keypad with a built-in video camera. Nile tapped in a code. There was an electronic buzz and the smaller door opened.

"Welcome back to school!" Nile announced.

Alex hesitated. The new term at Brookland would start in a few days' time. And here he was about to enter a school of a very different kind. But it was too late for second thoughts. He was following the path his father had mapped out for him.

Nile was waiting. Alex went in.

He found himself in a open courtyard with cloisters on three sides and the bell tower rising up above the fourth. The ground was a neat rectangle of grass with two cypress trees side by side at one end. A tile roof slanted in, covering the cloisters, like an old-fashioned tennis court. Five men dressed in white robes stood around an instructor, an older man dressed in black. As Alex and Nile entered, they stepped forward as one, lashed out with their fists and shouted – the *kiai* that Alex knew from karate.

"Sometimes, with the silent kill, it is not possible to shout out," the instructor said. He spoke with a Russian or Eastern European accent. "But remember the power of the silent *kiai*. Use it to drive your chi into the strike zone. Do not underestimate its power at the moment of the kill."

"That's Professor Yermalov," Nile told Alex. "He

taught me when I was here. You don't want to get on the wrong side of him, Alex. I've seen him finish a fight with a single finger. Fast as a snake and about as friendly..."

They crossed the courtyard and went through an archway into a vast room with a multicoloured mosaic floor, ornate windows, pillars and intricate wooden angels carved into the walls. This might once have been a place of worship; now it was used as a refectory and meeting place, with long tables, modern sofas and a hatch leading into a kitchen beyond. The ceiling was domed and carried the faint remnants of a fresco. There had been angels here too but they had long ago faded.

There was a door on the far side. Nile went over to it and knocked.

"*Entrez!*" The voice, speaking French, was friendly.

They went into a tall, octagonal room. Books lined five of the eight walls. The ceiling, painted blue with silver stars, was at least twenty metres high. There was a ladder on wheels reaching up to the top shelves. Two windows looked out onto more woodland but much of the light was blocked out by leaves, and an iron chandelier with about a dozen electric bulbs hung down on a heavy chain. The centre of the room was taken up by a solid-looking desk with two antique chairs in front of it and one behind. This third chair was occupied by a small, plump man in a suit and waistcoat. He was working at a laptop, his stubby fingers typing at great speed. He was peering at the screen through gold-rimmed glasses. He had a neat black beard that tapered to a point under his chin. The rest of his hair was grey.

"Alex Rider! Please ... come in." The man looked up from his computer with obvious pleasure. "I would have recognized you at once. I knew your father very well and you look just like him." Apart from a slight French accent, his English was perfect. "My name is Oliver d'Arc. I am, you might say, the principal of this establishment – the head teacher, perhaps. I was just looking at your personal details online."

Alex sat down on one of the antique chairs. "I wouldn't have thought they'd be posted on the Internet," he commented.

"It depends which search engine you use." D'Arc gave Alex a sly smile. "I know Mrs Rothman told you that your father was an instructor here. I worked with him and he was a good friend to me, but I never dreamt that I would one day meet his son. And it is Nile who brings you here. Nile graduated from here a few years ago. He was a brilliant student – the number two in his class."

Alex glanced at Nile and for the first time saw a flicker of annoyance cross the man's face. He remembered what Mrs Rothman had said ... something about Nile having a weakness ... and he wondered what it was that had prevented him becoming number one.

"Are you thirsty after your journey?" d'Arc asked. "Can I get you anything? A *sirop de grenadine*, perhaps?"

Alex started. The red fruit juice was his favourite drink when he was in France. Had d'Arc got that off the Internet too?

"It was what your father always drank," d'Arc explained, reading his thoughts.

"I'm all right, thank you."

"Then let me tell you the programme. Nile will introduce you to the other students who are here at Malagosto. There are never more than fifteen and at the moment there are only eleven. Nine men and two women. You will join in with them and over the next few days we will examine your progress. Eventually, if I consider you have the ability to become part of Scorpia, I will write a report and your real training will begin. But I have no doubts, Alex. You are very young, only fourteen. But you are John Rider's son and he was the very best."

"There's something I have to tell you," Alex said.

"Please. Go ahead." D'Arc sat back, beaming.

"I want to join Scorpia. I want to be part of what you do. But you might as well know now that I don't think I could kill anybody. I told Mrs Rothman and she didn't believe me. She said I'd only be doing what my dad had done, but I know how I am inside and I know I'm different to him."

Alex hadn't been sure how d'Arc would react. But he seemed completely unconcerned. "There are a great many Scorpia activities that do not involve killing," he said. "You could be very useful to us, for example, for blackmail. Or as a courier. Who would suspect that a fourteen-year-old on a school trip was carrying drugs or plastic explosives? But these are early days, Alex. You have to trust us. We will discover what you can and can't do and we will find the work that suits you best."

"I was eighteen when I killed my first man," Nile added. "That's only four years older than you are now."

"But, Nile, you were always exceptional," d'Arc purred.

There was a knock at the door and a moment later a woman came in. She was Thai, slender and delicate and several inches shorter than Alex. She had dark, intelligent eyes and lips that could have been drawn with an artist's pencil. She stopped and made the traditional greeting of the Thai people, bringing her hands together as if in prayer and bowing her head.

"*Sawasdee*, Alex," she said. "It is very nice to meet you." She had a very gentle voice and, like the principal, her English was excellent.

"This is Miss Binnag," d'Arc said.

"My name is Eijit. But you can call me Jet. I have come to take you to your room."

"You can rest this afternoon and I will see you

again at dinner." D'Arc stood up. He was very short. His pointed beard only just rose above the level of the desk. "I'm so glad you're here, Alex. Welcome to Malagosto."

The woman called Jet led Alex out of the room, back across the main hall and down a corridor with a high vaulted ceiling and bare plaster walls.

"What do you do here?" Alex asked.

"I teach botany."

"Botany?" He couldn't keep the surprise out of his voice.

"It is a very important part of the syllabus," Jet retorted. "There are many plants that can be useful to our work. The oleander bush, for example. You can extract a poison similar to digitalis from the leaves and this will paralyse the nervous system and cause immediate death. The berries of the mistletoe can also be fatal. You must learn how to grow the rosary pea. Just one pea can kill an adult in minutes. Tomorrow you can come to my greenhouse, Alex. Every flower there is another funeral."

She spoke in a way that was completely matter-of-fact. Again Alex felt a sense of unease. But he said nothing.

They passed a classroom that might once have been a chapel, with more faded frescos on the walls, and no windows. Another teacher, with ginger hair and a ruddy, weather-beaten face, was standing in front of a whiteboard, talking to half a dozen students, two of them women. There was a complicated diagram on the board and each student had what looked like a cigar box on the desk in front of them.

"...and you can lead the main circuit through the lid and back into the plastic explosive," he was saying. "And it's right here, in front of the lock, that I always put the trembler switch..."

Jet had paused briefly at the door. "This is Mr Ross," she whispered. "Technical specialist. He's from your country, from Glasgow. You'll meet him tonight."

They moved on. Behind him, Alex heard Mr Ross speaking again.

"Do try and concentrate, please, Miss Craig. We don't want you blowing us all up..."

They left the main building and walked over to the nearest apartment block that Alex had seen from the boat. Again, the building looked dilapidated from the outside but it was elegant and modern inside. Jet showed Alex to an air-conditioned room on the second floor. It was on two levels, with a king-sized bed overlooking a large living space with sofas and a desk. There were french windows with a balcony and a sea view.

"I'll come back for you at five," Jet told him. "You have an appointment with the nurse. Mrs Rothman wants you to have a complete examination. We meet for drinks at six and dinner is early, at seven. There's a night exercise tonight; the students are diving. But don't worry. You won't be taking part."

She bowed a second time and backed out of the room. Alex was left alone. He sat down on one of the sofas, noticing that the room had a fridge, a television and even a PlayStation – presumably put in for his benefit.

What had he got himself into? Had he done the right thing? Dark uncertainties rose up in his mind and he deliberately forced them back again. He remembered the film he had been shown, the terrible images he had seen. Mrs Jones mouthing those two words into the radio transmitter. He closed his eyes.

Outside, the waves broke against the island shore and the students in their white robes went once again through the motions of the silent kill.

Just over seven hundred miles away, the woman who had been so much in Alex's thoughts was examining a photograph. There was a single sheet of paper attached to it and both were stamped with the words TOP SECRET in red. The woman knew what the photo meant. There was only one course of action open to her. But for once – and for her it really was a first – she was reluctant. She couldn't allow emotion to get in the way. That was when mistakes were made, and in her line of work that could be disastrous. But even so...

Mrs Jones took off her reading glasses and

rubbed her eyes. She had received the photograph and report a few minutes ago. Since then she had made two calls, hoping against hope that there might have been a mistake. But there could be no doubt. The evidence was right there in front of her. She reached out and pressed a button on her phone, then spoke.

"William – is Mr Blunt in his office?"

In an outer office her personal assistant, William Dearly, glanced at his computer screen. He was twenty-three, a Cambridge graduate; he was in a wheelchair. "He hasn't left the building yet, Mrs Jones."

"Any meetings?"

"Nothing scheduled."

"Right. I'm going there now."

It had to be done. Mrs Jones took the photograph and the typed sheet and walked down the corridor on the sixteenth floor of the building that pretended to be an international bank but which was in fact the headquarters of MI6 Special Operations. Alan Blunt was her immediate superior. She wondered how he would react to the news that Alex Rider had joined Scorpia.

Blunt's office was at the very end of the corridor with views overlooking Liverpool Street. Mrs Jones entered without knocking. There was no need. William would have rung to say she was coming. And sure enough, Blunt registered no surprise as she came in. Not that his round, strangely featureless face ever showed any emotion. He too had been reading a report, several centimetres thick. She could see he had made neat notes using a fountain pen and green ink for instant recognition.

"Yes?" he asked as she sat down.

"This just came in from SatInt. I thought you should see it." SatInt was satellite intelligence. She passed it across.

Mrs Jones watched Alan Blunt carefully as he read the single page. She had been his deputy for seven years and had worked with him for another ten before that. She had never been to his home. She had never met his wife. But she probably knew him better than anyone in the building. And she was worried about him. Quite recently he had made a huge mistake, refusing to believe Alex when it came to that business with Damian Cray. As a result, Cray had come within minutes of destroying half the world. Blunt had been given a severe dressing down by the home secretary, but it wasn't just that he was finding hard to live with. It was the fact that he, the head of Special Operations, had been bettered by a fourteen-year-old-boy. Mrs Jones wondered how much longer he would stay.

Now he examined the photograph, his eyes unblinking behind his steel-framed spectacles. It showed two figures, a man and a boy, getting out of a boat. It had been taken above Malagosto and blown up many times. Both faces were blurred.

"Alex Rider?" Blunt asked. There was a dead tone to his voice.

"The picture was taken by a spy satellite," Mrs Jones said. "But Smithers ran it through one of his computers and it's definitely him."

"Who is the man with him?"

"We think it could be a Scorpia agent called Nile. It's hard to tell. The photograph is black and white, but so is he. I've downloaded his details for you."

"Are we to infer that Rider has decided to switch sides?"

"I've spoken to his housekeeper, the American girl ... Jack Starbright. It seems that Alex disappeared four days ago from a school trip to Venice."

"Disappeared where?"

"She didn't know. It's very surprising that he hasn't been in touch with her. She's his closest friend."

"Is it possible that the boy has somehow become involved with Scorpia and has been taken by force?"

"I'd like to believe it." Mrs Jones sighed. It couldn't be avoided any longer. "But there was always a chance that Yassen Gregorovich managed to speak to Alex before he died. When I met Alex after the Cray business, I knew something was wrong. I think Yassen must have told him about John Rider."

"Albert Bridge."

"Yes."

"That's very unfortunate."

There was a long silence. Mrs Jones knew that Blunt would be turning over a dozen possibilities in his mind, considering and eliminating each one in a matter of seconds. She had never met anyone with such an analytical brain.

"Scorpia haven't been very active recently," he said.

"It's true. They've been very quiet. We think they may have been involved in a piece of sabotage at Consanto Enterprises, near Amalfi, yesterday evening."

"The biomedical people?"

"Yes. We've only just received the reports and we're looking into them. There may be a link."

"If Scorpia have turned Alex, they'll use him against us."

"I know."

Blunt took a last look at the photograph. "This is Malagosto," he said. "And that means he isn't their prisoner. They're training him. I think we should step up your security rating with immediate effect."

"And yours?"

"I wasn't on Albert Bridge." He laid the photograph down. "I want all local agents in Venice placed on immediate alert, and we'd better contact airports and all points of entry into the UK. I want Alex Rider brought in."

"Unharmed." The single word was spoken as a challenge.

Blunt looked at her with empty eyes. "Whatever it takes."

THE BELL TOWER

"So tell me, Alex. What do you see?"

Alex was sitting in a leather chair in a plain, whitewashed room at the back of the monastery. He was on one side of a desk, facing a smiling middle-aged man who sat on the other. The man's name was Dr Karl Steiner and, although he spoke with a slight German accent, he had come to the island from South Africa. He was a psychiatrist and looked it – with silver-framed glasses, thinning hair and eyes that were always more inquisitive than friendly. Dr Steiner was holding a white card with a black shape on it. The shape looked like nothing at all; it was just a series of blobs. But Alex was meant to be able to interpret it.

He thought for a moment. He knew that this was called a Rorschach test; he had seen it once in a film. He supposed it must be important. But he wasn't sure that he saw anything in particular on the card. Eventually he spoke.

"I suppose it's a man flying through the sky," he suggested. "He's wearing a backpack."

"That's excellent. Very good!" Dr Steiner put the card down and picked up another. "How about this one?"

The second shape was easier. "It's a football being pumped up," Alex said.

"Good, thank you."

Dr Steiner laid the second card down and there was a brief silence in the office. Outside, Alex could hear gunfire. The other students were down on the shooting range. But there was no view of the range out of the window. Perhaps the psychiatrist had chosen this room for that reason.

"So how are you settling in?" Dr Steiner asked.

Alex shrugged. "OK."

"You have no anxieties? Nothing you wish to discuss?"

"No. I'm fine, thank you, Dr Steiner."

"Good. That's good." The psychiatrist seemed determined to be positive. Alex wondered if the interview was over, but then the man opened a file. "I have your medical report here," he said.

For a moment Alex was nervous. He had been physically examined on his first day on the island. Stripped down to his underwear, he had been put through a whole series of tests by an Italian nurse who spoke little English. Blood and urine samples had been taken, his blood pressure and pulse measured, his sight, hearing and reflexes checked. He wondered now if they had found something wrong.

But Dr Steiner was still smiling. "You're in very good shape, Alex," he commented. "I'm glad you've been looking after yourself. Not too much fast food. No cigarettes. Very sensible."

He opened a drawer in his desk and took out a hypodermic syringe and a little bottle. As Alex watched, he inserted the needle into the bottle and filled the syringe.

"What's that?" Alex asked.

"According to your medical report, you're a little run-down. I suppose it's to be expected after all you've been through. And I'm sure it's very demanding, being here on this island. The nurse has suggested a vitamin booster. That's all this is." He held the needle up to the light and squirted a little of the amber-coloured liquid out of the tip. "Would you mind rolling up your sleeve?"

Alex hesitated. "I thought you were a psychiatrist," he said.

"I'm perfectly qualified to give you an injection," Dr Steiner said. He raised an accusing finger. "You're not going to tell me you're afraid of a little prick?"

"I wouldn't call you that," Alex muttered. He rolled up his left sleeve.

Two minutes later, he was back outside.

He had been missing gun practice because of his

medical appointment and he joined the other students on the firing range. This was on the western side of the island – the side that faced away from Venice. Although Scorpia were legally permitted to be on Malagosto, they hadn't wanted to draw attention to themselves with the sound of gunfire, and the woodland provided a natural screen. There was a strip of the island that was long and flat with nothing growing apart from wild grasses, and the school had built a cut-out town, with offices and shops that were nothing more than fronts, like a film set. Alex had already been through it twice, using a handgun to shoot at paper targets – black rings with a red bull's-eye – that popped up in the windows and doors.

Gordon Ross, the ginger-haired technical specialist who seemed to have picked up most of his skills in Scotland's tougher jails, was in charge of the shooting range. He nodded as Alex approached.

"Good afternoon, Mr Rider. How was your visit to the shrink? Did he tell you you're mad? If not, I wonder what the hell you're doing here!"

A number of other students stood around him, unloading and adjusting their weapons. Alex knew all of them by now. There was Klaus, a German mercenary who had trained with the Taliban in Afghanistan. Walker, who had spent five years with the CIA in Washington before deciding he could earn more working for the other side. One of the two women there had become quite close to Alex, and he wondered if she had been specially chosen to look after him. Her name was Amanda and she had been a soldier with the Israeli army in the occupied Gaza Strip. Seeing him, she raised a hand in greeting. She seemed genuinely pleased to see him.

But then they all did. That was the strange thing. He had been accepted into the day-to-day life of Malagosto without any problem. That in itself was remarkable. Alex remembered the time MI6 had sent him for training with the SAS in Wales. He had been an outsider from the day he arrived, unwanted and unwelcome, a child in an adult world. He was by far the youngest person here too, but that didn't seem to matter. Quite the opposite. He was accepted and even admired by the other students. He was John Rider's son. Everyone knew what that meant.

"You're just in time to show us what you can do before lunch," Gordon Ross announced. His Scottish accent made almost everything sound like a challenge. "You got a high score the day before yesterday. In fact, you were second in the class. Let's see if you can do even better today. But this time I may have built in a little surprise!"

He handed Alex a gun, a Belgian-made FN semi-automatic pistol. Alex weighed it in his hand, trying to find the balance between himself and his weapon. Ross had explained that this was essential to the technique he called instinctive firing.

"Remember – you have to shoot instantly. You can't stop to take aim. If you do, you're dead. In a real combat situation you don't have time to mess around. You and the gun are one. And if you believe that you can hit the target, you will hit the target. That's what instinctive firing is all about."

Now Alex stepped forward, the gun at his side, watching the mocked-up doors and windows in front of him. He knew there would be no warning. At any time, a target could appear. He would be expected to turn and fire.

He waited. He was aware of the other students watching him. Out of the corner of his eye he could just make out the shape of Gordon Ross. Was the teacher smiling?

A sudden movement.

A target had appeared in an upper window and immediately Alex saw that the bull's-eye targets with their impersonal rings had been replaced. A photograph had appeared instead. It was a life-sized colour picture of a young man. Alex didn't know who he was – but that didn't matter. He was a target.

There was no time to hesitate.

Alex raised the gun and fired.

Later that day, Oliver d'Arc, the principle of Scorpia's Training and Assessment Centre, sat in his office on Malagosto, talking to Julia Rothman.

Her image filled the screen of the laptop on his desk just as his own image would be appearing somewhere in the Widow's Palace across the water, in Venice. Neither of them would ever have used a commercial instant messaging system. It would have been far too dangerous. Instead, Scorpia had developed its own Secure Real-time Transport Protocol and its servers were kept in a closely guarded vault in Switzerland. They were confident that none of their conversations could be intrecepted or monitored.

For the same reason, Mrs Rothman never came to the island. She knew it was under surveillance by both the American and British intelligence services, and one day they might be tempted to target the island with a non-nuclear ballistic missile. It was too dangerous.

It was only the second occasion they had spoken since Alex had arrived. The time was exactly seven o'clock in the evening. Outside, the sun had begun to set.

"How is he progressing?" Mrs Rothman asked. Her face on the screen looked cold and a little colourless.

D'Arc considered. He ran a thumb and a single finger down the sides of his chin, stroking his beard. "The boy is certainly exceptional," he murmured. "Of course, his uncle, Ian Rider, trained him all his life, almost from the moment he could walk. I have to say, he did a good job."

"And?"

"He is very intelligent. Quick-witted. Everyone here genuinely likes him. Unfortunately, though, I have my doubts about his usefulness to us."

"I am very sorry to hear that, Professor d'Arc. Please explain."

"I will give you two examples, Mrs Rothman. Today Alex returned to the shooting range. We've been putting him through a course of instinctive firing. It's something he's never done before and, I have to say, it takes many of our students several weeks to master the art. After just a few hours on the range, Alex was already achieving impressive results. At the end of his second day he scored seventy-two per cent."

"I don't see anything wrong with that."

D'Arc shifted in his seat. In his formal suit and tie, shrunk to fit Mrs Rothman's computer screen, he looked rather like a ventriloquist's dummy. "Today we switched the targets," he explained. "Instead of black and red rings, Alex was asked to fire at photographs of men and women. He was supposed to aim at the vital areas: the heart ... between the eyes."

"How did he do?"

"That's the point. His score dropped to forty-six per cent. He missed several targets altogether." D'Arc took off his glasses and polished them with a cloth. "I also have the results of his Rorschach psychological test," he went on. "He was asked to identify certain shapes—"

"I do know what a Rorschach test is, Professor."

"Of course. Forgive me. Well, there was one shape that every student who has ever come here has identified as a man lying in a pool of blood. But not Alex. He said he thought it was a man flying through the air with a backpack. Another shape, which is invariably seen as a gun pointing at someone's head, he believed to be someone pumping up a football. At our very first meeting, Alex told me that he couldn't kill for us, and I have to say that, psychologically speaking, he seems to lack what might be called the killer instinct."

There was a long pause. The image on the computer screen flickered.

"It's very disappointing," d'Arc went on. "Having met Alex, I must say that a teenage assassin would be extremely useful to us. The possibilities are almost limitless. I think we should make it a high priority to find one of our own."

"I doubt there are many teenagers quite as experienced as Alex."

"That's what I began by saying. But even so..."

There was another pause. Mrs Rothman came to a decision. "Did Alex see Dr Steiner?" she asked.

"Yes. Everything was done exactly as you instructed."

"Good." She nodded. "You say that Alex won't kill for us, but you could still be proved wrong.

It's just a question of giving him the right target – and this time I'm not talking about paper."

"You want to send him on an assignment?"

"As you know, Invisible Sword is about to enter its final, critical phase. Introducing Alex Rider into the mix right now might provide an interesting distraction, at the very least. And if he *did* succeed, which I believe he might, he could be very useful indeed. All in all, the timing couldn't be better."

Julia Rothman leant forward so that her eyes almost filled the screen.

"This is what I want you to do..."

There were two hundred and forty-seven steps to the top of the bell tower. Alex knew because he had counted every one of them. The bottom of the tower was empty, a single chamber with bare brick walls and a smell of damp. It had clearly been abandoned years ago. The bells themselves either had been stolen or had fallen down and been lost. The stairs were made of stone and twisted round, following the edges of the tower, and small windows allowed just enough light to see. There was a door at the top. Alex wondered if it would be locked. The tower was used occasionally during camouflage exercises, when the students had to creep from one side of the island to the other. It was a useful lookout post. But he hadn't been up here before himself.

The door was open. It led to a square platform, about ten metres wide, out in the open air. Once there might have been a balustrade enclosing the platform and making it safe. But at some point it had been removed and now the stone floor simply ended. If Alex took three more paces he would step into nothing. He would fall to his death.

Cautiously Alex walked to the edge and glanced down. He was right above the monastery courtyard. He could see the *makiwara* which had been set up earlier in the afternoon. This was a heavy pole with a thick leather pad wrapped around it at head height. It was used to practise kick-boxing and karate strikes. There was nobody in sight. Lessons for the day had ended and the other students were resting before dinner.

He looked across the woodland that surrounded the monastery, already dark and impenetrable. The sun was sinking into the sea, spilling the last of its light over the black water. In the distance he could see the twinkling lights of Venice. What was happening there right now? Tourists would be leaving their hotels, searching out the restaurants and bars. There might be concerts in some of the churches. The gondoliers would be tying up their boats. Winter might be a long way off but already it was too cold for most people to set out on an evening cruise. Alex still found it hard to believe that this island with all its secrets could exist so close to one of the world's most popular holiday destinations. Two worlds. Side by side. But one of them was blind, utterly unaware of the existence of the other.

He stood there unmoving, feeling the breeze rippling through his hair. He was wearing only a long-sleeved shirt and jeans and he was conscious of the evening chill. But somehow it was distant. It was as if he had become part of the tower – a statue or a gargoyle. He was on Malagosto because he had nowhere else to go; he no longer had any choice.

He thought back over the last couple of weeks. How long had he been on the island? He had no idea. In many ways it was just like being at school. There were teachers and classrooms and separate lessons, and one day more or less blurred into the next. Only the subjects here were nothing like the ones he had studied at Brookland.

First there was history – also taught by Gordon Ross. But his version of history had nothing to do with kings and queens, battles and treaties. Ross specialized in the history of weapons.

"Now, this is the double-edged commando knife, developed in the Second World War by Fairbairn and Sykes. One was a silent killing specialist, the other a crack shot with the rifle. Isn't it a beauty? You'll see it has a seven and a half inch blade with a crosspiece and a ribbed centre on both sides. It's designed to fit exactly in your palm. You may find it a little heavy, Alex, as your hand isn't fully developed. But this is still the greatest murder weapon ever invented. Guns are noisy; guns can jam. But the commando knife is a true friend. It will do its job instantly and it will never let you down."

Then there were practical lessons with Professor Yermalov. As Nile had said, he was the least friendly member of the staff at Malagosto: a scowling, silent man in his fifties who had little time for anyone. But Alex soon found out why. Yermalov was from Chechnya and had lost his entire family in the war with Russia.

"Today I am going to show you how to make yourself invisible," he said.

Alex couldn't resist a faint smile.

Yermalov saw it. "You think I am making a joke with you, Mr Rider? You think I am talking about children's books? A cloak of invisibility, perhaps? You are wrong. I am teaching you the skills of the ninjas, the greatest spies who ever lived. The ninja assassins of feudal Japan were reputed to have the ability to vanish into thin air. In fact they used the five elements of escape and concealment – the *gotonpo*. Not magic but science. They might hide underwater, breathing through a tube. They might bury themselves a few centimetres below the surface of the earth. Wearing protective clothing, they might hide inside a fire. To vanish into the air, they carried a rope or even a hidden ladder. And there were other possibilities. They developed the art of sight removers or eye blinders. Blind your enemy with smoke or chemicals and you will become invisible. That is what I will show you now, and this afternoon Miss Binnag will be demonstrating how to make a blinding powder from hot peppers..."

There had been other exercises too. How to assemble and dismantle an automatic pistol while blindfolded (Alex had dropped all the pieces, much to the amusement of the other students). How to use fear. How to use surprise. How to target aggression. There were textbooks – including a manual on the most vulnerable parts of the human body, written by a Dr Three – as well as blackboards and even written exams. They sat in classrooms with ordinary desks. There was just one difference. This was a school for assassination.

And then there had been the demonstration. It was something Alex would never forget.

One afternoon the students had assembled in the main courtyard, where Oliver d'Arc was standing with Nile, who was dressed in white judo robes with a black belt around his waist. It was odd how often the two colours seemed to surround him, as if perpetually mocking his disease.

"Nile was one of our best students," d'Arc explained. "Since his time here, he has risen up the ranks of Scorpia with successful assignments in Washington, London, Bangkok, Sydney – all over the world, in fact. He has kindly agreed to show you a few of his techniques. I'm sure you'll all learn something from him." He bowed. "Thank you, Nile."

In the next thirty minutes, Alex saw a display of strength, agility and fitness he would never forget. Nile smashed bricks and planks with his elbows, fists and bare feet. Three students with long wooden staffs closed in on him. Unarmed, he beat them all, weaving in and out, moving so fast that at times his hands were no more than a blur. Then he proceeded to demonstrate a variety of ninja weapons: knives, swords, spears and chains. Alex watched him throw a dozen *hira shuriken* at a wooden target. These were the deadly, star-shaped projectiles that spun through the air, each steel point razor sharp. One after another they thudded into the wood, hitting the inner circle. Nile never missed. And this was a man with some sort of secret weakness? Alex couldn't see it – and he understood now how he had been defeated so easily at the Widow's Palace. Against a man like Nile he wouldn't stand a chance.

But they were on the same side.

Alex reminded himself of that now as he stood at the top of the bell tower, watching the night draw in and darkness take hold. He had made his choice. He was part of Scorpia now.

Like his father.

Had he made the right decision? At the time, it had all seemed very simple. Yassen Gregorovich had told the truth; Mrs Rothman had shown it to him on film. But he still wasn't sure. There was a voice whispering to him in the evening breeze that this was all a terrible mistake, that he shouldn't be here, that it wasn't too late to get away. But where would he go? How could he return to England, knowing what he did? Albert Bridge. He couldn't erase the images from his mind. The three Scorpia agents waiting. Mrs Jones talking into the radio transmitter. The betrayal. John Rider pitching forward and lying still.

Alex felt hatred welling up inside him. It was stronger than anything he had ever experienced in his life. He wondered if it would be possible to live an ordinary life again one day. There seemed to be nowhere for him to go. Maybe it would be better for everyone if he just took one more step. He was already standing on the very edge. Why couldn't he just let the night take him?

"Alex?"

He hadn't heard anyone approach. He looked round and saw Nile standing in the doorway, one hand resting against the frame.

"I've been looking for you, Alex. What are you doing?"

"I was just thinking."

"Professor Yermalov said he thought he saw you come up here. You shouldn't really be here."

Alex expected Nile to come forward, but he stayed where he was.

"I just wanted to be alone," Alex explained.

"I think you should come down. You could fall."

Alex hesitated. Then he nodded. "All right."

He followed Nile back down the twisting staircase and at last they emerged at ground level.

"Professor d'Arc wants to see you," Nile said.

"To fail me?"

"What gave you that idea? You've done extremely well. Everyone is very pleased with you. You've been here less than a fortnight but you've already made great progress."

They walked back together. A couple of students passed them and murmured a greeting. Only the day before, Alex had seen them fight a ferocious duel with fencing swords. They were deadly killers; they were his friends. He shook his head and followed Nile into the monastery and through to d'Arc's study.

As usual, the principal was sitting behind his desk. He was looking as neat as ever, his beard perfectly trimmed.

"Do, please, sit down, Alex," he said. He tapped on his keyboard and glanced at the screen through his gold-rimmed spectacles. "I have some of your results here," he went on. "You'll be pleased to know that all the teachers speak very highly of you." He frowned. "We do have one small problem, however. Your psychological profile..."

Alex said nothing.

"This business of killing," d'Arc said. "I heard

what you said when you first came to my office and, as I told you, there are many other things you could do for Scorpia. But here's the problem, my dear boy. You're afraid of killing, so you're afraid of Scorpia. You are not quite one of us – and I fear you never will be. That is not satisfactory."

"Are you asking me to leave?"

"Not at all. I'm asking you only to trust us a little more. I'm searching for a way to make you feel that you belong with us completely. And I think I have the answer."

D'Arc shut down his computer and walked round from behind the desk. He was dressed in another suit – he wore a different suit every day. This one was brown, with a herringbone pattern.

"You have to learn to kill," he said suddenly. "You have to do it without any hesitation. Because, when you've done it once, you'll see that actually it wasn't such a big deal. It's the same as jumping into a swimming pool. As easy as that. But you have to cross the psychological barrier, Alex, if you are to become one of us." He raised a hand. "I know you are very young; I know this isn't easy. But I want to help you. I want to make it less painful for you. And I think I can.

"I am going to send you to England tomorrow. That same evening you will carry out your first mission for Scorpia and, if you succeed, there will be no going back. You will know that you are truly one of us and we will know that we can trust you.

But here is the good news." D'Arc smiled, showing teeth that didn't look quite real. "We have chosen the one person in the world who – we think you'll agree – most deserves to die. It is someone you have every reason to despise, and we hope that your hatred and your anger will drive you on, removing any last doubts you may have.

"Mrs Jones. The deputy head of MI6 Special Operations. She was the one responsible for the death of your father.

"We know where she lives; we will help you get to her. She is the one we want you to kill."

"DEAR PRIME MINISTER..."

Just before four o'clock in the afternoon, a man got out of a taxi in Whitehall, paid with a brand-new twenty-pound note, and began to walk the short distance to Downing Street. The man had started his journey at Paddington, but that wasn't where he lived. Nor had he come into London on a train. He was about thirty years old with short, fair hair, and he was wearing a suit and tie.

It is not possible to walk into Downing Street, not since Margaret Thatcher erected huge anti-terrorist gates. Britain is the only democracy whose leaders feel the need to hide behind bars. As always, there was a policeman there, just coming to the end of his eight-hour shift.

The man walked up to him, at the same time producing a plain white envelope made from the very finest paper. Later, when the envelope was analysed, it would be found to have come from a supplier in Naples. There would be no fingerprints, even though the man who had delivered it was not wearing gloves. He had no fingerprints: they had been surgically removed.

"Good afternoon," he said. He had no accent of any kind. His voice was pleasant and polite.

"Good afternoon, sir."

"I have a letter for the prime minister."

The policeman had heard it a hundred times. There were cranks and pressure groups, people with grievances, people needing help. Often they came here with letters and petitions, hoping they would reach the prime minister's desk. The policeman was friendly. As he was trained to be.

"Thank you, sir. If you'd like to leave it with me, I'll see it goes through."

The policeman took the letter – and his would be the only fingerprints that would show up later. Written on the front of the envelope in neat, flowing handwriting were the words: *For the attention of the Prime Minister of Great Britain, First Lord of the Treasury, 10 Downing Street*. He carried it into the long, narrow office which is little more than a Portakabin and which all members of the public must pass through before they can enter the famous street. This was as close as the letter would normally get to number ten. It would be re-routed to an office where a secretary – one of many – would open and read it. If necessary, it might be passed on to the appropriate department.

More likely, after a few weeks, the sender would receive a standard, word-processed reply.

This letter was different.

When the duty officer received it, he turned it over, and that was when he saw the silver scorpion embossed on the other side. There are many symbols and code words used by criminal and terrorist organizations. They are designed to make themselves instantly identifiable so that the authorities will treat them seriously. The duty officer knew at once that he was holding a communication from Scorpia, and pressed the panic button, alerting half a dozen policemen outside.

"Who delivered this?" he demanded.

"It was just someone..." The policeman was old and approaching the end of his career. After today, that end would be considerably nearer. "He was young. Fair-haired. Wearing a suit."

"Get out there and see if you can find him."

But it was too late. Seconds after the man in the suit had delivered the letter, another taxi had drawn up and he had got in. This taxi was not in fact licensed and its number plate was fake. After less than half a mile the man had got out again, disappearing into the crowds pouring out of Charing Cross Station. His hair was now dark brown; he had discarded his jacket and was wearing sunglasses. He would never be seen again.

By five thirty that evening the letter had been photographed, the paper analysed, the envelope checked for any trace of biochemical agents. The prime minister was not in the country. He had gone to Mexico City to join other world leaders at a summit meeting about the environment. He had been in the middle of a photo session but had been called outside and told about the letter. Already he was on his way home.

Meanwhile, two men were sitting in his private office. One was the permanent secretary to the Cabinet Office. The other was the director of communications. They each had a copy of the letter – three typewritten sheets, unsigned – in front of them.

This was what they had read:

Dear Prime Minister,

It is with regret that we must inform you that we are about to bring terror to your country.

We are acting on the instructions of an overseas client who wishes to make certain adjustments to the balance of world power. He makes four demands:

1. The Americans must withdraw all their troops and secret service personnel from every country around the world. Never again will the Americans act as international policemen.

2. The Americans must announce their intention to destroy their entire

nuclear weapons programme as well
as their long-range conventional
weapons systems. We will allow six
months for this process to be put into
effect and completed. By the end of
that time, the United States must have
disarmed.

3. The sum of one billion dollars must be
   paid to the World Bank, this money to
   be used to rebuild poor countries and
   countries damaged by recent wars.
4. The president of the United States
   must resign immediately.

Prime Minister, you may wonder why
this letter is addressed to you when our
demands are directed entirely at the
American government.

The reason for this is simple. You are
the Americans' best friend. You have
always supported their foreign policy.
Now it is time to see if they will be as
loyal to you as you have been to them.

Should they fail, it is you who will
pay the price.

We will wait two days. To be more
precise, we are prepared to give you
forty-eight hours, starting from the
moment this letter was delivered. During
this time, we expect to hear the president
of the United States agree to our terms.

If he fails to do so, we will inflict a terrible punishment on the people of Britain.

We must inform you, Prime Minister, that we have developed a new weapon which we have called Invisible Sword. This weapon is now primed and operational. If the president of the United States chooses not to respond to all four of our demands in the allotted time, then – at exactly four o'clock on Thursday afternoon – many thousands of schoolchildren in London will die. Let me assure you, most sincerely, that this cannot be avoided. The technology is in place; the targets have been selected. This is not a hollow threat.

Even so, we understand that you may doubt the power of Invisible Sword.

We have therefore arranged a demonstration. This evening the England reserve football squad will be returning to Britain from Nigeria, where they have been playing a number of exhibition games. When you read this letter, they will already be in the air. They are due to arrive at Heathrow Airport at five minutes past seven.

At exactly seven fifteen, all eighteen members of this squad, including the

coaches, will be killed. You cannot save
them; you cannot protect them: you can
only watch. We hope, by this action, you
will understand that we are to be taken
seriously and thus you will act quickly to
persuade the Americans to comply. By
doing so, you will avoid the terrible and
pointless massacre of so many of your
young people.

We have taken the liberty of
forwarding a copy of this letter to the
American ambassador in London. We
will be watching the news channels on
television, where we will be expecting
an announcement to be made. You will
receive no further communication from
us. We repeat: these demands cannot be
negotiated. The countdown has already
begun.

Yours faithfully,
SCORPIA

There was a long silence, broken only by the ticking
of an antique clock, as both men studied the letter
for a fourth and then a fifth time. Each was aware
of the other, wondering how he would react. The
two men could not have been more different. Nor
could they have disliked each other more.

Sir Graham Adair had been a civil servant for as
long as anyone could remember, not part of any

government but always serving it, advising it and (some people said) controlling it. He was now in his sixties and had silvery-grey hair and a face accustomed to disguising its emotions. He was dressed, as always, in a dark, old-fashioned suit. He was the sort of man who was sparing in his movements and who never said anything until he had thoroughly considered it first. He had worked with six prime ministers in his lifetime and had different opinions about them all. But he had never told anyone, not even his wife, his innermost thoughts. He was the perfect public servant. One of the most powerful people in the country, he was delighted that very few people knew his name.

The director of communications hadn't even been born when Sir Graham had first entered Downing Street. Mark Kellner was one of the many "special advisers" with whom the prime minister liked to surround himself – and he was also the most influential. He had been at university – studying politics and economics – with the prime minister's wife. For a time he had worked in television, until he had been invited to try his luck in the corridors of power. He was a small, thin man with glasses and too much curly hair. He was also wearing a suit, and there was dandruff on his shoulders.

It was Kellner who broke the silence with a single four-letter word. Sir Graham glanced at him. He never used that sort of language himself.

"You don't believe any of this rubbish, do you?" Kellner demanded.

"This letter came from Scorpia," Sir Graham replied. "I have had direct dealings with them in the past, and I have to tell you that they're not known to make idle threats."

"You accept that they've invented some sort of secret weapon? An invisible sword?" Mark Kellner couldn't hide the scorn in his voice. "So what's going to happen? They're going to wave some sort of magic wand and everyone's going to fall down dead?"

"As I've already said, Mr Kellner, in my opinion Scorpia would not have sent this letter if they did not have the means to back it up. They are probably the most dangerous criminal organization in the world. Bigger than the Mafia, more ruthless than the triads."

"But you tell me: what sort of weapon could target children? Thousands of schoolchildren – that's what they say. So what are they going to do? Set off some sort of dirty bomb in the playground? Or maybe they're going to go round schools with hand grenades!"

"They say the weapon is primed and operational."

"The weapon doesn't exist!" Kellner slammed his hand down on his copy of the letter. "And even if it did, these demands are ridiculous. The American president is not going to resign. His popularity ratings have never been better. And as for this suggestion that the Americans dismantle their weapons systems – do Scorpia really think for a single minute that they'll even consider it? The Americans love weapons! They've got more weapons than just about anyone else in the world. We show this letter to the president, and he'll laugh at us."

"MI6 aren't prepared to rule out the possibility that the weapon exists."

"You've spoken to them?"

"I had a telephone conversation with Alan Blunt earlier this evening. I have also sent him a copy of the letter. He believes, like me, that we should treat this matter with the utmost seriousness."

"The prime minister has cut short his visit to Mexico," Kellner muttered. "He's flying home as we speak. You don't get much more serious than that!"

"I'm sure we're all grateful to the prime minister for interrupting his conference," Sir Graham retorted drily. "But I would have said it's the aircraft carrying these football players that we should be considering. I've also spoken to British Airways. Flight 0074 was delayed in Lagos earlier today and only left this afternoon, just before half past twelve our time. It should be touching down at Heathrow at five past seven, just like the letter says. And the England reserve football squad *are* on board."

"So what are you suggesting we do?" Kellner demanded.

"It's very simple. The threat to the plane is at Heathrow. Scorpia's helped us at least by giving us the place and the time. We must therefore re-route the plane at once. It can land at Birmingham or Manchester. Our first priority is to make sure the players are safe."

"I'm afraid I don't agree."

Sir Graham Adair glanced at the director of communications, his eyes filled with an icy contempt. He had spoken at length with Alan Blunt. Both of them had been expecting this.

"Let me tell you my way of thinking," Kellner continued. He held his two index fingers in the air, as if to frame what he had to say. "I know you're scared of Scorpia; you've made that much clear. Well, I've read their demands and personally I think they're a bunch of idiots. But either way, they've given us a chance to call their bluff. Redirecting this football team is the last thing we want to do. We can use the arrival of the plane to test this so-called Invisible Sword. And by sixteen minutes past seven we'll know it doesn't exist and we can put Scorpia's letter where it deserves to be – in the bin!"

"You're willing to risk the lives of the players?"

"There *is* no risk. We'll throw a security blanket around Heathrow Airport, making it impossible for anyone to get near them. The letter states that the players are going to be hit at exactly seven fifteen. We can find out exactly who's on the plane. Then we can make sure that there are a hundred armed soldiers surrounding it when it lands. Scorpia can bring out their weapon and we'll see exactly what it is and how it works. Anyone tries to set foot in the airport, we'll arrest them and throw them in jail. End of story; end of threat."

"And how are you going to put a hundred extra armed guards into Heathrow Airport?" Sir Graham asked. "You'll start a national panic."

Kellner grinned. "You think I can't make up some sort of spin to take care of that? I'll say it's a training exercise. Nobody'll even blink."

The permanent secretary sighed. There were times when he wondered if he wasn't getting too old for this sort of work – and this was definitely one of them. There remained one final question. But he already knew the answer.

"Have you put this to the prime minister?" he asked.

"Yes. While you were speaking to MI6, I was talking to him. And he agrees with me. So I'm afraid on this matter you're overruled, Sir Graham."

"He's aware of the risks?"

"We don't believe there are any risks, actually. But it's really very simple. If we don't act now, we'll lose the chance to see this weapon in action. If we do this my way, we force Scorpia to show their hand."

Sir Graham Adair stood up. "There doesn't seem to be anything more to discuss," he said.

"You'd better get on to MI6."

"Of course." Sir Graham moved to the door. He stopped and turned round. "And what happens if you're wrong?" he enquired. "What happens if these players do somehow get killed?"

Kellner shrugged. "At least we'll know what we're dealing with," he said. "And they lost every single one of their games while they were in Nigeria. I'm sure we can put together another team."

The plane landing at Heathrow was a Boeing 747 – flight number BA 0074 from Lagos. It had been in the air for six hours and thirty-five minutes. It had departed late. There had been a seemingly endless delay in Lagos: some sort of technical fault. Scorpia had arranged that, of course. It was important the plane followed the schedule that they had imposed. It had to land by five past seven. In fact it hit the runway at five minutes to.

The eighteen members of the football squad were sitting in business class. They were blank-faced and bleary-eyed, not just from the long flight but from the series of defeats they had left behind them. The tour had been a disaster from start to finish. These were only exhibition games. The results weren't meant to matter, but the trip had been something of a humiliation.

As they gazed out of the windows, looking at the grey light and the grey tarmac of a Heathrow twilight, the captain's voice came over the intercom.

"Well, good evening, ladies and gentlemen, and welcome to Heathrow. Once again, I'm sorry for the late running of this aircraft. I'm afraid I've just spoken to the control tower and for some reason we're being re-routed away from the main terminal, so we're going to be out here a little longer. Please remain in your seats with your seat belts fastened, and we'll have you out of here as soon as we possibly can."

And here was something strange. As the plane taxied forward, two army jeeps appeared from nowhere, one on each side, escorting them along the runway. There were soldiers with machine guns in the back. Following instructions from the control tower, the plane turned off and began to move away from the main buildings. The two jeeps accompanied it.

Alan Blunt stood behind an observation window, watching the 747 through a pair of miniature binoculars. He didn't move as the plane trundled towards a square concrete holding area. When he lowered the binoculars, his eyes still remained fixed on the distance. He hadn't spoken for several minutes; he'd barely even breathed. There is nothing more dangerous than a government that does not trust its own intelligence and security services. Unfortunately, as Blunt was only too well aware, the prime minister had made his dislike of both

MI5 and MI6 clear almost from the first day he had come to power. This was the result.

"So what now?" Sir Graham Adair was standing next to him. The permanent secretary to the Cabinet Office knew Alan Blunt very well. They met once a month, formally, to discuss intelligence matters. But they were also members of the same club and occasionally played bridge together. Now he was watching the sky and the runway as if expecting to see a missile streaking towards the slowly moving plane.

"We are about to watch eighteen people die."

"Kellner is a bloody fool, but even so I can't see how they're going to do it." Sir Graham didn't want to believe him. "The airport has been sealed off since six. We've trebled the security. Everyone is on the highest possible alert. You looked at the passenger list?"

Blunt knew just about everything about every man, woman and child who had boarded the plane in Lagos. Hundreds of agents had spent the past hour checking and cross-checking their details, looking for anything remotely suspicious. If there were assassins or terrorists on the plane, they would have to be under deep cover. At the same time, the pilots and cabin staff had been alerted to look out for anything amiss. If anyone so much as stood up before the squad had disembarked, they would raise the alarm.

"Of course we did," Blunt said irritably.

"And?"

"Tourists. Businessmen. Families. Two weather forecasters and a celebrity chef. Nobody seems to have any understanding of what we're up against."

"Tell me."

"Scorpia will do what they said they would do: it's as simple as that. They never fail."

"They may not find it so easy this time." Sir Graham looked at his watch. It was nine minutes past seven. "It's still possible they made a mistake warning us."

"They only warned you because they knew there was nothing you could do."

The plane came to a halt with the two jeeps on either side. At the same time, more armed soldiers appeared. They were everywhere. Some were in clusters on the ground, watching the plane through the telescopic sights of their automatic weapons. There were snipers dotted about on the roofs, all of them linked by radio. Armed policemen with sniffer dogs waited at the entrance to the main terminal. Every door was guarded. Nobody was being allowed in or out.

Sixty more seconds had passed. There were just five minutes to the deadline: quarter past seven.

On the plane the captain switched off the engines. Normally the passengers would already be standing up, reaching for their bags, anxious to leave. But by now they all knew something was wrong. The plane seemed to have stopped in the middle of nowhere.

Powerful spotlights had been trained on it, as if pinning it down. There was no tunnel connecting the door with the terminal. A vehicle edged slowly forward, bringing with it a flight of steps. Armed soldiers in khaki uniforms with helmets and visors crept along beside it. Whatever window the passengers looked out of, they could see armed forces totally surrounding the plane.

The captain spoke again, his voice deliberately calm and matter-of-fact.

"Well, ladies and gentlemen, it seems we have a situation here at Heathrow, but the control tower assures me that it's all routine ... there's nothing to worry about. We're going to be opening the main door in a moment, but I must ask you to remain in your seats until you're given instructions to leave. We're going to be disembarking our passengers in business class first, starting with those in rows seven to nine. The rest of you will be allowed to leave very shortly. Please can I ask for your patience for just a few minutes more."

Rows seven to nine. The captain had already been told. These were the rows occupied by the football squad. None of the players had been informed of what was happening.

There were four minutes left.

The players stood up and began to collect their hand luggage, a variety of sports bags and souvenirs: brightly coloured clothes and wooden carvings. They were glad they had been chosen to leave first. Some of them were thinking that it was all quite fun.

The steps connected with the side of the plane and Blunt watched as a man in orange overalls ran up to stand next to the door. The man looked like an airport technician but in fact he worked for MI6. A dozen soldiers sprinted forward and formed a circle around the steps, their guns pointing outwards so that they resembled a human porcupine. Every angle was covered. The nearest building was more than fifty metres away.

At the same time, a bus appeared. The bus was one of two kept at Heathrow for exceptional circumstances such as this. It looked ordinary but its shell was made of reinforced steel and its windows were bulletproof. Blunt had been in charge of all these preparations, working with the police and airport authorities. As soon as all the players were on board, it would leave the airport, not bothering with customs or passport control. Fast cars were waiting on the other side of the perimeter fence. The players, two or three in each, would be whisked to a secret location in London. By then they would be safe.

Or so everyone hoped. Blunt alone was less sure.

"There's nothing," Sir Graham murmured. "There's nobody even close."

It was true. The area surrounding the plane was empty. There were maybe fifty soldiers and policemen in view. But nobody else.

"Scorpia will have been expecting this."

"Maybe one of the soldiers..." Sir Graham hadn't thought of this until now – when it was too late.

"They've all been checked," Blunt said. "I went through the list personally."

"Then for heaven's sake—"

The door of the plane opened.

A stewardess appeared at the top of the steps, blinking nervously in the glare of the spotlights. Only now could she fully appreciate how serious the situation must be. It was as if the plane had landed in a battlefield. It was totally surrounded. There were men with guns everywhere.

The MI6 agent in the orange overalls spoke briefly with her and she went back inside. Then the first of the players appeared, a sports bag slung over his shoulder.

"That's Hill-Smith," Sir Graham said. "He's the team captain."

Blunt looked at his watch. It was fourteen minutes past seven.

Edmund Hill-Smith was dark-haired, a well-built man. He looked around him, obviously puzzled. He was followed by the other squad members. A black player in sunglasses. His name was Jackson Burke; he was the goalie. Then one of the strikers, a man with blond hair. He was holding a straw hat, something he must have bought in a Nigerian market. One by one they appeared in the doorway and began to walk down the stairs to the waiting bus.

Blunt said nothing. A tiny pulse was beating in his temple. All eighteen men were out in the open now. Sir Graham looked left and right. Where was the attack going to come from? There was nothing anybody could do. Hill-Smith and Burke had already reached the bus. They were safely inside.

Blunt twisted his wrist. The seconds hand on his watch passed the twelve.

One of the players, the last to leave the plane, seemed to stumble. Sir Graham saw one of the soldiers turn, alarmed. On the bus Burke suddenly jerked backwards, his shoulders slamming into the glass. Another player, halfway down the stairs, dropped his bag and clutched his chest, his face distorted with pain. He toppled over, knocking into the two men in front of him. But they too appeared to have been gripped by some invisible force...

One after another the players crumpled. The soldiers were shouting, gesticulating. What was happening was impossible. There was no enemy. Nobody had done anything. But eighteen healthy athletes were collapsing in front of their eyes. Sir Graham saw one of the soldiers speaking frantically into a radio transmitter and a second later a fleet of ambulances appeared, lights blazing, speeding towards the plane. So somebody had been prepared for the worst. Sir Graham glanced at Blunt and knew it had been him.

The ambulances were already too late. By the time they arrived, Burke was on his back, gasping his last few breaths. Hill-Smith had joined him, dropping to the floor of the bus, his lips mauve, his eyes empty. The steps were strewn with bodies, one or two feebly kicking, the others deadly still. The man with the blond hair was lost in a tangle of bodies. The straw hat had rolled away, blown across the runway by the breeze.

"What?" Sir Graham rasped. "How?" He couldn't find the words.

"Invisible Sword," Blunt said.

At that exact moment, a quarter of a mile away in Terminal Two, passengers were just arriving on a flight from Rome. At passport control the officer noticed a mother and a father with their son. The boy was fourteen years old. He was overweight, with black curly hair, thick glasses and terrible skin. There was a slight moustache on his upper lip. He was Italian; his passport gave his name as Federico Casali.

The passport officer might have looked more closely at the boy. There was some sort of alert out for a fourteen-year-old called Alex Rider. But he knew what was happening out on the main runway. Everyone knew. The whole airport was in a state of panic and right now he was distracted. He didn't even bother comparing the face in front of him with the picture that had been circulated.

What was happening outside was much more important.

Scorpia had timed it perfectly.

The boy took his passport and slouched away, through customs and out of the airport.

Alex Rider had come home.

PIZZA DELIVERY

Spies have to be careful where they live.

An ordinary person will choose a house or a flat because it has nice views, because they like the shape of the rooms, because it feels like home. For spies, the first consideration is security. There's a comfortable sitting room – but will the window offer a target for a possible sniper's bullet? A garden is fine – so long as the fence is high enough and there aren't too many shrubs providing cover for an intruder. The neighbours, of course, will be checked. So will the postman, the delivery man, the window cleaner and anyone else who comes to the front door. The front door itself may have as many as five separate locks and there will be alarm systems, night cameras and panic buttons. Someone once said that an Englishman's home is his castle. For a spy, it can be his prison too.

Mrs Jones lived in the penthouse flat on the

ninth floor of a building in Clerkenwell, not far from the old meat market at Smithfields. There were forty flats altogether and the security check run by MI6 had shown that the majority of the residents were bankers or lawyers, working in the City. Melbourne House was not cheap. Mrs Jones had two thousand square metres and two private balconies on the top floor – a great deal of space, particularly as she lived alone. On the open market it would have cost her many millions of pounds when she bought it seven years ago. But as it happened, MI6 had a file on the developer. The developer had seen it and had been glad to do a deal.

The flat was secure. And from the moment Alan Blunt had decided his second in command might need protection, it had become more so.

The front doors opened onto a long, rather stark reception area with a desk, two fig trees and a single lift at the far end. There were CCTV cameras above the desk and outside in the street, recording everyone who entered. Melbourne House had porters working twenty-four hours, seven days a week, but Blunt had replaced them with agents from his own office. They would remain there for as long as necessary. He had also installed a metal detector next to the reception desk, identical to the sort you would find in an airport. All visitors had to pass through it.

The other residents hadn't been particularly

happy about this, but they had been assured it was only temporary. Reluctantly they had agreed. They all knew that the woman who lived alone on the top floor worked for some government department. They also knew that it was better not to ask too many questions. The metal detector arrived; it was installed. Life went on.

It was impossible to get into Melbourne House without passing the two agents on the front desk. There was a goods entrance at the back but it was locked and alarmed. The building couldn't be climbed. The walls had no footholds of any sort; anyway, there were four more agents on constant patrol. Finally there was an agent on duty outside Mrs Jones's front door, and he had a clear view of the corridor in both directions. There was nowhere to hide. The agent – in radio contact with those downstairs – was armed with a high-tech, finger-print-sensitive automatic weapon. Only he could fire it, so if – impossibly – he was overpowered, his gun would be useless.

Mrs Jones had protested about all these arrangements. It was one of the very few times she had ever argued with her superior.

"For heaven's sake, Alan! We're talking about Alex Rider."

"No, Mrs Jones. We're talking about Scorpia."

There had been no more discussion after that.

At half past eleven that night, just hours after the deaths at Heathrow Airport, two agents were sitting behind the front desk. Both were in their twenties, dressed in the uniform of security guards. One was plump, with short, fair hair and a childish face that looked as if it would never need a shave. His name was Lloyd. He had been thrilled to get into MI6 straight from university, but he was fast becoming disappointed. This sort of work, for example. It wasn't what he had expected. The other man was dark and looked foreign; he could have been mistaken for a Brazilian footballer. He was smoking a cigarette, even though it wasn't allowed in the building, and this annoyed Lloyd. His name was Ramirez. The two men had started their night shift a few hours ago. They would be there until seven the next morning, when Mrs Jones left.

They were bored. As far as they were concerned, there was no chance of anyone getting anywhere near their boss on the ninth floor. And as if to add insult to injury, they had been told to look out for a fourteen-year-old boy. They had been given a photograph of Alex Rider, and they both agreed that it was crazy. Why would a schoolboy be gunning for the deputy head of Special Operations?

"Maybe she's his aunt," Lloyd mused. "Maybe she's forgotten his birthday and he's out for revenge."

Ramirez blew a smoke ring. "You really believe that?"

"I don't know. What do you think?"

"I don't care. It's just a waste of time."

They had been talking about the events at Heathrow. Even though they were part of MI6, they were too junior to be told what had really happened to the football squad. According to the radio, the players had picked up a rare disease in Nigeria. Quite how they had all managed to die at the same moment hadn't so far been explained.

"It was probably malaria," Lloyd guessed. "They've got these new mosquitoes out there."

"Mosquitoes?"

"Super-mosquitoes. Genetically modified."

"Yeah. Sure!"

Just then the front doors swung open and a young black man swaggered into the reception area, dressed in motorbike leathers, a helmet in one hand and a canvas bag slung over his shoulder. There was a logo on his chest, repeated on the bag:

Perelli's Pizzas
Grab yourself a pizza the action

The agents ran their eyes over him. About seventeen or eighteen years old. Short, frizzy hair and a wispy beard. A gold tooth. And lots of attitude. He was smiling crookedly as if he wasn't just delivering fast food to a fancy flat. As if he lived here.

Lloyd stopped him. "Who are you delivering to?"

The delivery man looked taken aback. He dug into his top pocket and pulled out a grubby sheet of paper. "Foster," he said. "A pizza wanted on the sixth floor."

Ramirez was also taking an interest. It was going to be a long night. Nobody had come in or out yet. "We're going to have to take a look in that bag," he said.

The delivery man rolled his eyes. "Are you kidding me, man? It's just a ham and cheese pizza, that's all. What *is* this place? Fort Knox or something?"

"We need to take a look inside," Lloyd informed him.

"Yeah. OK. Jesus!"

The delivery man opened the bag and took out a litre bottle of Coca-Cola which he set upright on the desk.

"I thought you said you only had a pizza," Lloyd complained.

"One pizza. One bottle of Coke. You want to call my office?"

The two agents exchanged glances. "What else have you got in there?" Lloyd asked.

"You want to see everything?"

"Yes. As a matter of fact, we do."

"OK! OK!"

The delivery man put down his helmet next to the bottle. He produced a handful of drinking straws, still in their paper wrappers. Next out was a rectangular card, about fifteen centimetres long.

Lloyd took it. "What's this?"

"What does it look like?" The delivery man sighed. "I'm meant to leave it behind. It's like ... a promotion. Can't you read?"

"You want to come into this place, you mind your manners."

"It's a promotion. We leave them all over town."

Lloyd examined the card. There were pictures of pizzas on both sides and a series of special offers. Family-sized pizza, Coke and garlic bread for just nine pounds fifty. Order before seven and get a pound off.

"You want to order pizza?" the delivery man asked.

He was rubbing the two agents up the wrong way. "No," Lloyd said. "But we want to see the pizza you're delivering."

"You can't do that, man! That's not hygienic."

"We don't see it; you don't deliver it."

"OK. Whatever you say. You know, I've been delivering all over London and I've never had this before."

With a scowl he took out a cardboard box, warm to the touch, and laid it on the reception desk. Lloyd lifted the lid and there was the pizza – a four seasons, with ham, cheese, tomato and black olives. The smell of melted mozzarella wafted upwards.

"You want to taste it too?" the delivery man asked sarcastically.

"No. What else have you got in there?"

"There *is* nothing else. It's empty." The delivery man yanked open the canvas bag to show them. "You know, if you're so worried about security, why don't you deliver it yourself?"

Lloyd closed the box. He knew he should do just that. But he was a secret agent, not a pizza boy! And anyway, the pizza was only going as far as the sixth floor. He could see the lift from where he was standing. There was a steel panel next to the door, marked with the letter G and then the numbers from one to nine. Each number lit up as the lift travelled and if the pizza delivery man tried to go any further, he would see. As for the stairs between the floors, they had been equipped with pressure pads and security cameras. Even the air-conditioning ducts running through the building had been alarmed.

It was safe.

"OK," he decided. "You can take it up. You go straight to floor number six. You do not go any-where else. Do you understand that?"

"Why should I want to go anywhere else? I've got pizza for someone called Foster and she's on the sixth floor."

The delivery man reloaded the bag and walked away.

"You go through the metal detector," Ramirez ordered.

"You got a metal detector? I thought this was

a block of flats, not Heathrow Airport."

The delivery man handed his helmet to Ramirez and, with the canvas bag over his shoulder, walked through the metal frame. The machine was silent.

"There you are!" he said. "I'm clean. Now can I deliver the pizza?"

"Wait a minute!" The fair-haired agent sounded threatening. "You forgot the Coke – and your pro-motions card." He picked the two items up from the reception desk and handed them over.

"Yeah. Thanks." The delivery man began to walk towards the lift.

He had known he would be stopped.

Behind the wig and the black latex mask, Alex Rider heaved a sigh of relief. The disguise had worked. Nile had told him it would and he'd had no reason to doubt it. He had been careful to make his voice sound older, with an authentic accent. The motorbike leathers had thickened out his build and he was wearing special shoes that had added three centimetres to his height. He hadn't been worried about his bag being searched. The moment he'd set eyes on them Alex had known that Lloyd and Ramirez were new to the game, with little field experience.

If they had taken him up on his offer and demanded to call the pizza company, Alex would have given them a business card with the phone number. But it would have been Scorpia who answered. If they had been smart, the two agents might have telephoned up to the sixth floor. But Sarah Foster – the owner of the flat – was away. Her line had been switched from outside. The call would be redirected ... again to Scorpia.

Everything had gone exactly as planned.

Alex had been taken from Malagosto to Rome, where he had boarded a flight with two Scorpia people he had never seen before. They had been with him at Heathrow, accompanying him through passport control to ensure there was no problem. How could there have been? Alex was in disguise; he had a false passport. And there seemed to be some sort of security alert at the airport – everyone was running around in circles. Doubtless it had been engineered by Scorpia.

From Heathrow he had been taken to a house in the middle of London, catching only a glimpse of the front door and the quiet, leafy road before he was whisked inside. Nile had been waiting for him there, sitting on an antique chair with his legs crossed.

"Federico!" He greeted Alex by the name on his fake passport.

Alex said little. Nile swiftly briefed him. He was given another disguise – the pizza delivery man costume – as well as everything he needed to break into Mrs Jones's flat and kill her. How he got out again would be his problem.

"It'll be easy," Nile said. "You'll just walk out the way you came in. And if there is any trouble,

I'm sure you'll cope, Alex. I have every faith in you."

Scorpia had already reconnoitred the flat. Nile showed him the plans. They knew where the cameras were, how many pressure pads had been installed, how many agents had been commandeered. And everything had been worked out, right down to the Coke bottle which Alex had deliberately left on the reception desk and which had been handed back to him *without being passed through the metal detector frame*. It was simple psychology. A plastic bottle filled with liquid. How could it possibly contain anything metallic?

Alex reached the lift and stopped. This was the vital moment.

He had his back to the two agents. He was standing between them and the lift, blocking their line of vision. He had already slipped the special offers card out of the canvas bag as he walked, and he was holding it in both hands. In fact, one side of the card peeled off to reveal a thin silver plate engraved with the letter G and the numbers one to nine. It was identical to the plate beside the lift. The other side was magnetic. Casually, Alex leant forward and placed the fake panel over the real one. It was held in place immediately. Sticking it there had also activated it. Now it was just a matter of timing.

The lift doors opened and he entered. As he turned round, he saw the two agents watching him. He reached out and pressed the button for the ninth floor. The lift doors slid shut, cutting off his view. A second later, the lift jerked and moved up.

The two agents saw the numbers changing beside the lift door. Ground ... one ... two... What they didn't realize was that they weren't following the real progress of the lift. A tiny chip and a watch battery inside the silver plate were illuminating the fake numbers. The real numbers were blocked out behind.

Alex arrived at the ninth floor.

The silver panel showed he had stopped at floor six.

It had taken him thirty seconds to travel up from the ground floor. In that time, Alex had discarded the motorbike leathers to reveal, underneath, clothes that were loose, light-wearing and black: the uniform of the ninja assassin. He tugged off his wig and grabbed hold of the latex covering his face. It came off almost in one piece. Finally, he removed the gold tooth. The doors slid open. Once again he was himself.

He had already been shown a floor plan of the entire building. Mrs Jones's flat was to the right – and there were two unforgivable lapses of security. Although there were CCTV cameras in the fire escapes, there were none in the corridor. And the agent standing in front of the door could see all the way from one end to the other, but he couldn't see into the lift. Two blind spots. Alex was about to take advantage of them both.

The agent on the ninth floor had heard the lift arrive. Like Lloyd and Ramirez downstairs, he was new to the job. He wondered why they had sent the lift up. Perhaps he should radio down and find out. Before he could make any decision, a boy with fair hair and death in his eyes stepped out. Alex Rider was holding one of the drinking straws that the two agents had seen but not examined. He had unwrapped it, and it was already between his lips. He blew.

The *fukidake* – or blowgun – was another lethal weapon used by the ninjas. A needle-sharp dart fired into a major artery could kill instantly. But there were also darts that had been hollowed out and filled with poison. A ninja could hit a man over a distance of twenty metres or more without making any sound at all. Alex was much closer than that. Fortunately for the agent, the dart that he fired out of the straw contained only a sleeping draught. It hit the side of his cheek. The agent opened his mouth to cry out, stared stupidly at Alex, then collapsed.

Alex knew he had to move quickly. The two agents downstairs would allow him a couple of minutes but then they would expect him to return. He grabbed the Coke bottle and opened it – not turning the lid but the bottle itself. The bottle came apart in half. Dark brown liquid poured out, soaking into the carpet. Inside the bottle was a package, wrapped in brown plastic, the same colour as the Coke. With the label covering most of it, the package had been completely invisible. Alex tore it open. There was a gun inside.

It was a Kahr P9, double-action semi-automatic, manufactured in America. It was six inches long and, with its stainless steel and polymer construction, it weighed just eighteen ounces, making it one of the smallest, lightest pistols in the world. The in-line magazine could have held seven bullets; to keep the weight down, Scorpia had provided just one. It was all Alex would need.

Carrying the canvas bag with the pizza, he went past the sleeping agent and over to Mrs Jones's door. It had three locks, as he had been told. He lifted the pizza box lid and removed three of the black olives from the top, squeezing each one against a lock. The canvas bag had a false bottom. He opened it and trailed out three wires which he connected to the olives. A plastic box and a button were built into the bottom of the bag. Crouching down, Alex pressed it. The olives – which weren't olives at all – exploded silently, each one a brilliant flare, burning into the locks. The sharp smell of molten metal rose in the air. The door swung open.

Holding the gun tightly, Alex walked into a large room with grey curtains draped along the far wall, a dining table with four chairs, and a suite of leather sofas. It was lit by a soft yellow glow radiating from a single lamp. The room was modern and sparsely furnished; there was little in it that told him any more about Mrs Jones than he already knew. Even the pictures on the walls were abstracts, blobs of colour that gave nothing away. But there were clues. He saw a photograph on a shelf, a younger Mrs Jones – actually smiling – with two children, a boy and a girl aged about six and four. A nephew and a niece? They looked a lot like her.

Mrs Jones read books; she had a fifty-five inch, wall mounted TV and an expensive, wireless home music system. A chessboard stood on a slender table to one side. She was halfway through a game. But who with? Alex wondered. Nile had told him she lived alone. He heard a soft purring and noticed a Siamese cat stretched out on one of the sofas. That was a surprise. He hadn't expected the deputy head of MI6 Special Operations to need companionship of any sort.

The purring grew louder. It was as if the cat were trying to warn its owner that he was there; and, sure enough, a door opened on the other side of the room.

"What is it, Q?"

Mrs Jones walked in. Approaching the cat, she suddenly saw Alex and stopped.

"Alex!"

"Mrs Jones."

She was wearing a grey silk dressing gown. Alex suddenly saw a snapshot of her life and the emptiness at the heart of it. She came home from work, had a shower, ate dinner on her own. Then there was the chess game ... maybe she was playing over the Internet. *News at Ten* on the television. And the cat.

She paused in the middle of the room. She didn't seem alarmed. There was nothing she could do – certainly no panic button or alarm she could reach. Her hair was still wet from the shower; Alex noticed her bare feet. He raised his hand and she saw the gun.

"Did Scorpia send you?" she asked.

"Yes."

"To kill me."

"Yes."

She nodded as if she understood why this should be so. "They told you about your father," she said.

"Yes."

"I'm sorry, Alex."

"Sorry you killed him?"

"Sorry I didn't tell you myself."

She didn't try to move; she simply stood there, facing him. Alex knew he didn't have much time. Any moment now the lift might return to the ground floor. As soon as the agents saw he wasn't in it, they would raise the alarm. They might already be on their way up.

"What happened to Winters?" she asked. Alex

didn't know whom she meant. "He was outside the door," she explained.

Winters was the third agent.

"I knocked him out."

"So you got past the two downstairs. You came up here. And you broke in." Mrs Jones shrugged. "Scorpia have trained you well."

"It wasn't Scorpia who trained me, Mrs Jones: it was you."

"But now you've joined Scorpia."

Alex nodded.

"I can't quite picture you as an assassin, Alex. I realize you don't like me – or Alan Blunt. I can understand that. But I know you. I don't think you have any idea what you've got yourself into. I bet Scorpia were all smiles; I'm sure they were delighted to see you. But they've been lying to you—"

"Stop it!" Alex's finger tightened on the trigger. He knew that she was trying to make it difficult for him. He had been warned that this was what she would do. By talking to him, by using his first name, she was reminding him that she wasn't just a paper cut-out, a target. She was sowing doubts in his mind. And, of course, she was playing for time.

Nile had told him to do it quickly, the instant they met. Alex realized that this was already going wrong; she had already gained the upper hand – even though he was the one with the gun. He reminded himself of what Mrs Rothman had shown him in Positano. Albert Bridge. The death of his father. He was facing the woman who had given the order to shoot.

"Why did you do it?" he demanded. His voice had become a whisper. He was trying to channel the hatred through him, to give him the strength to do what he had been sent here for.

"Why did I do what, Alex?"

"You killed my father."

Mrs Jones looked at him for a long moment and it was impossible to tell what was going on in those black eyes. But he could see that she was making some sort of calculation. Of course, her entire life was a series of calculations – and once she'd worked out the figures, someone would usually die. The only difference here was that the death would be her own.

She seemed to come to a decision.

"Do you want me to apologize to you, Alex?" she asked, suddenly hard. "We're talking about John Rider, a man you never knew. You never spoke to him; you have no memory of him. You know nothing about him."

"He was still my dad!"

"He was a killer. He worked for Scorpia. Do you know how many people he murdered?"

Five or six. That was what Mrs Rothman had told him.

"There was a businessman working in Peru;

he was married with a son your age. There was a priest in Rio de Janeiro; he was trying to help the street children, but unfortunately he'd made too many enemies so had to be taken out. There was a British policeman. An American agent. Then there was a woman; she was about to blow the whistle on a big corporation in Sydney. She was only twenty-six, Alex, and he shot her as she was getting out of her car—"

"That's enough!" Now Alex was holding the gun with both hands. "I don't want to hear any of this."

"Yes, you do, Alex. You asked me. You wanted to know why he had to be stopped. And that's what you're going to do, isn't it? Follow in your father's footsteps. I'm sure they'll send you all over the world, making you kill people you know nothing about. And I'm sure you'll be very good at it. Your father was one of the best."

"You cheated him. He was your prisoner and you said you were letting him go. You were going to swap him for someone else. But you shot him in the back. I saw..."

"I always wondered if they filmed it," Mrs Jones murmured. She gestured and Alex stiffened, wondering if she was trying to misdirect him. But they were still alone. The cat had gone to sleep. Nobody was approaching the room. "I'll give you some advice," she said. "You'll need it if you're going to work with Scorpia. Once you join the other side, there are no rules. They don't believe in fair play.

Nor do we.

"They had kidnapped an eighteen-year-old." Alex remembered the figure on the bridge. "He was the son of a British civil servant. They were going to kill him; but they were going to torture him first. We had to get him back – so, yes, I arranged the exchange. But there was no way I was ever going to release your father. He was too dangerous. Too many more people would have died. And so I arranged a double-cross. Two men on a bridge. A sniper. It worked perfectly and I'm glad. You can shoot me if it really makes you feel any better, Alex. But I'm telling you: you didn't know your father. And if I had to do it all again, I'd do it exactly the same."

"If you're saying my father was so evil, what do you think that makes me?" Alex was trying to will himself to shoot. He had thought anger would give him strength, but he was more tired than angry. So now he searched for another way to persuade himself to pull the trigger. He was his father's son. It was in his blood.

Mrs Jones took a step towards him.

"Stay where you are!" The gun was less than a metre from her, aiming straight at her head.

"I don't think you're a killer, Alex. You never knew your father. Why do you have to be like him? Do you think every child is 'made' the moment they're born? I think you have a choice..."

"I never chose to work for you."

"Didn't you? After Stormbreaker you could have walked away. We never needed to meet again. But if you remember, you *chose* to get tangled up with drug dealers and we had to bail you out. And then there was Wimbledon. We didn't make you go undercover. You agreed to go – and if you hadn't locked a Chinese gangster in a deep freeze, we wouldn't have had to send you to America."

"You're twisting everything!"

"And finally Damian Cray. You went after him on your own and we're very grateful to you, Alex. But you ask me – what do I think you are? I think you're too smart to pull that trigger. You're not going to shoot me. Now or ever."

"You're wrong," Alex said. She was lying to him, he knew that. She had always lied to him. He could do this. He had to do it.

He held the gun steady.

He let the hatred take him.

And fired.

The air in front of him seemed to explode into fragments.

Mrs Jones had tricked him. She had been tricking him all along, and he hadn't seen it. The room was divided into two parts. A huge pane of transparent, bulletproof glass ran from one corner to the other, stretching from the floor to the ceiling. She had been on one side; he had been on the other. In the half-light it had been invisible, but now the glass frosted, a thousand cracks spiralling outwards from the dent made by the bullet. Mrs Jones had almost disappeared from sight, her face broken up as if she had become a smashed picture of herself. At the same time, an alarm rang, the door flew open and Alex was grabbed and thrown sideways onto the sofa. The gun went flying. Somebody shouted something in his ear but he couldn't understand the words. The cat snarled and leapt past him. His arms were wrenched behind him. A knee pressed into his back. A bag was pulled over his head and he felt cold steel against his wrists. There was a click. He could no longer move his hands.

Now he could make out several voices in the room.

"Are you all right, Mrs Jones?"

"We're sorry, ma'am..."

"We've got the car waiting outside..."

"Don't hurt him!"

Alex was jerked off the sofa with his hands cuffed behind him. He felt wretched and sick. He had failed Scorpia. He had failed his father. He had failed himself.

He didn't cry out. He didn't resist. Limp and unmoving, he allowed himself to be dragged out of the room, back down the corridor and into the night.

COBRA

The room was a bare white box, designed to intimidate. Alex had measured out the space: ten paces one way, four across. There was a narrow bunk with no sheets or blankets, and, behind a partition, a toilet. But that was all. The door had no handle and fitted so flush to the wall that it was almost invisible. There was no window. Light came from behind a square panel in the ceiling and was controlled from outside.

Alex had no idea how long he had been here. His watch had been removed.

After he had been taken from Mrs Jones's flat, he had been bundled into a car. The black cloth bag was still over his head. He had no idea where he was going. They drove at speed for what seemed like half an hour, then slowed down. Alex felt his stomach sink and knew they were heading down some sort of ramp. Had they taken him to the basement of the Liverpool Street HQ? He had been here once before but this time he was to be given no chance to take his bearings. The car stopped. The door opened and he was grabbed and dragged out. Nobody spoke to him. He was marched along – pinned between two men – and down a flight of stairs. Then his hands were unlocked, and the bag was pulled off. He just had time to glimpse Lloyd and Ramirez – the two agents from the reception desk – as they walked out. Then the door closed and he was on his own.

He lay on his back, remembering the final moments in the flat. He was amazed that he hadn't seen the glass barrier until it was too late. Had Mrs Jones's voice been amplified in some way? It didn't matter. He had tried to kill her. He had finally found the strength to pull the trigger, proving that Scorpia had been right about him all along.

He was a killer. Do you know how many people he murdered?

Alex remembered what Mrs Jones had said about his father. She was the one who had given the order for John Rider's death; she had arranged it. She deserved to die.

Or so he tried to persuade himself. But the worst thing was, he half understood what she meant. Suppose his father hadn't been killed on Albert Bridge. Suppose Alex had grown up with him and somehow found out what his father did.

How would he have felt about it? Would he have been able to forgive him?

Sitting on his own in this cruel white room, Alex thought back to the moment when he had fired the gun. He felt again the shudder in his hand. Saw the invisible glass screen crack but not break. Good old Smithers! It was almost certainly the MI6 gadget master who had fixed it up. And, despite everything, Alex was glad. He was glad he hadn't killed Mrs Jones.

He wondered what would happen to him now. Would MI6 prosecute? More likely, they would interrogate him. They would want to know about Malagosto, about Mrs Rothman and Nile. But maybe after that, at last, they would leave him alone. After what had happened, they would never trust him again.

He fell asleep – not just exhausted but drained. It was a black and empty sleep, without dreams, without any feeling of comfort or warmth.

The sound of the door opening woke him up. He opened his eyes and blinked. It was disconcerting having no idea of the time. He could have slept for a few hours or all night. He wasn't feeling rested; there was a crick in his neck. But without a window it was impossible to say.

"You need the toilet?"

"No."

"Then come with me."

The man at the door wasn't Lloyd or Ramirez or

anyone Alex had ever met at MI6. He had a blank, uninteresting face and Alex knew that if they met the next day, he would already have forgotten him. He got off the bunk and walked towards the door, suddenly nervous. Nobody knew he was here. Not Tom, not Jack Starbright … nobody. MI6 could make him disappear. Permanently. Nobody would ever find out what had happened to him. Maybe that was what they had in mind.

But there was nothing he could do. He followed the agent along a curving corridor with a steel mesh floor and fat pipes following the line of the ceiling. He could have been in the engine room of a ship.

"I'm hungry," he complained. He was. But he also wanted to show this agent that he wasn't afraid.

"I'm taking you to breakfast."

Breakfast! So he had slept through the night.

"Don't worry," Alex said. "You can drop me off at a McDonald's."

"I'm afraid that's not possible. In here…"

They had arrived at a second door and Alex went through into a strange, curving room – obviously they were still underground. There were thick glass panels built into the ceiling and he could see the forms of people – commuters – walking overhead. The room was beneath a pavement. Feet of different sizes and shapes touched, briefly, against the glass. Above them the commuters were like ghosts, twisting, rippling, moving soundlessly by as they made their way to work.

There was a table on which were arranged fruit salad, cereal, milk, croissants and coffee. Alex welcomed the sight of breakfast but lost some of his appetite when he saw whom he was supposed to share it with. Alan Blunt was waiting for him, sitting in a chair on the other side of the table, dressed in yet another of his neat, grey suits. He really did look like the bank manager that he had once pretended to be, a man in his fifties, more comfortable with figures and statistics than with human beings.

"Good morning, Alex," he said.

Alex didn't reply.

"You can leave us, Burns. Thank you."

The agent nodded and backed out. The door swung shut. Alex approached the table and sat down.

"Are you hungry, Alex? Please. Help yourself."

"No thanks." Alex *was* hungry. But he wouldn't feel comfortable eating in front of this man.

"Don't be stupid. You need your breakfast. You have a very busy day ahead of you." Blunt waited for Alex to respond. Alex said nothing. "Do you realize how much trouble you're in?" Blunt demanded.

"Perhaps I will have some Weetabix after all," Alex said.

He helped himself. Blunt watched him coldly.

"We have very little time," Blunt said as Alex

ate. "I have some questions for you. You will answer them fully and honestly."

"And if I don't?"

"What do you think? Do you think I'll give you a truth serum or something? You'll answer my questions because it's in your interest to do so. Right now, I don't think you have any idea what's at stake. But believe me when I tell you that this meeting is vital. We have to know what you know. More lives than you can imagine may depend on it."

Alex lowered his spoon and nodded. "Go on."

"You were recruited by Julia Rothman?"

"You know who she is?"

"Of course we do."

"Yes. I was."

"You were taken to Malagosto?"

"Yes."

"And you were sent to kill Mrs Jones."

Alex felt a need to defend himself. "She killed my dad."

"That's not the issue."

"Not for you."

"Just answer the question."

"Yes. I was sent to kill Mrs Jones."

"Good." Blunt nodded. "I need to know who brought you to London. What you were told. And what you were to do when you completed your mission."

Alex hesitated. If he told Blunt all this, he knew he would be betraying Scorpia. But suddenly he didn't care. He had been drawn into a world where everyone betrayed everyone. He just wanted to get out.

"They had a layout of her flat," he said. "They knew everything, except for the glass screen. All I had to do was wait for her to appear. Two of their agents took me through Heathrow. We came in as an Italian family; they never told me their real names. I had a fake passport."

"Where did they take you?"

"I don't know. A house somewhere. I didn't get a chance to see the address." Alex paused. "Where is Mrs Jones?"

"She didn't want to see you."

Alex nodded. "I can understand that."

"After you killed her, what were you supposed to do?"

"They gave me a phone number. I was meant to ring it the moment I'd done what they wanted. But they'll know you've got me now. I expect they were watching the flat."

There was a long silence. Blunt was examining Alex minutely, like a scientist with an interesting lab specimen. Alex squirmed uncomfortably in his chair.

"Do you want to work for Scorpia?" Blunt demanded.

"I don't know." Alex shrugged. "I'm not sure it's any different to working for you."

"You don't believe that. You can't believe that."

"I don't want to work for either of you!" Alex cut in. "I just want to go back to school. I don't want to see any of you ever again."

"I wish that were possible, Alex." For once, Blunt actually sounded sincere. "Let me tell you something that may surprise you. It's been six ... seven months since we first met. In that time, you've proved yourself to be remarkably useful. You've been more successful than I could possibly have calculated. And yet, in truth, I wish we had never met."

"Why?"

"Because there has to be something wrong – seriously wrong – when the security of the entire country rests on the shoulders of a fourteen-year-old boy. Believe me, I would be very glad to let you walk out of here. You don't belong in my world any more than I belong in yours. But I can't let you go back to Brookland, because in approximately thirty hours every child in that school could be dead. Thousands of children in London could have joined them. This is what your friends in Scorpia have promised, and I have no doubt at all that they mean what they say."

"Thousands?" Alex had gone pale. He hadn't expected anything like this. What had he walked into?

"Maybe more. Maybe many thousands."

"How?"

"We don't know. You may. All I can tell you now

is that Scorpia have made a series of demands. We cannot give them what they want. And they're going to make us pay a heavy price."

"What do you want from me?" Alex asked. All the strength seemed to have drained out of him.

"Scorpia have made one mistake. They've sent you to us. I want to know everything you've seen – everything Julia Rothman told you. We still have no idea what we're up against, Alex. You may at least be able to give us a clue."

Thousands of children in London.

Assassination, Alex. It's part of what we do.

That was what she had said.

This was what she meant.

"I don't know anything," Alex said, his head bowed.

"You may know more than you think. You're all that stands between Scorpia and an unimaginable bloodbath. I know what you think of me; I know how you feel about MI6. But are you willing to help?"

Alex slowly raised his head. He examined the man sitting opposite him and saw something he would never have believed.

Alan Blunt was afraid.

"Yes," he said. "I'll help you."

"Good. Then finish your breakfast, have a shower and get changed. The prime minister has called a meeting of Cobra. I want you to attend."

* * *

Cobra.

The acronym stands for Cabinet Office Briefing Room A, which is where, at 10 Downing Street, the meetings take place. Cobra is an emergency council, the government's ultimate response to any major crisis.

The prime minister is, of course, present when Cobra sits. So are most of his senior ministers, his director of communications, his chief of staff and representatives from the police, the army and the intelligence and security services. Finally there are the civil servants, men in dark suits with long and meaningless job titles. Everything that happens, everything that's said, is recorded, minuted and then filed away for thirty years under the Official Secrets Act. Politics may be called a game, but Cobra is deadly serious. Decisions made here can bring down a government. The wrong decision could destroy the entire country.

Alex Rider had been shown into another room and left to shower and change into fresh clothes. He recognized the faded jeans and World Cup rugby shirt: they were his own. Somebody must have been round to his home to fetch them, and seeing them laid out on a chair he felt a pang of guilt. He hadn't spoken to Jack since he had left for Venice. He wondered if anyone from MI6 had told her what was happening. He doubted it. MI6 never told anyone anything unless they had to.

But as he pulled on the jeans, he felt something

rustle in one of the back pockets. He dipped his hand in and took out a folded sheet of paper. He opened it and recognized Jack's handwriting.

Alex,

What have you got yourself mixed up in this time? Two secret agents (spies) waiting downstairs. Suits and sunglasses. Think they're smart, but I bet they don't look in the pockets.

Thinking of you. Take care of yourself. Try and come home in one piece.

Love you,
Jack

That made him smile. It seemed it had been a long time since anything had happened to cheer him up.

As he had thought, the cell and interrogation room were beneath the MI6 headquarters. He was led out to a car park where a navy blue Jaguar XJ6 was waiting, and the two of them were driven up the ramp and out into Liverpool Street itself. Alex settled into the leather seat. He found it strange to be sitting so close to the head of MI6 Special Operations without a table or a desk between them.

Blunt was in no mood to talk.

"You'll be brought up to date at the meeting," he muttered briefly. "But while we're driving there, I want you to think of everything that happened to you while you were with Scorpia. Everything you overheard. If I had more time, I'd debrief you myself. But Cobra won't wait."

After that he buried himself in a report which he took from his briefcase, and Alex might as well have been alone. He looked out of the window as the chauffeur drove them west, across London. It was quarter past nine. People were still hurrying to work. Shops were opening. On one side of the glass, life was going on as normal. But once again Alex was on the wrong side, sitting in this car with this man, heading into God knows what.

He watched as they arrived at Charing Cross and stopped at the lights at Trafalgar Square. Blunt was still reading. Suddenly there was something Alex wanted to know.

"Is Mrs Jones married?" he asked.

Blunt looked up. "She was."

"In her flat I saw a photograph of her with two children."

"They were hers. They'd be about your age now. But she lost them."

"They died?"

"They were taken."

Alex digested this. Blunt's replies were leaving him hardly any the wiser. "Are *you* married?" he asked.

Blunt turned away. "I don't discuss my personal life."

Alex shrugged. Frankly he was surprised Blunt had one.

They drove down Whitehall and then turned right, through the gates that were already open to receive them. The car stopped and Alex got out, his head spinning. He was standing in front of probably the most famous front door in the world. And the door was open. A policeman stepped forward to usher him in. Blunt had already disappeared ahead. Alex followed.

The first surprise was how large 10 Downing Street was inside. It was two or three times bigger than he had expected, opening out in all directions, with high ceilings and a corridor stretching improbably into the distance. Chandeliers hung from the ceiling. Works of art, lent by major galleries, lined the walls.

Blunt had been greeted by a tall, grey-haired man in an old-fashioned suit and striped tie. The man had the sort of face that would not have looked out of place in a Victorian portrait. It belonged to another world, and like an old painting it seemed to have faded. Only the eyes, small and dark, showed any life. They flickered over Alex and seemed to know him at once.

"So this is Alex Rider," the man said. He held out a hand. "My name is Graham Adair."

He was looking at Alex as if he knew him – but

Alex was sure the two of them had never met before.

"Sir Graham is permanent secretary to the Cabinet Office," Blunt explained.

"I've heard a great deal about you, Alex. I have to say, I'm pleased to meet you. I owe you a great deal. More, I think, than you can imagine."

"Thanks." Alex was puzzled. He didn't know what Sir Graham meant, and wondered if the man had been involved in some way in one of his previous assignments.

"I understand you're joining us at Cobra. I'm very glad – although I should warn you that there may be one or two people there who know less about you and may resent your presence."

"I'm used to it," Alex said.

"I'm sure. Well, come this way. I hope you can help us. We're up against something very different and none of us is quite sure what to do."

Alex followed the permanent secretary along the corridor, through an archway and into a large, wood-panelled room with at least forty people gathered around a huge conference table. Alex's first impression was that they were all middle-aged and, with only a few exceptions, male and white. Then he realized how many faces he recognized. The prime minister was sitting at the head of the table. The deputy prime minister – fat and jowly – was next to him. The foreign secretary was fiddling nervously with his tie. Another man who might have been the defence secretary was opposite him. Most of the men were in suits but there were also uniforms – army and police. Everyone in the room had a thick file in front of them. Two elderly women, dressed in black suits and white shirts, sat in the corners, their fingers poised over laptops, ready to type anthing that was said.

Blunt waved Alex to an empty chair at the table and sat down next to him. Sir Graham took his seat on the other side. Alex noticed a few heads turn in his direction but nobody said anything.

The prime minister stood and Alex felt the same buzz he'd experienced when he first met Damian Cray – the realization that he was seeing, close up, a face known all over the world. The prime minister looked older and shabbier than he did on television. Here there was no make-up, no subtle lighting. He looked defeated.

"Good morning," he said, and everyone in the room fell silent.

The meeting of Cobra had begun.

REMOTE CONTROL

They had been talking for three hours.

The prime minister had read out the contents of Scorpia's letter, and copies had been placed in every file around the table. Alex had read his with a feeling of sick disbelief. Eighteen innocent people had already died and nobody in the room had any idea how it had happened. Would Scorpia go ahead with the threat to target children in London? Alex was in no doubt, but nobody had asked his opinion and the first hour had been taken up discussing the question over and over again. At least half the people in the room thought it was a bluff. The other half wanted to put pressure on the Americans – to make them agree to Scorpia's demands.

But there was no chance of that happening. The foreign secretary had already met with the American ambassador. The prime minister had spent several hours on the telephone with the president of the United States. This was the American position: Scorpia were asking the impossible. The Americans considered their demands to be laughable, quite possibly insane. The president had offered the help of the FBI to track Scorpia down. Two hundred American agents were already on their way to London. But there was nothing more he could do. Britain was on its own.

This response caused a great deal of anger at Cobra. The deputy prime minister crashed his fist against the table.

"It's incredible! It's a bloody scandal. We help the Americans; we're their closest allies. And now they turn round and tell us to jump in the lake!"

"That's not quite what they've said." The foreign secretary was more cautious. "And I don't know what else they could do. The president has a point. These demands are impossible."

"They could try to negotiate!"

"But the letter says there will be no negotiation—"

"That's what it says. But they could still try!"

Alex listened as the two men argued, neither really listening to what the other had to say. So this was how government worked!

Next up was a medical officer with a report on how the footballers had died.

"They were all poisoned," he announced. He was a short man, bald, with a round, pink face.

He had put on a crumpled suit for the meeting but somehow Alex could tell he spent most of his life in a white coat. "We found traces of cyanide which seem to have been delivered straight to the heart. The amounts were very small – but they were enough."

"How were they administered?" someone – a police chief – asked.

"We don't yet know. They hadn't been shot, that's for sure. There were no unexplained perforations on their skin and there's only one thing we've come up with that's rather odd. We found tiny traces of gold in their blood."

"Gold?" The director of communications spoke for the first time and Alex noticed him sitting next to the prime minister. He was the smallest – and in many ways seemed to be the least imposing – man in the room. And yet, at his single word, every head turned.

"Yes, Mr Kellner. We don't believe the gold particles contributed to their death. But every single one of the players was the same..."

"Well, it all seems pretty obvious to me," Kellner said, and there was a sneer in his voice. He stood up and looked around the crowded table with cold, superior eyes. Alex disliked him at once. He had seen kids like him at Brookland. Small and spiteful, always winding people up. But running in tears to the teachers the moment they got whacked. "All these people died at exactly the same time," he continued. "So it's pretty obvious they were all poisoned at the same time. When could that have been? Well, obviously when they were on the plane! I've already checked. The flight lasted six hours and thirty-five minutes and they were given a meal shortly after they left Lagos. There must have been cyanide in the food and it kicked in just after they arrived at Heathrow."

"Are you saying there is no secret weapon?" the deputy prime minister asked. He blinked heavily. "What do Scorpia mean by Invisible Sword then?"

"It's a trick. They're trying to make us think they can kill people by some sort of remote control..."

Remote control. That meant something to Alex. He remembered something he had seen when he'd been inside the Widow's Palace. What was it?

"...but there *is* no Invisible Sword. They're just trying to frighten us."

"I'm not sure I agree with you, Mr Kellner." The medical officer seemed nervous of the director of communications. "They could all have taken the poison at the same time, I suppose. But each one of those men had his own metabolism. The poison would have reacted more quickly in some than in others."

"They were all athletes. Their metabolisms would have been more or less the same."

"No, Mr Kellner. I don't agree. There were also two coaches and a manager..."

"To hell with them. There *is* no Invisible Sword. These people are playing games with us. They make demands they know the Americans can't possibly meet, and they threaten us with something that simply isn't going to happen."

"That isn't normally Scorpia's way."

Alex was surprised to see that it was Blunt who had spoken. The head of MI6 Special Operations was sitting on his left. His voice was quiet and very even.

"We've had dealings with them before and they've never yet made a hollow threat."

"You were at Heathrow, Mr Blunt. What do you think happened?"

"I don't know."

"Well, that's very helpful, isn't it? Secret intelligence comes to the table and doesn't have any intelligence to offer. And since you're here" – Mark Kellner seemed to have noticed Alex for the first time – "I'd be fascinated to know why you've brought along a schoolboy. Is he your son?"

"This is Alex Rider." This time it was Sir Graham Adair who spoke. His dark eyes settled on the director of communications. "As you know, Alex has helped us on several occasions. He also happens to be the last person to have had contact with Scorpia."

"Really? And how was that?"

"I sent him to Venice, undercover," Blunt said, and Alex was surprised at how fluently he lied.

"Scorpia have a training school on the island of Malagosto and we needed to know certain details. Alex trained there for a while."

One of the politicians coughed. "Is that really necessary, Mr Blunt?" he asked. "I mean, if it was known that the government was using school-age children for this sort of work, it might not look very good for us."

"I hardly think that's relevant right now," Blunt retorted.

The police chief looked puzzled. He was an elderly man in a blue uniform with brightly polished silver buttons. "If you know about Scorpia, if you even know where to find them, why can't you take them out?" he asked. "Why can't we just send in the SAS and kill the whole lot of them?"

"The Italian government might not be too amused to have their territory invaded," Blunt replied. "And anyway, it's not as simple as that. Scorpia's a worldwide organization. We know some of the leaders, but not all of them. If we eliminate one branch, another one will simply take over the operation. And then they'll come for revenge. Scorpia never forgive or forget. You have to remember: they may be the ones who are threatening us, but they'll be working for a client and it is the client who is our real enemy."

"And what did Alex Rider find out when he was on Malagosto?" Kellner sneered. He wasn't going to allow himself to be knocked off his pedestal.

Not by Alan Blunt. And certainly not by a fourteen-year-old boy.

Alex felt all eyes on him. He shifted uncomfortably. "Mrs Rothman took me out for dinner and she mentioned Invisible Sword," he said. "But she wouldn't tell me what it was."

"Who exactly is Julia Rothman?" Kellner demanded.

"She sits on the executive board of Scorpia," Blunt said. "She is one of nine senior members. Alex met her when he was in Italy."

"Well, that's very helpful," Kellner said. "But if that's all Alex has to offer, we really don't need him here any more."

"There was something about a cold chain," Alex added, remembering the conversation he had overheard at the Widow's Palace. "I don't know what that means, but it may have something to do with it."

In one corner of the room a young, smartly dressed woman with long, black hair sat up in her chair and looked at Alex with sudden interest.

But Kellner had already moved on. "We're being asked to believe that Scorpia can somehow poison thousands of children and arrange for them all to keel over at exactly four o'clock tomorrow afternoon..."

"They'll all be coming out of school," one of the army men said.

"It can't be done! The football squad was a

stunt. They want to panic us into going public with this, and if we do that the entire credibility of the government will be undermined. Maybe that's what they want."

"Then what are you suggesting we do?" Sir Graham Adair asked. The permanent secretary was trying hard to keep the contempt out of his voice. He remembered what he had seen at Heathrow Airport; he didn't want to see it again all over London.

"Ignore them. Tell them to get lost."

"We can't!" Like almost everyone else, the foreign secretary was clearly afraid of Kellner. But he was determined to have his say. "We can't take that risk!"

"There *is* no risk. Think about it for a minute. The footballers were poisoned with cyanide. They were all on the same plane at the same time. It wasn't difficult. But if you wanted to poison thousands of kids, how could you possibly do it?"

"Injections," Alex said.

Everyone looked at him again.

He had worked it out in a split second. It had suddenly come to him, as if spoken by someone else. He had been thinking about a trip he had once made to South America, a long time ago. And then he had remembered what he had seen at Consanto. The little test tubes. All that machinery ... everything utterly sterile. What was it for? Now he understood the link with Dr Liebermann. And there was something else. When he was in the restaurant with Julia Rothman, she had made a joke about the scientist.

You could say his death was a shot in the arm for us all.

A shot in the arm. An injection.

"Every schoolchild in London gets injected at some point," Alex said. He was aware that he was now the centre of attention. The prime minister, half the Cabinet, the police and army chiefs, the civil servants – all the most powerful people in the country were here, in this room. He was surrounded by them. And they were all listening to him. "When I was at Consanto, I saw test tubes with liquid in them," he went on. "And there were trays with what looked like eggs."

"Some vaccines are grown in eggs," the medical officer explained. "And Consanto do supply vaccines all over the world." He nodded as he was struck by another thought. "That would also explain what you heard. Of course! The cold chain. It refers to the transportation of vaccines. They have to be kept at a certain temperature all the time. If you break the chain, the vaccine is no use."

"Go on, Alex," Sir Graham Adair urged.

"I saw them kill a man called Dr Liebermann," Alex said. "He worked at Consanto and Julia Rothman told me she'd paid him a lot of money to help them with something. Maybe he put something in a whole load of vaccines. Some sort of poison. It would be injected into school kids. There are always injections at the start of term..."

Adair glanced at the medical officer, who nodded. "It's true. There were BCG injections in London last week."

"Last week!" Mark Kellner cut in. His tone of voice hadn't changed; he wasn't accepting any of it. "If they were injected with cyanide a week ago, how come they haven't all dropped dead already? How is this Julia Rothman going to arrange for the poison to work tomorrow afternoon on the dot of four?" A few heads around the table nodded in agreement and he went on. "And I don't suppose the football squad had BCG injections while they were away. Or are you going to tell me I'm wrong?"

"Of course they'd have had injections," the permanent secretary snapped, and Alex saw that he was no longer able to hide his anger. He wasn't even trying. "They were in Nigeria. They wouldn't have been allowed into the country without being inoculated."

"Yes!" The medical officer couldn't keep the excitement out of his voice. "They'd have been inoculated against yellow fever."

"A month ago!" Kellner insisted.

"Then the question isn't how did they administer the poison," Sir Graham said; "the question is – how do they prevent it working until a time of their choosing? That's the secret of Invisible Sword."

"What else can you tell us, Alex?" Blunt asked.

"You were talking about remote control," Alex said. "Well, Mrs Rothman kept a Siberian tiger in her office. It attacked me and I thought I was going to be killed—"

"Are you seriously asking us to believe this?" Kellner enquired.

Alex ignored him. "But then someone came in and pressed a button on a machine. It looked like a remote control ... you know, for a TV. The tiger just lay down and went back to sleep."

"Nanoshells."

The young woman who was sitting in a corner and who had been examining Alex earlier had spoken the single word. She obviously hadn't been considered important enough to be given a place at the table, but now she stood up and walked forward. She looked about thirty – after Alex, the youngest person in the room – slim and pale, wearing a suit with a white shirt and a silver chain around her neck.

"What the hell are nanoshells?" the deputy prime minister demanded. "And, for that matter, who are you?"

"This is Dr Rachel Stephenson," the medical officer said. "She's a writer and a researcher ... a specialist in the field of nanotechnology."

"Oh, so now we're moving into science fiction," Kellner complained.

"There's no fiction about it," Dr Stephenson

replied, refusing to be intimidated. "Nanotechnology is about manipulating matter at the atomic level and it's already out there in more ways than you would believe. Universities, food companies, drug agencies and, of course, the military are all spending billions of pounds a year on development programmes and they all agree. In less time than you think, the life of every human being on this planet is going to change for ever. There are some amazing breakthroughs on the way and if you don't believe that, it's time you woke up."

Kellner took this as a personal insult. "I don't see—" he began.

"Tell us about nanoshells," the prime minister said, and it occurred to Alex that it was a while since he had spoken.

"Yes, sir." Dr Stephenson collected her thoughts. "I was already thinking about nanoshells when I heard about the gold particles, but Alex has made it all clear. It's quite complicated and I know we don't have a lot of time, but I'll try to make it as simple as I can.

"Injections *must* be the answer. What these people have done is to inject first the football players and then goodness knows how many children with gold-coated nanoshells." She paused. "What we're talking about here are tiny bullets – and by tiny I mean about a hundred nanometres across. Just so you know, one nanometre is a billionth of a metre. Or to put it another way, a single hair on your head is about one hundred thousand nanometres wide. So each one of these bullets is a thousand times smaller than the tip of a human hair."

She leant forward, resting her hands on the table. Nobody moved. Alex couldn't hear anyone so much as breathe.

"What might these bullets consist of?" Dr Stephenson continued. "Well, it's anyone's guess. But if you imagine a Malteser, it would be a bit like that. The inside would be what we call a polymer bead and might be made of something not very different to a supermarket carrier bag. Don't forget, though, I'm only talking about a few molecules. The polymer would hold everything together and it would be quite easy to mix in the cyanide. When the polymer and the cyanide are released, the person dies.

"And what stops it being released? Well, that's the chocolate on the outside of the Malteser – except what we're talking about here is gold. A solid gold shell, but so tiny you could never see it. All of this would have been done by Dr Liebermann, the man who was killed, using highly advanced colloidal chemistry." She stopped again. "I'm sorry. I'm probably making it sound more complicated than it really is. Basically, what you've got is a bullet with the poison inside, and after that you fix a protein onto the outside, onto the shell."

"What does the protein do?" someone asked.

"It guides the whole thing, a bit like a heat-seeking missile. It would take too long to explain how it works, but proteins can find their way around the human body. They know exactly where to go. And once the nanoshell was injected, the right protein would direct it straight to the heart."

"How many of these nanoshells would you need to inject?" Blunt asked.

"That's impossible to answer," Dr Stephenson replied. "They'd be sitting right inside the heart. Once the poison was released, it would act almost immediately and you wouldn't need very much of it. As a matter of fact, we've studied the effect of nanoshells on the human body, developing them as a cure for cancer. Of course, this is rather different because Scorpia are only interested in killing, but let me see..." She thought for a moment. "There's not very much liquid in a BCG injection. Only about a fiftieth of a teaspoon. At a guess, I'd say you'd only need to add one part cyanide for every one hundred parts of the actual vaccine." She worked it out and nodded. "That adds up to about one billion nanoshells," she said. "Just enough to cover the head of a pin."

"But you said that the poison is safe. It's protected by the gold."

"Yes. But I'm afraid that's where these people have been so very clever. The polymer and poison mix is contained in the gold. It's sitting inside the heart and it's not doing anyone any harm. If you leave it alone, it'll just pass out of the system in a little while and nobody will be any the wiser.

"But Scorpia can break up the gold. And they can do it, like Alex said, by remote control. Have you ever put an egg in a microwave? After a few moments, it explodes. It's exactly the same here. It could be microwave technology that they're planning to use." Stephenson shook her head, her long hair swaying. "No. Microwaves would be too low frequency. I'm sorry. I'm not really an expert on plasmon resonance." She hesitated. "A terahertz beam might be the answer."

"I'm sorry, Dr Stephenson," the foreign secretary said, "but you're losing me. What are terahertz beams?"

"They're not much used yet. They sit between the infrared and the microwave bands of the electromagnetic spectrum and they're being developed for medical imaging and satellite communications."

"So you're saying that Scorpia could send out a signal using a satellite and it would break up the gold, releasing the poison..."

"Yes, sir. Except they wouldn't actually need to use a satellite. In fact, they couldn't. The beams wouldn't be strong enough. If you ask me, when those poor men got off the plane at Heathrow, there must have been some sort of satellite dish erected. It was probably put there a long time ago, on one of the buildings or perhaps up a mast, and they'll have taken it down by now. But all they had to do was throw a switch, the terahertz beams would have broken down the gold and ... well, you know the result."

"Is there any chance that the nanoshells could be broken up accidentally?" Sir Graham Adair asked.

"No. That's what's so brilliant about the whole thing. You'd need to know the exact thickness of the gold. That tells you what frequency to use. It's just like when you shatter a glass by singing the right note. If you ask me, Alex saw that same technology at work with that tiger. The animal must have had some sort of sedative in its bloodstream. They just had to press a button and it fell asleep."

"So if they're not using a satellite, what are we looking for?"

"A saucer. It would look much the same as a satellite dish, only bigger. They've said they're targeting London kids, so it will have to be somewhere in London. Probably mounted on the side of an office building. They may call it Invisible Sword, but I'd say it's more like invisible arrows being fired out of satellite dishes. They shoot out in a straight line."

"And how long will it take for the gold to break up once the switch is thrown?"

"A few minutes. Maybe less. Once the gold breaks, the children will die."

Dr Stephenson backed away from the table and sat down again. She had nothing more to say. Immediately everyone began to speak at once.

Alex noticed some of the civil servants talking into mobile phones. The two women in black and white were typing furiously, trying to keep up with the babble of conversation. Meanwhile, the permanent secretary had leant across Alex, talking quickly and quietly to Alan Blunt. Alex saw the spy chief nod. Then the prime minister held up a hand for silence.

It took a few moments for the clamour to die down.

The prime minister glanced at his director of communications, who was looking down, biting his nails. Everyone was waiting for him to speak.

"All right," Kellner said. "We know what we're up against. We know about Invisible Sword. The question is – what are we going to do?"

DECISION TIME

"**Y**ou have to evacuate London."

It was Sir Graham Adair who made the sugges-tion. This was the result of his swift conversation with Alan Blunt. His voice was soft and measured, but Alex could sense the tension. The permanent secretary was as brittle as ice.

"Scorpia has planned this at exactly the right moment. Four o'clock. Thousands of children will be out of school – on their way home. We have no way of knowing how far these terahertz beams can reach. There may be several dishes, mounted on buildings throughout the capital ... near schools, near tube stations. No child in London will be safe. But as Dr Stephenson has just told us, provided they don't come into contact with the beams, the poison will pass out of their systems eventually. We can keep them out of the city for as long as it takes."

"An evacuation on that scale?" The police chief shook his head. "Do you have any idea how much organization that will take? All of this is meant to be happening at four o'clock tomorrow afternoon. We couldn't possibly arrange everything in time."

"You could try..."

"Forgive me, Sir Graham. But what reason, exactly, are you going to give? You'll be closing down every school in the capital. Whole families will have to move. Where are they going to go? What are you going to tell them?"

"We'll tell them the truth."

"I don't think so." Alex wasn't surprised that the director of communications had chosen this moment to re-enter the conversation. "You tell the British public that their kiddies have all been injected with some sort of nanoparticles, you'll start a panic that will turn into a mass stampede," he said.

"Better that than the streets filled with corpses," Blunt muttered.

"And how do you know that Scorpia won't throw the switch anyway?" Kellner continued. "If you go on television and announce you're evacuating the capital, maybe they'll decide to go ahead with their threat a few hours early."

"There is no alternative," Sir Graham said. "We can't leave the children in danger. If we do nothing..." He shook his head. "The nation would never forgive us."

Alex glanced at the prime minister sitting at the far end of the table. He seemed to have shrunk in the last few minutes. There was even less colour in his face than there had been when the meeting started. The deputy prime minister was chewing furiously; the foreign secretary was polishing his glasses. Everyone was waiting for the three men to make a decision, but they looked completely out of their depth. The prime minister glanced from Kellner to Adair.

At last he spoke. "I think Mark is right."

"Prime Minister..." Sir Graham began.

"If we had more time, maybe we could do something. But we have just over twenty-four hours. And it's true. If we go public, we'll terrify people. We'll also alert Scorpia. Thanks to—" – the prime minister nodded briefly in Alex's direction but seemed unwilling to mention his name – "we know what this weapon is that we're fighting. Invisible Sword. That's the only advantage we have. We can't risk losing that by going on TV."

"So what are we going to do?" the deputy prime minister demanded.

Mark Kellner turned to Dr Stephenson. There was a dull light in his eyes, magnified by his round, wire-framed glasses. Alex knew his mind was already made up. "Satellite dishes," he said.

"Yes." Dr Stephenson nodded.

"You said they would be quite big. Would we be able to recognize them?"

Dr Stephenson thought briefly. "I suppose they could be disguised," she said slowly. "Lots of buildings in London have satellite dishes for one reason or another. But I'm sure it would be possible to find out if they weren't meant to be there."

"And you think they'd have to be high up."

"Yes, probably. I'd say about one hundred metres. But that's only a rough guess."

"That would make it easier." Kellner had forgotten that only a few minutes ago he had doubted the very existence of Invisible Sword. Once again he was in control. "If you're right, we're looking for unauthorized satellite dishes that have been mounted on any tall structures in the last two or three months," he announced. "All we have to do is find them and disconnect them. At the same time, we can find out exactly who received inoculations developed by Consanto. Every single name and address. That may also give us a clue as to where these dishes are located – which areas of London."

"Forgive me, Prime Minister." Sir Graham was exasperated. "You say it would be difficult to evacuate London. But what's being suggested here – it's impossible. A vast game of hide-and-seek, and we have no idea how many we're looking for. If even one of these dishes remains undetected, children will still die."

"We have no alternative," Kellner insisted. "If we go public with this, the children will die anyway."

"I can have twenty thousand officers working around the clock," the police chief said. "The Metropolitan Police. The Home Counties. I can bring in every man and woman in the south of England."

"We can supply troops." This was a soldier's contribution.

"And you think the sight of all these people climbing up and down buildings won't panic people?" Sir Graham exclaimed.

The prime minister raised his hands for silence. "We'll start the search at once," he ordered. "We'll keep it low-key; we can say it's a terrorist alert. It doesn't matter what we say. No one has to know."

"They won't be hard to find," Kellner muttered. "There can't be that many tall buildings in London. All we're looking for is a dish stuck on the side."

"And there is one other possibility," the prime minister added. He glanced at Blunt. "This woman, Julia Rothman. She knows where the dishes are located. Can you find her?"

Blunt showed no emotion at all. He didn't look at anyone in the room. His eyes were empty slits. "It is possible," he said. "We can try."

"Then I suggest you get on to it straight away."

"Very well, Prime Minister."

Blunt got to his feet. Sir Graham nodded and Alex stood up too. He was suddenly feeling very tired, as if he had been in this room for days.

"It's been very good to finally meet you, Alex," the prime minister said. "Thank you for all you've done."

He could have been thanking Alex for serving tea and biscuits. A moment later Alex was forgotten. He and Blunt left the room.

Alex knew what they would want him to do.

He said nothing as he and Blunt were driven back to Liverpool Street. Blunt didn't speak either, apart from once, just as they were pulling out of Downing Street.

"You did very well in there, Alex," he said.

"Thank you."

It was the first time the head of MI6 Special Operations had ever complimented him.

And finally they entered the room on the sixteenth floor, the office Alex knew all too well. Mrs Jones was waiting for them. It was the first time Alex had seen her since he had tried to kill her. She looked exactly the same as he always remembered her. It was as if nothing had happened between them. She was dressed in black, her legs crossed. She was even sucking one of her peppermint sweets.

There was a brief silence as Alex came in.

"Hello, Alex," she said.

"Mrs Jones." Alex felt uncomfortable, unsure what to say. "I'm sorry about what happened," he muttered.

"I think there's something you should know, Alex. It's important." She glanced at Blunt. "Did you tell him?"

"No."

She sighed and turned back to Alex. "I know you think you took a shot at me, but you didn't. We've worked out the angles. The bullet wouldn't have come close. You were less than two metres away from me and there was no way you could have missed accidentally, so – as far as I can see – something stopped you at the last second. As much as you hate me – and I suppose you've every right to – you weren't able to shoot me in cold blood."

"I don't hate you," Alex said. It was true. He felt nothing.

"Well, you don't need to hate yourself either. Whatever Scorpia may have told you, you're not one of them."

"Shall we get down to business?"

Blunt took his place behind his desk. Briefly he outlined what had happened at Cobra. "They've made all the wrong decisions," he concluded. "They're going to look for the dishes – as if they have any hope of finding them. They think an evacuation would be too difficult."

"Kellner." Mrs Jones spoke the name with a heavy voice.

"Of course. The prime minister always does what he says. And the trouble is, Kellner's completely out of his depth. It seems to me we have only one hope."

"You want me to go back," Alex said.

It was obvious. Blunt had been told to find Julia

Rothman. But he had already admitted that he didn't know where she was. Nobody did. Only Alex might be able to find her. He had a phone number; they were expecting his call.

"They'll know I failed," he said. "At least, they'll know I was taken prisoner by you."

"You could escape," Mrs Jones suggested. "Scorpia won't know if I'm alive or dead. You could tell them you killed me and that you managed to escape from us later."

"They might not believe it."

"You'll have to make them." Mrs Jones hesitated. "I know it's a lot to ask, Alex," she went on. "After everything that's happened, I'm sure you never want to see any of us again. But you know the stakes now. If there was any other way..."

"There isn't," Alex said. He had made up his mind before he had even left Downing Street. "I can call them. I don't know if it'll work; I don't know if they'll even answer. But I can try."

"We'll just have to hope that they take you to Julia Rothman. It's our only chance of finding her, and maybe she'll lead us to the dishes." Blunt reached out and pressed a button on his phone. "Please could you send Smithers up," he murmured into the machine.

Smithers. Alex almost smiled. It struck him that Alan Blunt and Mrs Jones had already planned this. They had known they would be sending him back and they had already told Smithers to come up with whatever gadgets he would need. That was typical of MI6. They were always one step ahead. Not just planning the future but controlling it.

"This is what I want you to do," Blunt explained. "We'll arrange an escape for you. If we make it spectacular enough, we can even get it on the evening news. You'll make the call to Scorpia. You can tell them that you shot Mrs Jones. You'll sound nervous, on the edge of panic; you'll ask them to bring you in."

"You think they'll come?"

"Let's hope so. If you can somehow make contact with Julia Rothman, you may be able to find out where the dishes are located. And the moment you know, you get in contact with us. We'll do the rest."

"You'll have to be very careful," Mrs Jones warned. "Scorpia aren't stupid. They sent you to us and when you go back, they'll be very suspicious indeed. You'll be searched, Alex. Everything you do and say will be examined. You'll have to lie to them. Do you think you can get away with it?"

"How will I get in touch with you?" Alex asked. "I doubt if they'll let me use a phone."

As if in answer to his question, the door opened and Smithers came in. In a strange way Alex was pleased to see him. Smithers was so fat and jolly that it was hard to believe he was part of MI6 at all. He was wearing a tweed suit that was at least fifty years out of date. With his bald head, black moustache, several chins and his open, smiling face, he could have been anybody's uncle, the sort who liked to do magic tricks at parties.

And yet, for once, even he was serious. "Alex, my dear boy," he exclaimed. "This is all a bit of a mess, isn't it! How are you keeping? Are you in good shape?"

"Hello, Mr Smithers," Alex said.

"I'm sorry to hear you've been tangling with Scorpia. They're a very, very nasty piece of work. Worse than the Russians ever were. Some of the things they get up to – well, quite frankly it's criminal." He was out of breath and sat down heavily in an empty seat. "Sabotage and corruption. Intelligence and assassination. Whatever next?"

"What have you got for us, Smithers?" Blunt asked.

"Well, you always ask the impossible, Mr Blunt, and this time it's even worse. There are all sorts of gadgets I'd like to give young Alex. I'm always working on new ideas. I've just finished work on a pair of Rollerblades with real blades! They're hidden in the wheels and they'll cut through anything. I've got a very nice tennis ball hand grenade. But as I understand it, these people aren't going to let him keep anything when he turns up again. If there's anything remotely suspicious, they're going to examine it, and then they'll know he's working with us."

"He needs to have a homing device," Mrs Jones said. "We have to be able to track him wherever he goes. And he has to be able to signal to us when it's time for us to move in."

"I know," Smithers said. He reached into his pocket. "And I think I may have come up with the answer. It's the last thing they'd expect ... but at the same time, it's exactly what you'd expect a teenage boy to have."

He took out a clear plastic bag and inside it Alex saw a small metal and plastic object. He couldn't help smiling. The last time he had seen one of these had been at the dentist's.

It was a brace. For his teeth.

"We may have to make a few adjustments, but it should fit snugly into your mouth." Smithers tapped the bag. "The wire going over your teeth is transparent, so it won't be noticed. It's actually a looped radio aerial. The brace will begin transmitting the moment you put it in." He turned the bag over in his pudgy fingers and pointed to the bottom. "There's a little switch here," he continued. "You activate it with your tongue. As soon as you do that, you send out a distress signal and we can come rushing in."

Mrs Jones nodded. "Well done, Smithers. That's first-rate."

Smithers sighed. "I feel really terrible sending Alex in without any weapons. And I've got a marvellous new device for him too! I've been working on an anti-perspirant that will knock you out at ten paces. It stinks!"

"No weapons," Blunt said.

"We can't take the risk," Mrs Jones agreed.

"You're right." Smithers dragged himself slowly to his feet. "Just take care, Alex, old bean. You know how I worry about you. Don't you dare get yourself killed. I want to see you again."

He left, closing the door behind him.

"I'm sorry, Alex," Mrs Jones said.

"No." Alex knew she was right. Even if he could persuade Scorpia that he had carried out his assignment, they still wouldn't trust him. They would search him from head to toe.

"Activate the tracking device as soon as you've found the dishes," Blunt ordered.

"It's always possible they won't take you to them," Mrs Jones added. "In that event, if you can't slip away, if you feel yourself to be in any danger, activate it anyway. We'll send special forces in to pull you out."

That surprised Alex. She had never shown very much concern for him in the past. It was as if his breaking into her flat had somehow changed things between them. He glanced at her sitting bolt upright, neat and contained, chewing slowly on the peppermint, and guessed that there was something she wasn't telling him. Well, that made two of them.

"Are you quite sure about this, Alex?" she asked.

"Yes." Alex paused. "Can you really make them believe I escaped?"

Blunt gave a thin, humourless smile. "Oh yes," he said. "We'll make them believe it."

It happened in London and made the six o'clock news.

A car had been driving at speed on the Westway, one of the main roads leading out of the city. The car was high up – this part of the road was suspended on huge concrete pillars. All of a sudden it lost control. Witnesses saw it swerve left and right, careering into the other traffic. At least a dozen other cars were involved in the resulting pile-up. There was a Fiat Uno, crumpled up like paper. A BMW had one side torn off. A van full of flowers, unable to stop in time, crashed into them. Its doors swung open and suddenly – bizarrely – the road was covered with roses and chrysanthemums. A taxi, trying to avoid the chaos, hit the crash barrier and catapulted over the edge, smashing into an upstairs window of someone's house.

It was a miracle nobody was killed, although a dozen people were rushed to nearby hospitals. The aftermath of the accident had been recorded by traffic policemen in a helicopter, and there it was on television. The road was closed. Smoke was still rising from a burnt-out car. There was shattered metal and glass everywhere.

A number of witnesses were interviewed and

they described what they had seen. There had been a boy in the front car, they said, the one that had started it all. They had seen him get out the moment it was all over. He had run back down the road and disappeared through the traffic. There had been a man – in a dark suit and sunglasses – who had tried to follow him. But the man had obviously been hurt. He had been limping. The boy had escaped.

Two hours later the road was still closed. The police said they were looking for the boy urgently, to interview him. But apart from the fact that he was about fourteen years old and dressed in black, there was no description. They didn't have a name. The traffic in west London had come to a stand-still. It would take days to clear up the damage.

Sitting in a hotel room in Mayfair, Julia Rothman saw the report and her eyes narrowed. She knew who the boy was, of course. It couldn't be any-one else. She wondered what had happened. More to the point, she wondered when Alex Rider would get in touch.

In fact, it wasn't until seven o'clock that evening that Alex made the call. He was in a phone box near Marble Arch. He was already wearing the brace, giving his mouth time to get used to it. But still he found it hard to stop slurring his words.

A man answered. "Yes?"

"This is Alex Rider."

"Where are you?"

"I'm in a call box on the Edgware Road."

This was true. Alex was dressed once again in the black ninja outfit which Scorpia had supplied him with. The phone box was outside a Lebanese restaurant. He had no doubt that Scorpia would be using sophisticated equipment to trace the call. He wondered how long it would take them to reach him.

He thought back to the car crash. He had to admit that MI6 had stage-managed it brilliantly. No fewer than twenty cars had been involved and they had only had a couple of hours, working with a team of stuntmen, to get it right. Not a single member of the public had been injured. But looking at the television footage and hearing the reports, Scorpia would have to admit that it looked real. That was what Blunt had said from the start. The bigger the pile-up, the less reason there would be for doubt. The front page of the *Evening Standard*'s final edition carried a photograph of the taxi embedded in the window of the house.

None of this mattered to the voice at the other end of the line.

"Is the woman dead?" it asked. *The woman*. Scorpia didn't call her Mrs Jones any more. But then, corpses don't need names.

"Yes," Alex answered.

When they came to him, they would find the Kahr P9 back in his pocket with the one bullet fired. If they examined his hands (Blunt was sure they would) there would be traces of gunpowder on his fingers. And there was a bloodstain on the sleeve of his shirt. The same blood type as Mrs Jones. She had supplied the sample.

"What happened?"

"They caught me on the way out. They took me to Liverpool Street and asked me questions. This afternoon they were taking me somewhere else but I managed to get away." Alex allowed a little panic to enter his voice. He was a teenager; he had just made his first kill; and he was on the run. "Look. You said you'd bring me in once I'd done it. I'm in a phone box. Everyone's looking for me. I want to see Nile..."

A brief pause.

"All right. Make your way to Bank tube station. There's an intersection. Seven roads. Be outside the main entrance at nine o'clock exactly and we'll come and collect you."

"Who will—" Alex began. But the phone had gone dead.

He hung up and stepped out of the telephone box. Two police cars sped past, their lights flashing. But they weren't interested in him. Alex took his bearings and started off, heading east. Bank tube station was on the other side of London and it would take him at least an hour to walk there. He had no money on him and couldn't risk being arrested for fare-dodging on a bus. And when he got there – seven roads! Scorpia were being careful. They could come for him from any direction. If this was a set-up and MI6 were following him, they would have to divide themselves seven ways.

He set off along the crowded pavements, keeping to the shadows, trying not to think what he was letting himself in for. The night was already drawing in. He could see a hard, white moon, dead in the sky. Everything would end, one way or another, the next day. Just over twenty hours remained until Scorpia's deadline.

It was his deadline too.

That was the one thing he hadn't told Mrs Jones.

He remembered what had happened on Malagosto. On his last day there he had been sent to see a psychiatrist – an inquisitive, middle-aged man – who had put him through certain tests and then produced his medical report. What was it that Dr Steiner had said? He was a little run-down. He needed more vitamins.

And he had given Alex an injection.

Alex had absolutely no doubt that he had been injected with the same nanoshells that were about to kill thousands of other children in London. He could almost feel them in his bloodstream, millions of golden bullets swirling around in his heart, waiting to release their deadly contents. There was a sour taste in his mouth. Scorpia had tricked him. They had been laughing at him from the very start.

Even as Mrs Rothman sipped her champagne in Positano, she must have been thinking of how to get rid of him.

He hadn't told Mrs Jones because he didn't want her to know. He didn't want anyone to know what a fool he had been. And, at the same time, he was utterly determined. Once the switch was thrown, he would die. But there would be time before that.

Scorpia had told him that it was good to get revenge.

That was exactly what Alex Rider intended to do.

THE CHURCH OF FORGOTTEN SAINTS

The search had already begun.

Hundreds of men and women were working their way across London, with hundreds more acting as back-up: on the telephone, on computers, searching and cross-referencing, trawling through the records. Government scientists had confirmed Dr Stephenson's prediction that the terahertz dishes would have to be at least one hundred metres above the ground to be effective – and that did indeed make it easier. A search of the city's basements, cellars and twisting alleyways would have been impossible, even for the country's entire police force and army. But they were looking for something that had to be high up and in plain view. The clock was ticking but it could be done.

Every satellite dish in London was noted, photographed, authenticated and then eliminated from the search. Whenever possible, the original planning application was found and checked against the actual dish itself. Telecommunications experts had been called in and wherever there was any doubt they were taken up to the relevant floor to see for themselves.

If people were puzzled by the sudden buzz of activity in apartment blocks and offices, nobody said anything. The few journalists who started to ask questions were quietly pulled aside and threatened with such ferocity that they soon decided there were other, less dangerous stories to pursue. Word went round that there was a crackdown on television licences. And every hour, across the city, more technicians poked and probed, examining the dishes, making sure they had a right to be there.

And then, just after ten o'clock on Thursday morning, six hours before Scorpia's deadline, they found them.

There was a block of flats on the edge of Notting Hill Gate with amazing views over the whole of west London. It was one of the tallest blocks in the city – famous for both its height and its ugliness. It had been designed in the sixties by an architect who must have been relieved he would never have to live in it.

The roof contained a number of brick structures: the cables for the lifts, air-conditioning units, emergency generators. It was on the side of one of these that the inspectors found three brand-new satellite dishes facing north, south and east.

Nobody knew what they were for. Nobody had any record of their being placed there. Within minutes there were a dozen technicians on the roof and more circling in helicopters. The cables were found to lead to a radio transmitting device, programmed to begin emitting high frequency terahertz beams at exactly four o'clock that afternoon.

Mark Kellner took the phone call at 10 Downing Street.

"We've done it!" he exclaimed. "A block of flats in west London. Three dishes. They're disconnecting them now."

Cobra was still in session. Around the table there was a murmur of disbelief that swelled in volume and became a roar of triumph.

"We're going to keep looking," Kellner said. "There's always a faint chance that Scorpia put other dishes in place as back-up. But if there are any others, we'll find them too. I think we can say that the immediate crisis is over."

At Liverpool Street Alan Blunt and Mrs Jones were also told the news.

"What do you think?" Mrs Jones asked.

Blunt shook his head. "Scorpia are more clever than that. If these dishes have been found, it's only because they were meant to be found."

"So Kellner is wrong again."

"The man's a fool." Blunt glanced at his watch. "We don't have much time."

Mrs Jones looked at him. "All we have is Alex Rider."

Alex was on the other side of London, a long way from the satellite dishes.

He had been picked up outside Bank Station at the agreed time the night before – but not by car. A scruffy young woman he had never seen before walked past him, whispering two words as she went by, and thrusting a tube ticket into his hand.

"Follow me."

She led him into the station and onto a train. She didn't speak to him again, standing some distance away in the carriage, her eyes vacant, as if she was nothing to do with him. They changed trains twice, waiting until the last moment as the doors slid shut and then suddenly stepping out onto the platform. If anyone were following them, she would see. Finally they emerged at King's Cross Station. She left Alex standing in the street, signalling for him to wait. A few minutes later a taxi pulled up.

"Alex Rider?"

"Yes."

"Get in."

It was all done very smoothly. As they moved off, Alex knew that it would have been impossible for any MI6 agents to have followed them. Which was, of course, exactly what Scorpia had planned.

He was taken to a house – a different house to

the one he had visited when he first arrived back in London. This one was on the edge of Regent's Park. A man and woman were waiting for him, and he recognized them as the fake Italian parents who had accompanied him through Heathrow. They led him upstairs and showed him into a shabby bedroom with a bathroom attached. There was a late supper waiting for him on a tray. They left him there, locking the door behind them. There was no telephone. Alex checked the window. That was locked too.

And now it was half past one the next day and Alex was sitting on the bed, looking out of the window at the trees and Victorian railings of the park. He was feeling a little sick. He had begun to think that Scorpia simply planned to leave him here until four o'clock, that they wanted him to die with the other children in London. And that reminded him of the nanoshells which he knew were inside him, resting inside his heart. He remembered the prick of the needle, the smiling face of Dr Steiner as he injected him with death. The thought of it made his skin crawl. Was he really doomed to spend the last hours of his life here, in this room, sitting on an unmade bed, alone?

The door opened.

Nile walked in, followed by Julia Rothman.

She was wearing an expensive coat, grey with a white fur collar, buttoned up to her neck – another designer label. Her black hair was immaculate, her make-up as much a mask as the ones that had been worn at her party at the Widow's Palace. Her smile was a brilliant red. Her eyes seemed more dazzling than ever, highlighted by perfectly applied black eyeliner.

"Alex!" she exclaimed. She sounded genuinely delighted to see him, but Alex knew now that everything about her was fake: nothing was to be trusted.

"I wondered if you were going to come," Alex commented.

"Of course I was going to come, my dear. It's just that this is rather a busy day. How are you, Alex? I am so pleased to see you."

"Did you really kill her?" Nile asked. He was casually dressed in a loose jacket and jeans, trainers and a white sweatshirt.

Mrs Rothman scowled. "Nile, do you have to be so direct?" She shrugged. "He's talking about Mrs Jones, of course. And I suppose we do need to know what happened. The mission was a success?"

"Yes." Alex nodded. This was the most dangerous part. He knew he couldn't talk too much; he was afraid of giving himself away. And he was horribly conscious of the brace. It fitted well, but it had to be distorting his speech, at least a bit. The wire across his teeth was transparent but, even so, surely Mrs Rothman would notice it.

"So what happened?" Nile asked.

"I managed to get inside her flat. It all went

exactly like you said. I used the gun..."

"And then?"

"I took the lift back down and I was just on my way out when the two guys behind the desk grabbed me." Alex had spent half the night rehearsing this. "I don't know how they found out it was me. But before I could do anything they had me on the floor with my hands cuffed behind my back."

"Go on." Mrs Rothman was gazing at him. Her eyes could have been trying to suck him in.

"They took me somewhere. A cell." This part was easier – Alex was actually telling a version of the truth. "It was underneath Liverpool Street. They left me there overnight and then Blunt saw me the next day."

"What did he say?"

"Not a lot. He knew I was working for you. They'd got satellite photographs of me arriving at Malagosto."

Nile glanced at Mrs Rothman. "That makes sense," he said. "I've always had a feeling we've been under surveillance."

"He didn't want to know very much," Alex went on. "He didn't really want to talk to me. He said I was going to be questioned somewhere out of London. I was left hanging around there for a bit, then a car came to collect me."

"You were handcuffed?" Mrs Rothman asked.

"Not this time. That was their mistake. It was

just an ordinary car. There was the driver in the front, and an MI6 man in the back with me. I didn't know where they were taking me and I didn't want to go. I didn't really care what happened. I didn't even care if I was killed. I waited until they got a bit of speed up and then I threw myself at the driver. I managed to put my hands over his eyes. There was nothing much he could do. He lost control and the car crashed."

"Quite a few cars crashed," Mrs Rothman remarked.

"Yeah. But I was lucky. Everything sort of went upside down, but the next thing I knew, we'd stopped and I was able to get out and run away. Eventually I reached a phone box and called the number you gave me – and here I am."

Nile had been watching him closely through all this. "How did it feel, Alex?" he asked. "Killing Mrs Jones."

"I didn't feel anything."

Nile nodded. "It was the same for me, the first time. But you will learn to enjoy it. That'll come with time."

"You've done very well, Alex." Mrs Rothman spoke the words, but she still sounded doubtful. "I have to say, I'm quite astonished by your daring escape. I saw it on the news and I could hardly believe it. But you've certainly passed the test. You really are one of us."

"Does that mean you'll take me back to Venice?"

"Not quite yet." Mrs Rothman thought for a moment and Alex could see she was coming to a decision. "We're just at the critical point in a certain operation," she revealed. "It might interest you to see the climax; it's going to be quite spectacular. What do you think?"

Alex shrugged. He mustn't look too keen. "I don't mind," he said.

"You met Dr Liebermann; you were there at Consanto when dear Nile dealt with him. It seems only right that you should see the fruits of his handiwork." She smiled again. "I'd like to have you with me, at the end."

So you can watch me die, Alex thought. "I'd like to be there," he replied.

Then her eyes narrowed and the smile seemed to freeze. "But I'm afraid we're going to have to search you," she said. "I do trust you, of course. But as you'll learn when you've been with Scorpia for a while, we don't leave anything to chance. You were taken prisoner by MI6. It's always possible that you were somehow contaminated without knowing it. So before we leave here, I want you to go into the bathroom with Nile. He'll give you a thorough examination. And we've got you a complete change of clothes. Everything has to come off, Alex. It's all a bit embarrassing, I know, but I'm sure you'll understand."

"I've nothing to hide," Alex said, but he couldn't help running his tongue over the brace. He was certain she'd see it.

"Of course you haven't. I'm just being over-cautious."

"Let's do it." Nile jerked a thumb in the direction of the bathroom. He seemed amused by the whole idea.

Twenty minutes later Alex and Nile came downstairs. Alex was now dressed in loose-fitting jeans and a round-necked jersey. Nile had brought the clothes with him, along with fresh socks, trainers and pants. Mrs Jones had been right. If he'd had so much as a penny on him, Nile would have found it. Alex had been thoroughly searched.

But Nile hadn't noticed the brace. Alex's mouth was the one place he hadn't looked.

"Well?" Mrs Rothman asked. She was in a hurry to leave.

"He's clean," Nile answered.

"Good. Then we can go."

There was a grandfather clock in the hall, standing in the corner on the black and white tiled floor. As Alex moved towards the front door, it struck the hour. Two o'clock.

"Is that the time already?" Mrs Rothman said. She reached out and stroked Alex's cheek. "You have just two hours left, Alex."

"Two hours until what?" he asked.

"In two hours' time you'll know everything."

She opened the door.

There was a car waiting for them outside. It took

them across London, heading south. They drove round the Aldwych and over Waterloo Bridge, and for a moment Alex gazed out over one of the most startling views of the capital: the Houses of Parliament and Big Ben, with the Millennium Wheel on the opposite bank. What would it look like two hours from now? Alex tried to imagine the ambulances and police cars screaming across London, the crowds staring in disbelief, the undersized bodies strewn over the pavements. It would be like another world war – but without a single shot being fired.

And then they were on the south bank of the river, making their way through Waterloo, heading east. The buildings they passed became older and dustier. It was as if they had travelled not just a few miles but a few hundred years. Alex sat in the back, next to Nile. Mrs Rothman was in the front with a blank-faced driver. Nobody spoke. It was warm inside the car – the sun was shining – but Alex could feel a tension that made the air cold. He was certain they were heading for some high point where Invisible Sword must be concealed, but he had no idea what to expect. An office block? Perhaps a building under construction? He stared out of the window, his head pressed against the glass, trying to stay calm.

They stopped.

The car had pulled up on a strange, empty stretch of road that ran for about fifteen metres before coming to a dead end. Mrs Rothman and Nile climbed out of the car and Alex followed, examining his surroundings with a sinking heart. It looked as if they hadn't taken him to the dishes after all. There were no tall buildings in sight, not for at least a mile around. The street – almost as wide as it was long – ran between two rows of dilapidated shops, the lower floors boarded up, the windows broken and discoloured. The street itself was covered with rubbish: scraps of newspaper, dented cans and old crisp packets.

But it was the building at the end that commanded his attention. The street led to a church that would have been more suited to Rome or Venice than London. It had obviously been abandoned long ago and had deteriorated badly, yet still it struggled to be magnificent. Two huge, cracked pillars supported a triangular roof over the main entrance. Marble steps led up to huge doors made of solid bronze, but green now rather than gold. The great bulk of the church rose up behind, surmounted by a dome which glinted in the afternoon sun. Statues lined the steps and stood dotted across the roof. But they had been brutalized by time and the elements. Some were missing arms; many had no faces. Once they had been saints and angels. Two hundred years standing in London had turned them into cripples.

"Why are we here?" Alex asked.

Mrs Rothman was standing next to him, looking

up at the church. "I thought you'd like to witness the conclusion of Invisible Sword."

"I don't know anything about Invisible Sword." Without giving himself away, Alex was searching for any sign of the satellite dishes. But there didn't seem to be anything on the dome and, anyway, as impressive as it was, it wasn't tall enough. The dishes had to be higher up. "What is this place?"

Mrs Rothman looked at him curiously. "You know, Alex, I'd swear there was something different about you."

Alex quietly closed his mouth, hiding the brace. He looked at her quizzically.

"Nile? Did you search him from top to bottom?"

"Yes. Just like you told me to."

"I would've thought you'd have trusted me by now," Alex protested, but this time he looked away so she wouldn't see his teeth. "I did exactly what you told me to. And I nearly got killed."

"I don't trust anyone, Alex. Not even Nile." She paused. "Since you ask, this building is the Church of Forgotten Saints. It's not actually a church; it's an oratory. It was built in the nineteenth century by a community of Catholic priests living in the area. They were rather odd. They worshipped a collection of saints who have all fallen into obscurity. You'd be amazed how many saints there are who we've completely forgotten about. St Fiacre, for example, is the patron saint of gardeners and taxi drivers. That must keep him busy! St Ambrose looks after bee-keepers, and where would tailors be without St Homobonus? Did you know that undertakers and perfume makers both have their own saints? They were worshipped here too. I suppose it's not surprising the church fell into disuse. It was bombed in the war and it's been empty ever since. Scorpia took it over a few years ago. As you'll see, we've made one or two interesting adjustments. Do you want to come inside?"

Alex shrugged. "Whatever you say."

He had no choice. For some reason, Julia Rothman had chosen to bring him here, and presumably he would still be here when the terahertz beams were fired across London. He glanced at the dome again, wondering if the surface would be enough to protect him. He doubted it.

The three of them walked forward. The car had left. Alex looked at the shops on either side. Not a single one was occupied. He wondered if he was being watched. It occurred to him that anyone wanting to enter the church would have to come this way, and it would be easy enough to keep them under surveillance with hidden cameras. They reached the main entrance, which sensed their arrival and opened electronically. That was interesting. Mrs Rothman had spoken of adjustments and it was already clear that the oratory wasn't quite as derelict as it first appeared.

They entered a grand hall, rectangular in shape, that served as an antechamber to the main body of the church. Everything was grey: the huge flagstones, the ceiling, the stone pillars that supported it. Alex looked around him as his eyes grew accustomed to the dim light. There were circular windows on both sides but the glass was so thick it seemed to block out most of the daylight rather than allow it in. Everything was faded and dusty. Two statues – more forgotten saints? – stood either side of a cracked and broken font. There was a faint smell of damp in the air. It was easy to believe that nobody had been here for fifty-odd years. Alex coughed and listened to the sound travel up. The chamber was utterly silent, and there seemed to be no obvious way forward. The street was behind them; a solid wall blocked the way ahead. But then Julia Rothman walked across the floor. Her stiletto heels rapped against the stone, creating echoes that flitted into the shadows.

Her movement had been some sort of signal. There was a loud buzz and, overhead, a series of arc lamps – concealed in the walls and ceiling – flashed on. Beams of brilliant white light crashed down from every direction. At the same time, five panels slid silently open, one after the other. They were part of the wall, built into it, disguised to look like brick. Now Alex saw that they were in fact solid steel. More light spilled out and with it came the sound of men moving, of machinery, of frantic activity.

"Welcome to Invisible Sword," Mrs Rothman

announced, and in that moment Alex knew why she had brought him here. She was proud of what she had done. She couldn't hide the pleasure in her voice. She wanted him to see.

Alex stepped through the opening and into a scene he would never forget.

It was a classical church, just like the monastery on Malagosto. Scorpia seemed to enjoy cloaking itself in religion. The floor was made up of black and white tiles. There were stained-glass windows, a richly carved wooden pulpit, even a few old pews. The remains of an organ clung to one wall but, looking at the pipes, some broken, others missing, Alex knew that it would never play again. The dome curved above his head, the underside painted with more saints, men and women holding the various objects with which they were associated: furniture, shoes, library books and loaves of bread. All of them had been forgotten. All of them were frozen together in a single great tableau overhead.

The church had been filled with electronic equipment: computers, TV monitors, industrial lights and a series of switches and levers that couldn't have been more out of place. Two steel gantries had been built, one on either side, with armed guards positioned at intervals. There must have been twenty or thirty people involved in the operation, at least half of them carrying machine guns. As Alex took all this in, a voice rang out, amplified through speakers bolted into the walls.

"Six minutes until launch. Six minutes and counting..."

Alex knew that he had arrived at the centre of the web, and even as he stared, his tongue travelled to the roof of his mouth and pressed the switch which Smithers had built into his brace. Mark Kellner, the prime minister's director of communications, had got it wrong again. Scorpia hadn't attached the terahertz dishes to any tall building.

They had attached them to a hot-air balloon.

Six men dressed in dark overalls were inflating it. There was plenty of floor space, and the dome was as high as a six-storey building. The balloon was painted blue and white. Once released, it would blend in with the sky. How were they going to release it? Alex wondered. The church was completely enclosed by the dome. Even so, that had to be their plan. There was a frame under the balloon with a single burner pointing upwards, and, beneath that, a platform about twenty metres square. The balloon was strangely old-fashioned, like something out of a Victorian adventure story. The platform couldn't have been more high-tech, though, built out of some sort of lightweight plastic with a low railing to protect the equipment it carried.

Alex recognized the equipment instantly. There were four dishes, one in each corner, facing the four points of the compass. They were dull silver in colour, about three metres in diameter, with thin metal rods forming a triangle that protruded from the centre. Wires connected the dishes to a series of complicated-looking boxes which took up most of the space in the centre of the platform. Black pipes ran up to the burner, carrying propane gas from the tanks which were stacked next to the boxes. The balloon was almost inflated. It had been lying spread out on the ground but even as Alex watched, the air in the envelope was heated by three men using a second burner device and it began to lift itself limply up.

More men ran forward to hold the platform steady. There were two ropes, one at each end. Alex saw that the whole thing had been tethered to a pair of iron rings set in the floor. Now he understood what Scorpia intended to do. Julia Rothman must have anticipated that government scientists would work out how the footballers at Heathrow Airport had died. She had known that they would be searching London for the satellite dishes. So she had kept them hidden until the last moment. The hot-air balloon would lift them up into the air. They would only need to stay there for a few minutes. By the time anyone realized what was happening, it would be too late. The golden nanoshells would have dissolved and thousands of children would be dead.

He noticed that Nile had taken off his jacket and was strapping something to his back. It was a leather harness with two lethal-looking weapons: not quite swords, not quite daggers, but something

301

in between. Alex remembered how Dr Liebermann had died and knew that Nile was an expert at *iaido*, the ninja art of sword fighting. He could slice with the swords or he could throw them. Either way, he was lightning fast – Alex knew he could deliver death in an instant.

There was nothing he could do but stand and watch. He had no gadgets, no hidden weapons. Mrs Rothman might have bought the story of his capture and escape, but her eyes were still on him. In truth they had never wavered. She was still suspicious. If he so much as sneezed without her permission, she would give the order and he would be cut down.

How long had it been since he had activated the homing device? Sixty seconds? Maybe more. Alex felt the wire running across his teeth and tried to imagine the signal being transmitted to MI6. How long would it take them to arrive?

Mrs Rothman stepped closer and laid a hand on his shoulder. Her fingers caressed the side of his neck. She ran her tongue, small and moist, over her lips.

"Let me explain to you what we're doing here, Alex," she began. "As a member of Scorpia, I'm sure you'd like to know."

"Are you going for a balloon ride?" Alex asked.

"No. I'm not going anywhere." She smiled. "Two days ago we made certain demands. These demands were directed against the American government but we made it clear that if they did not obey, it would be the British who would suffer the consequences. The deadline runs out" – she looked at her watch – "in less than fifteen minutes. The Americans have not done as we asked. And now it is time for the punishment to begin."

"What are you going to do?" Alex asked. He couldn't keep the horror out of his voice because, of course, he already knew.

"In a few minutes the balloon will be completely inflated and we will raise it above this church. The ropes will keep it tethered at exactly one hundred metres, and when it reaches that point, the machinery which you can see on the platform will activate immediately. High frequency terahertz beams will then be transmitted over London for exactly two minutes and, at that moment, I'm afraid a very large number of people will die."

"Why?" Alex could barely speak. "What did you ask the Americans? What did you want them to do?"

"As a matter of fact, we didn't want them to do anything. The demands we made were completely ridiculous. We asked them to disarm; we told them to pay a billion dollars. We knew they'd never agree."

"Then why ask?"

"Because what our client really wants is revenge. Revenge for the constant interference and bullying of the British and the Americans in matters that don't concern them. What he wants is to ensure that the special friendship between the two countries is destroyed for ever. And this is how it's going to happen.

"I'm afraid that a great many people are about to die in London. The deaths will be sudden and totally unexpected. It'll be as if they've been struck down by an invisible sword. The whole country will be in shock. And then the news will come out: they died because the Americans wouldn't agree to our demands. They died because the Americans refused to help the ally who always stands by them. Can you imagine what the newspapers will say? Can you imagine what people will think? By tomorrow morning the British will hate the Americans.

"And then, Alex, in a few months, Invisible Sword will strike again – but next time it will be in New York. And next time our demands will be more reasonable. We'll ask for less and the Americans will give us what we want, because they will have seen what happened in London and they won't want it to happen again. They'll have no choice. And that will be the end of the British–American alliance. Don't you see? The Americans couldn't care less about the British. They've only ever been concerned about themselves. That's what everyone will say, and you have no idea how much hatred will be created. One country humiliated; the other crushed. And Scorpia will have earned a hundred million pounds along the way."

She paused, as if waiting for him to congratulate her. Alex was meant to be a member of her organization, the newest recruit. His father would have been glad to stand at her side. But Alex couldn't do it. He simply couldn't find it in himself. He couldn't even pretend.

"You can't do it!" he whispered. "You can't kill children just to get rich."

The words were no sooner out of his mouth than he knew he had made a mistake. Julia Rothman's reaction was as fast as a snake ... as fast as a scorpion. One moment, that soft, casual smile had been on her lips; the next, she was rigid, alert, her whole consciousness focused on Alex.

Nile looked over, sensing something was wrong. Alex waited for the axe to fall. And then it came.

"Children?" Mrs Rothman murmured. "I never said anything about children."

"But there *will* be children." Alex tried frantically to backtrack. "Adults and children."

"No, Alex." Mrs Rothman seemed almost amused. "You know that children are the targets. I never told you that; so somebody else must have."

"I don't know what you're talking about..."

She was examining him minutely. Closing in on him. And suddenly she saw it. "I thought there was something different about you," she snapped. "What's that you've got on your teeth?"

It was too late to hide it. Alex opened his mouth. "I wear a brace."

"You weren't wearing a brace in Positano."

"I didn't have it in."

"Take it out."

"It doesn't come out."

"It will – with a hammer."

Alex had no choice. He reached into his mouth and took out the piece of plastic. Nile moved closer, his eyes full of curiosity.

"Let me see it, Alex."

Like a naughty boy caught eating gum, Alex held out his hand. The brace was resting in his palm. And it was obvious it was no ordinary brace. They could see some of the circuitry leading to the switch he had activated.

Had he pressed it in time?

"Drop it!" Mrs Rothman commanded.

Alex let the brace fall to the floor and she stepped forward. Her foot came down on it and Alex heard the sound of breaking plastic as she ground it into the tiles. When she removed her foot the brace was cracked in half, the wire bent. If it had been transmitting before, it certainly wasn't now.

Mrs Rothman turned to Nile. "You're a fool, Nile. I thought I told you to search him from top to bottom."

"His mouth..." Nile didn't know what to say. "It was the one place I didn't look."

But she had already turned back to Alex. "You didn't do it, did you, Alex?" Her voice was full of scorn. "You didn't kill her. Mrs Jones is still alive."

Alex said nothing. Mrs Rothman stared at him for what seemed like an eternity, and then she struck. She was faster and stronger than he would have guessed. Her hand slammed into the side of his face. The sound of it echoed all around. Alex staggered back, dazed. His whole head was ringing and he could feel his cheek glowing red. Mrs Rothman signalled and two guards with machine guns stepped forward to stand next to him, one on either side.

"We may be expecting company," she announced in a loud, clear voice. "I want units three, four and five to take up defensive positions."

"Units three, four and five to the perimeter." An amplified voice relayed the command and twenty of the men ran forward, their feet stamping on the metal gantries, heading for the front of the church.

Mrs Rothman gazed at Alex with eyes that had lost their disguise. They were utterly cruel. "Mrs Jones may be alive," she spat, "but you won't be. You have very little time left to live, Alex. Why do you think I brought you here? It's because I want to see it for myself. I had a special reason to want to kill you, and believe it or not, my dear, you're already dead."

She looked past him. The balloon was fully inflated, floating in the space between the floor and the dome. The platform with its deadly cargo was underneath it, hovering a metre above the ground. The ropes were ready. The dishes were set to automatic.

"Start the launch," Mrs Rothman commanded. "It's time London saw the power of Invisible Sword."

HIGH RESOLUTION

"Launch ... status red. Launch ... status red."

The disembodied voice rang out as one of the Scorpia technicians, sitting in front of a bank of machinery, reached out and pressed a button.

There was a single metallic click and then the hum of machinery as a wheel turned somewhere overhead. Alex looked up. At first glance it seemed to him that the saints and angels were flying apart, as if they had come to life and were drifting down to the pews to pray. Then, with a gasp, he saw what was actually happening. The entire roof was moving. The dome of the oratory had been reconstructed with hidden hydraulic arms that were slowly pulling it open. A crack appeared and widened. He could see the sky. An inch at a time, the great dome was folding back, splitting into two halves. Mrs Rothman was staring upwards, her face filled with delight. Only now did Alex see how much planning had gone into this operation. The entire church had been adapted – it must have cost millions – for this single moment.

And nobody had guessed. The police and the army had been searching all over London, examining every structure at least a hundred metres high. But the dishes had been hidden – at ground level. Only now would the hot-air balloon carry them above the city. Certainly someone would notice it. But by the time they made their way to this desolate area, it would be too late. The dishes would have done their work. Thousands of children would have died.

And Alex would be one of them. Mrs Rothman hadn't killed him, because she had no need to. She had said it herself: he was already dead.

"Raise the balloon." Mrs Rothman gave the order in a soft voice. But her words were quite clear in the vast space of the church.

The burner under the envelope was alight, sending a red and blue flame shooting up. Two men darted forward and pulled the release mechanism, and at once the platform began to rise. The entire roof had disappeared. It was as if the oratory had been peeled open like an exotic fruit. There was more than enough room for the balloon to begin its journey, and Alex watched it float smoothly up, travelling in a straight line, as if this had been rehearsed. There was no wind. Even the weather seemed to be on Scorpia's side.

Alex looked around him. His face was still smarting where Mrs Rothman had slapped him but he ignored the pain. He was horribly aware of the seconds ticking away, but there was nothing he could do. Nile was watching him with as much hatred as he had ever seen in a man's face. The two samurai swords protruded just above his shoulders, and Alex knew he was itching to use them. He had betrayed Scorpia and, worse, he had betrayed Nile. He had humiliated the man in front of Julia Rothman, and for that Nile would make him pay by cutting him to pieces. He needed only the tiniest excuse. The two armed guards still flanked Alex. Others watched him from the gantries and their positions at the entrance. He was helpless.

And where were MI6? He glanced at the broken pieces of the brace. He wished now that he had activated the trigger the moment he had seen the church. But how could he have known? How could anyone have known?

"Alex, before you die, there's something I want to tell you," Mrs Rothman confided.

"I'm not interested," Alex replied.

"Oh, I think you will be, my dear. Because, you see, it's about your father. And your mother. There's something you ought to know."

Alex didn't want to hear it. And he had come to a decision. He was going to die – but he wouldn't just stand there. Somehow he was going to hurt Julia Rothman. She had lied to him; she had manipulated him. Worse, she had almost made him betray everything he believed in. She had tried to make him part of Scorpia, like his father. But whatever his father had been, he would never be the same.

Alex tensed, about to throw himself at her, wondering if Nile would cut him down before the guards' bullets did.

And then one of the windows shattered and something exploded inside the church. Thick smoke billowed out, spreading across the black and white tiles, devouring everything. At the same time came the chatter of machine-gun fire and a second explosion, this one outside. Julia Rothman staggered and fell sideways. Nile twisted round, the white blotches on his face suddenly more livid than ever, his eyes wide and staring.

Alex moved.

He lashed out at the guard on his left, swinging his elbow into the man's stomach and feeling the bone sink into soft flesh. The man doubled up. The other guard turned and Alex pivoted on one foot, kicking hard with the other. His heel smashed into the barrel of the man's machine gun a fraction before it fired. Alex felt the bullets pass over his shoulder and heard a scream as one of the other guards was hit. Well, that made one less anyway! He charged, head down, and slammed into the man like a maddened bull. The guard cried out. Alex punched upwards, his fist driving into the man's throat. The guard was thrown off his feet and sent crashing to the floor.

Alex was free.

Everything was confused. Smoke coiled and twisted. More machine-gun fire, another explosion. Alex saw the balloon rise slowly above the church. It hadn't been hit; it had passed through the gaping roof and was continuing its journey up into the London sky. Suddenly he knew that whatever happened down here, that was where he had to be. The balloon carried equipment that was set to automatic. MI6 were here. They might invade the church and capture Julia Rothman; they might bring the balloon back down. But there could only be minutes left. It might already be too late.

There was only one thing Alex could do. The balloon was trailing the two ropes that would act as anchors when the platform reached the correct height. Alex sprinted towards them. A man blocked his way and Alex automatically dropped him with a roundhouse kick. He grabbed the nearest rope and felt a jerk as the balloon lifted him off the ground.

"Stop him!" Mrs Rothman screamed.

She had seen him but the smoke was still cloaking him from the other guards. There was a burst of machine-gun fire but it missed, slicing the rope a few metres below his feet. Alex looked down and saw that the ground was already quite a long way away. And then he was pulled out of the church, up into the open air, leaving Nile, Mrs Rothman and the swirling chaos behind.

Half blinded by the smoke and shocked by the suddenness of the attack, Mrs Rothman had to waste precious seconds forcing herself to calm down. She strode over to the television monitors, trying to make sense of the situation. She could see soldiers in black combat dress, their faces covered by helmets, taking up positions outside the church. Well, she could deal with them in her own time. Right now, the boy was all that mattered.

"Nile!" she snapped. "Get after him!"

Nile had been hit by flying fragments of glass from the first explosion. For once he seemed slow to react, confused.

"Now!" she screamed.

Nile moved. One rope still hung down, shivering in front of him. He grabbed hold of it and, like Alex, was jerked into the air.

The platform was now forty metres above ground level. It had another sixty metres to travel before the dishes would activate. The extra weight – Alex on one rope, Nile on the other – had slowed it down. But the burner was still heating the air inside the envelope. A digital display on one of the metal boxes was flickering and changing, measuring the distance. Forty-one ... forty-two... The machines knew nothing of what was taking place below. That didn't matter. They would do what they had been designed for. The dishes were waiting for the signal to start transmitting.

The balloon continued to rise. There were just four minutes left.

Mrs Jones had acted immediately. There had been five SAS teams on permanent standby in different parts of London, and as soon as Alex's signal had been received, she had alerted the team nearest to him, with the other four moving in as back-up.

Eight men were slowly closing in on the church – all of them dressed in full combat gear, including flameproof black overalls, belt kits, body armour, Kevlar vests and Mk 6 combat helmets complete with throat mikes. They were carrying a variety of weapons. Most of them had a Sig 9mm pistol strapped to their thigh. One had a sawn-off pump-action shotgun which would be used to blast open the church doors. Others carried axes, knives, Maglites and flashbang grenades; and each man was equipped with the same high-powered semi-automatic submachine gun, the Heckler & Koch 9mm MP5, the favourite assault weapon of the SAS. As they spread out across the seemingly empty street, they barely looked human. They could have been radio-controlled robots, sent from some future war.

They knew that the church was their target but this operation was every soldier's nightmare. Normally, when the SAS go in, they will have been briefed by the police and regular army. They will have access to a huge computer database giving them vital information about the building they're about to attack: the thickness of its walls, the position of windows and doors. If no information is available, they can still produce a three-dimensional computer image by simply inputting whatever details they can see outside. But this time there was nothing. The Church of Forgotten Saints was a blank. And there were only minutes left.

Their instructions were clear. Find Alex Rider and get him out. Find the dishes and destroy them. But even after everything that had happened, Alan Blunt had made sure they understood their priorities. The dishes mattered more.

The soldiers had arrived just in time to see the dome open and the balloon start to appear above the church. They were too late. If they had come equipped with Stingers – heat-seeking missiles – they could have brought it down. But this was the middle of London. They were prepared for what was essentially a hostage situation. They hadn't counted on a full-out war.

The balloon rose in front of their eyes and they were unable to stop it. They could see at once that they needed to get onto the roof of the oratory, but first they had to reach it. One of the men made a snap decision and shot a 94mm HEAT warhead rocket from a plastic firing tube. The missile looped towards the balloon but fell short, smashing through an upper window and detonating inside the church. This was the explosion that had given Alex his chance.

It was the signal for the Scorpia men to show themselves. Suddenly the SAS team found themselves under fire from both sides as a blazing torrent of bullets erupted from the abandoned shops. Somebody threw a grenade. A huge ball of flame and shattered concrete ripped through the air. One of the men was sent flying, his arms and legs limp. He crashed to the ground and lay still.

The SAS hadn't been expecting a war, but in seconds they found themselves in the middle of one. They were outnumbered. The church was seemingly impregnable. The balloon was still rising.

One of the soldiers had dropped to his knee and was talking furiously into his radio transmitter.

"This is Delta One Three. We have engaged the enemy and are coming under heavy fire. We need immediate back-up. Urgent. Satellite dishes have been located. Request immediate air strike to take them out fast. They are being carried by hot-air balloon over the target area. Repeat, they are in a balloon. We cannot reach them. An air strike must respond ... condition red. Over."

The message was relayed instantly to Headquarters Strike Command at RAF High Wycombe, thirty miles outside London. It took them a few precious seconds to understand what they were being told, and a few more precious seconds to believe it. But in less than a minute, two Tornado

GR4 fighter jets were taxiing towards the main runway. Each plane was equipped with Paveway II general-purpose bombs with built-in laser guidance systems and movable tail fins. The pilots were fully trained in low altitude precision attacks. Flying at just over seven hundred miles per hour, they would reach the church in less than five minutes. They would blast the balloon out of the sky.

That was the plan.

Unfortunately, they didn't have five minutes. This was the first real test for the Joint Rapid Reaction Force that had been created to tackle any major terrorist alert. But everything had happened too quickly. Scorpia had left it to the very last moment before revealing their hand.

By the time the planes got there, it would be too late.

Alex Rider pulled himself up the rope, one hand over the other, keeping a loop between his feet. He had done the same often enough in the school gym, but – he had no need to remind himself – this wasn't quite the same.

For a start, even when he stopped to rest, he still went up. The balloon was rising steadily. The hot air inside the envelope weighed twenty-one grams per cubic foot. The cooler air of the London sky weighed roughly twenty-eight grams per cubic foot. This was the simple arithmetic that made the balloon fly. And that was exactly what Alex was doing. If he had looked down, he would have seen the ground fifty metres below. He didn't look down. That was something else that was different from a school gym. If he fell from this height, he would die.

But the platform was less than ten metres above him. He could see the great rectangle, blocking out the sky. Above it the burner was still blazing, shooting a tongue of flame into the bulging blue and white envelope. Alex's shoulders and arms were aching. Worse than that, every movement sent pain shuddering through his bones. His wrists felt as if they were being torn apart. He heard another explosion and a sustained burst of machine-gun fire. He wondered if the SAS were shooting at him. If they had seen the balloon – and they must have – they would want to bring it down, no matter what the cost. What did his own life matter compared with the thousands who would die if the dishes reached one hundred metres?

The thought gave him new strength. If a stray bullet caught him while he was dangling from the rope, he would fall. For more than one reason he needed to be on that platform. He gritted his teeth and pulled himself up.

Sixty-five metres, sixty-six... The balloon was unstoppable. But the distance between Alex and his goal was shortening. There was a third explosion and he risked a glance down. Almost at once he wished he hadn't. The ground was a long way below. The

SAS men were the size of toy soldiers. He could see them taking up their positions in the street that led to the church, preparing to storm the front entrance. Scorpia's men were in the derelict shops on either side. The explosion that Alex had just heard must have come from a hand grenade.

But the battle meant nothing to him. He had seen something else that filled him with dread. A man was climbing the other rope and there could be no mistaking the white blotches on his face. It was Nile. He was moving slowly, as if out of breath. Alex was surprised by that. He knew how fit and strong Nile was. He could almost see the muscles rippling beneath the man's shirt as he reached up with one hand. He had to disable the dishes – permanently – before Nile arrived. After that, he wouldn't stand a chance.

Something struck his hand and he cried out. Alex had still been climbing, even with his eyes fixed on Nile – and he hadn't seen that he had at last reached the platform. He had hit his knuckles against the edge of one of the dishes. For a moment he wondered if he could reach out and pull the bloody thing off. Let it fall and smash somewhere below. But he could see at once that the dishes were well secured with metal braces. He would have to find another way.

And first, that meant climbing onto the platform itself. This wasn't going to be easy – and yet he had to move quickly, giving himself as much time as possible before Nile caught up with him.

He leant backwards and let go of the rope with one hand. His stomach lurched and he thought he was going to fall. But then he lunged and grabbed hold of the edge of the railing that ran all the way around the platform. With a last effort, he heaved himself up and over, toppling down the other side. He landed awkwardly, banging his knee on the edge of a propane gas cylinder. He let the pain ripple through him as he tried to work out what to do.

He examined the balloon.

There were two propane tanks feeding the burner less than a metre above his head. Thick black tubes made of rubber or plastic connected them, and Alex wondered if he could unfasten them and make the flame go out. Would the balloon sink? Or would there be enough hot air in the envelope to keep it rising?

He examined the large, black boxes that were clustered together in the centre of the platform. They were made of metal and each one had a single, blinking light – currently yellow. A tangled network of cables joined them all together. There were four of them and Alex realized that each one was connected to a satellite dish. The power was on. The dishes were primed. But the terahertz beams hadn't yet been activated. He noticed a fifth, smaller box. It had to be some sort of master control. It had a window set into the surface, a digital read-out. Seventy-seven ... seventy-eight

... seventy-nine... Alex watched as the altitude was measured and the balloon moved ever nearer to the point of detonation.

And suddenly he had the answer. Disconnect the dishes. Do it before the platform reached one hundred metres. Do it before Nile arrived. How much time did he have? Very briefly he considered somehow unfastening the rope that Nile was climbing. But even if it was possible, he would never be able to bring himself to do it, to kill someone in such a cold-blooded way. Anyway, it would take too long. No. The four twinkling lights were his targets. Somehow he had to turn them off.

He got unsteadily to his feet and took a small step, the platform swaying slightly beneath him. For a moment he was afraid. Was the platform even designed to hold his weight? Move too fast and it might tip up and throw him off. He grimaced and edged forward. Apart from the hiss of the gas feeding the flame, the hot-air balloon was absolutely silent. Somewhere inside him, Alex wished he could simply sit back and enjoy the ride. The majestic envelope, soaring into the sky. The views of London. But he had perhaps less than a minute before Nile got there. And how long until the balloon reached the right height?

Eighty-three ... eighty-four...

God. It was like being back in Murmansk again. Another digital counter, though that one had been going down, not up, and it had been attached to a nuclear bomb. Why him? Alex fell to his knees and reached out for the first of the cables.

He quickly examined it. It was thick, attached to the master control by a solid-looking socket. He tried unscrewing it but it didn't budge. He would have to tear it out, and in such a way that it would be impossible to reconnect. His hand closed around the cable and he pulled with all his might. Nothing happened. The connections were too strong: metal screwed into metal. And the cables themselves were too thick. He needed a knife or a pair of scissors; he had nothing.

Alex leant back and pressed his foot against the metal box. He strained, still gripping the cable, using his whole body weight. The balloon was still rising. A wisp of cloud slid past – or maybe it was smoke from the fight below. Alex swore through gritted teeth, his entire consciousness focused on the cable and its connection.

And suddenly it came free. Alex felt the cable tear. He fell back, his head slamming into the platform railing. Ignoring the new pain, he dragged himself back up. He could see the separate ends – the severed wires – sprouting out of his hands. There were deep welts in his palms, and he had hurt his head. But when he looked, he saw that one of the yellow lights had blinked out. One of the dishes was no longer functioning.

Ninety-three ... ninety-four...

There were three left. And Alex knew he didn't

have enough time to disconnect them all.

Even so, he lunged forward and grabbed hold of the second. What else could he do? Once again he pressed the flats of his feet against the side of the box. He took a deep breath...

...and something flashed in the corner of his eye. Instinctively Alex threw himself sideways. The samurai sword, half a metre long, sliced the air so close to his face that he felt it. He realized that it had been aimed at his throat. But for the sun reflecting off the blade, he would have been killed.

Nile had reached the platform. He was standing in the corner, holding the railing. There had been two swords strapped to his back – he had thrown only one of them. Now he reached for the other. Alex was lying flat. He couldn't move. There wasn't enough room to do anything. He was an easy target, wedged between the metal boxes and the side of the platform. Above him the flame burned, carrying the balloon the last few metres.

Ninety-seven ... ninety-eight ... ninety-nine...

The digital display flickered to the final figure. There was a buzzing sound inside the master control and the lights on the three remaining connected boxes changed from yellow to red. The system had been activated. Terahertz signals were being beamed all over London.

Alex knew that inside him, in his very heart, the golden nanoshells had begun to break up.

Nile unsheathed the second sword.

*   *   *

Inside the church Mrs Rothman was beginning to realize that the battle was lost. Her men had fought well and they outnumbered the enemy – but they were simply outclassed. There had been many casualties and two more SAS units had arrived, providing back-up for the first.

She could see the fighting outside. Everything was being relayed to her by a series of hidden cameras. It was right in front of her on the television monitors, one for every angle. The street had been torn apart. A wounded SAS man was being dragged away by two of his comrades, dust and debris leaping up as the surface was strafed by enemy fire. More soldiers were moving from doorway to doorway, lobbing grenades through the windows behind them. This was the sort of fighting the SAS had experienced in Northern Ireland and the Middle East.

The whole area had been cordoned off. Police cars had moved in from every direction. They couldn't be seen but their sirens filled the air. This was London. It was nearing the end of a working day. It was impossible to believe that something like this could really be happening here.

There was another explosion – closer this time. Thick smoke billowed over the open dome and paintwork rained down, flaking off the walls. Most of the Scorpia men had abandoned their positions, preferring to take their chances outside. A guard ran up to Mrs Rothman, blood streaking his face.

"They're inside the church," he rasped. "We're finished. I'm leaving."

"You'll stay at your post!" Mrs Rothman snapped.

"To hell with that." The guard spat and swore. "Everyone's going. We're all getting out of here."

Mrs Rothman looked nervous, afraid of being left on her own. "Please, let me have your gun," she begged.

"Sure. Why not?" The guard handed his weapon to her.

"Thank you," she said, and shot him with a single, short burst.

She watched the man go sprawling, then went over to the monitors. The SAS were in the outer chamber. She could see them laying plastic explosives against the fake brick wall. It was hard to be sure, but she fancied they would need rather more explosive than they were using. She had designed the wall herself and it was solid steel. Even so, they would get through it eventually. They would not relent.

She glanced up at the balloon, now straining at the one remaining rope, a hundred metres above London. She knew it had reached the correct height – the equipment inside the church had told her this. In just another minute or so it would all be over. She thought of Alex Rider somewhere up above. All in all, it had been a mistake bringing him here. Why had she? To see him die, of course. She hadn't been there when John Rider had died and she wanted to make up for it. Miss the father; catch the son. That was why she had risked everything to bring Alex to the church, and she knew the other members of the executive board of Scorpia would be less than pleased. But it didn't matter. The operation would succeed. The SAS were too late.

A huge explosion. The whole church shook. Three of the largest organ pipes keeled over and came crashing down. Brick and plaster fragments hung in the air. Half the television monitors went black. But the steel wall held. She had been right about that.

She threw the machine gun down and hurried to a door almost invisible in the wall of a side chapel. It was lucky that Mrs Rothman was the sort of person who prepared for every eventuality – including the need to slip out without being seen.

The guard she had killed had been right. It was definitely time to go.

Alex lay on his back, his shoulders pressing against the railing of the platform. The first sword that Nile had thrown had sliced into the plastic floor, centimetres from his head, and it was still there, quivering, just beside his neck. Nile had unsheathed the second sword and was balancing it in his hand. He was taking his time. Alex knew that he had no need to hurry. He had nowhere to hide. They were less than three metres apart. Alex had seen what Nile could do. There was no way he would miss.

And yet...

Why was he so slow? Taking his time with the sword, still clutching the railing with his other hand...

Alex looked at him, examining the handsome, flawed face, searching for something in the man's eyes.

And found it.

That look. He had seen it before. He remembered Wolf, the SAS soldier he had trained with. And suddenly everything made sense. The secret weakness that Mrs Rothman had mentioned. The reason why Nile had come second, not first, at Malagosto. He thought back to their meeting in the bell tower over the monastery. Nile had lingered at the door, unwilling to come forward, holding onto the frame in just the same way that he was holding onto the railing now. No wonder Nile had been so slow climbing up to the balloon.

Nile was afraid of heights.

But that wasn't going to save Alex. Fifteen seconds had passed since the lights had turned red. Already the nanoshells with their poisonous cargo would be oscillating inside his heart. All over London children would be walking home, waiting for buses, pouring into tube stations, unaware of what was about to happen.

Then Nile spoke.

"This is what I promised would happen to you if you betrayed us," he said. The smile on his face might have been forced, but there could be no doubting what he was about to do. He balanced the sword in the palm of his hand, feeling the weight before he aimed and threw. "I said I would kill you. And that's what I'm going to do, right now."

"Sure, Nile," Alex replied. "But how are you going to get back down?"

"What?" The smile faltered.

"Just look down, Nile," Alex went on. "Look how high we are." He glanced up at the flame and the envelope. "You know, I don't think this balloon is going to hold us both up."

"Shut up!" Nile hissed the words. The hand clutching the railing had gone whiter than ever. Alex could see the fingers clenching tighter and tighter.

"Look at the people; look at the cars. See how tiny they are!"

"Stop it!"

And that was when Alex made his move. He already knew what he was going to do. Nile was petrified, unable to react. All his speed and strength had vanished. With a gasp, Alex pulled out the first sword, freeing it from the plastic. In a single movement he swept it up and slashed through one of the rubber pipes that fed the burner.

After that, everything happened very quickly.

The severed pipe coiled left and right like a wounded snake. Propane gas in liquid form was still being pumped through, and as the severed end whipped past the burner, it ignited, becoming at once a huge ball of flame. The pipe twisted back again and spat its deadly payload in the direction of Nile.

Nile had just managed to raise the second sword in the start of what would be his final throw. He was aiming at Alex's chest. Then the fireball hit him. He screamed once and disappeared. One second he was there, the next he had been blown into the air, a spinning, burning puppet of a man, falling to his death one hundred metres below.

It looked as if Alex was about to follow him.

The entire platform was on fire, the plastic melting. There was burning liquid propane everywhere and it was dissolving everything it touched. Alex struggled to his feet as the flames licked towards him. What now? The burner had gone out but the balloon didn't seem to be falling. The platform, however, would – and very soon. The four ropes securing it to the envelope were made of nylon and all four of them were on fire. One of them snapped and Alex cried out as the platform tilted, almost throwing him over the edge. His eyes darted to the machinery. The electric cables must be fireproof. The little red lights showed him that the three remaining dishes were still transmitting. More than a minute must have passed since Nile had appeared, surely! Alex pressed a hand against his chest, expecting at any moment to feel the stab of pain as the poison broke free and entered his system.

But he was still alive, and he knew he had just seconds left to escape from the burning platform. No chance of jumping to safety. He was a hundred metres above the ground. He heard a snapping sound as a second rope began to break. The fire was out of control. It was burning him; it was burning everything.

Alex jumped.

Not down – but up. He leapt first onto the control box and then up so that his hands caught the metal frame surrounding the burner. He hauled himself up and stood. Now he could reach the circular skirt at the bottom of the envelope itself. It was incredible. Looking up, it felt as if he were standing inside a huge, circular room. The walls were fabric but they could have been solid. He was inside the balloon, imprisoned by it. He saw a nylon cord. It led all the way to the parachute valve at the very top. Would it take his weight?

And then the remaining ropes holding the platform gave way. The platform fell, taking the burner and the dishes with it, disappearing from under Alex's feet. Alex just had time to wind the nylon cord around one hand and grab hold of the fabric of the balloon with the other. Suddenly he was dangling. Once again his arms and wrists took the strain. He wondered if the balloon would crumple and fall. But most of the weight had gone; only he was left. It stayed where it was.

Alex looked down. He couldn't stop himself. And that was when he saw – in the middle of the fire and the smoke, the spinning platform and the falling ropes – the three red lights had gone out. He was sure of it. Either the flames had destroyed the machinery or the dishes had deactivated themselves the moment they dropped below one hundred metres.

The terahertz beams had stopped. Not a single child would die.

Nobody was sure where the bag lady had appeared from. Perhaps she had been dossing in the small cemetery behind the Church of Forgotten Saints. But now she had wandered into what, until a few minutes ago, had been a full-scale battle.

She was lucky. The SAS men had taken control of the church and the immediate area. Most of the Scorpia people were dead; the remainder had put down their weapons in surrender. A final explosion had breached the entrance of the church itself. SAS soldiers were already pouring in, searching for Alex.

The bag lady was clearly confused by all this activity; possibly she was also drunk. There was a bottle of cider in one of her hands and she stopped to force the neck between her rotten teeth and drink. She had a repulsive, withered face and grey hair that was long and knotted. She was dressed in a filthy coat, tied around her bulging waist with string. Her other hand clutched two dustbin bags close to her, as if they contained all the treasure in the world.

One of the soldiers saw her. "Get out of here!" he yelled. "You're in danger."

"All right, love!" The bag lady giggled. "What's the matter, then? It's like bleeding World War Three."

But she shuffled off, out of harm's way, while the SAS men rushed past her, heading for the church.

Underneath the wig, the make-up and the costume, Mrs Rothman smiled to herself. It was almost incredible that these stupid SAS soldiers should let her walk away, slipping between them in plain daylight. She had a gun hidden under her coat and she would use it if anyone tried to stop her. But they were so busy rushing into the church, they had barely noticed her.

And then one of them called out.

"Stop!"

She had been seen after all. Mrs Rothman hurried on.

But the soldier hadn't been trying to detain her: he had been trying to warn her. A shadow fell across her face and she looked up just in time to see a blazing rectangle fall out of the sky. Julia Rothman opened her mouth to scream but the sound didn't have time to reach her lips. She was crushed, driven into the pavement, flattened like a creature in some hideous cartoon. The SAS man who had shouted could only gaze at the burning wreckage in horror. Then, slowly, he looked up to see where it had come from.

But there was nothing there. The sky was clear.

Freed from the platform and the mooring ropes, the balloon had been blown north, with Alex still clinging beneath it. He was limp and exhausted; his legs and the side of his chest had been burnt. It was as much as he could do simply to hang on.

But the air inside the envelope had cooled and the balloon was coming down. Alex had been lucky that the fabric of the balloon was flame-resistant.

Of course, he might still be killed. He had no control of the balloon at all and the wind might choose to steer him into a high voltage wire. He had already crossed the river and could see Trafalgar Square with Nelson's Column looming up in front of him. It would be a sick joke to land there and end up getting run over.

Alex could only hang on and wait to find out what was going to happen. Despite the pain in his arms, he was aware of a sense of inner peace. Somehow, against all the odds, he had come through everything alive. Nile was dead. Mrs Rothman was probably a prisoner. The nanoshells were no longer a threat.

And what about him? The wind had changed. It was carrying him to the west. Yes. There was Green Park – just fifty-odd metres below. He could see people pointing up at him and shouting. He silently urged the balloon on. With a bit of luck he might make it all the way to Chelsea, to his house, where Jack Starbright would be waiting. How much further could it be? Did the balloon have the strength to take him there?

He hoped so, because that was all he cared about now.

He just wanted to go home.

DEEP COVER

It ended – inevitably, it seemed to Alex – in Alan Blunt's office in Liverpool Street.

They had left him alone for a week but then the telephone call had come on Friday evening, asking him to come in. Asking, not telling. That was at least a change. And they had chosen a Saturday, so he wouldn't have to miss school.

The balloon had dropped him on the edge of Hyde Park, lowering him to the grass as gently as an autumn leaf. It was the end of the day and by that time there were few people in the park. Alex had been able to slip away quietly, five minutes before a dozen police cars had come roaring in. It was a twenty-minute walk home and he had more or less fallen into Jack's arms before taking a hot bath, wolfing down dinner and going to bed.

He wasn't badly hurt. There were burns on his arms and chest and his wrist was swollen where he had dangled from the balloon. Mrs Rothman had also left her mark on his cheek. Looking at himself in the mirror, he wondered how he was going to explain the very obvious-shaped bruise. In the end he told everyone he had been mugged. In a way, he felt, he had.

He had been back at Brookland for five days. Mr Grey was one of the first people to see him crossing the school yard before assembly, and he shook his head warily but said nothing. The teacher had taken it as a personal insult that Alex had disappeared on his school trip to Venice, and although Alex felt terrible, he couldn't tell him the truth. On the other hand, Tom Harris was overjoyed.

"I knew you'd be OK," he said. "You sounded a bit down when I spoke to you on the phone. That was after that place had blown up. But at least you were still alive. And a couple of days later, Jerry got an envelope stuffed with cash for a new parachute. Except it was about five times too much. He's in New Zealand now, thanks to you. BASE jumping off some building in Auckland. Just what he's always wanted!" Tom took out a newspaper cutting. "Was this you?" he demanded.

Alex looked at it. It was a photograph of the hot-air balloon drifting over London. He could see a tiny figure clinging to it. Fortunately the picture had been taken from too far away to identify him. Nobody knew what had happened at the Church of Forgotten Saints. And nobody knew he was involved.

"Yes," Alex admitted. "But, Tom – you mustn't tell anyone."

"I've already told Jerry."

"No one else."

"Yeah. I know. Official secrets and all that." Tom frowned. "Maybe I should join MI6. I'm sure I'd make a great spy."

Alex thought of his friend now as he sat down opposite Alan Blunt and Mrs Jones. He lowered himself slowly into the chair, wondering what they were going to say to him. Jack hadn't wanted him to come here at all.

"The moment they know you're capable of walking, they'll probably have you parachuting into North Korea," she had said. "They're never going to leave you alone, Alex. I don't even want to know what happened to you after Venice. But just promise me you won't let it happen again."

Alex agreed with her. He would rather have stayed at home. But he knew he had to be here. If nothing else, he owed it to Mrs Jones after what had happened in her flat.

"It's good to see you, Alex," Blunt said. "Once again, you've done a very good job."

Very good. The highest praise Blunt knew.

"I'll just bring you up to date," Blunt went on. "I don't need to tell you that Scorpia's plot was a complete failure, and I very much doubt that they'll try anything on this scale again. They lost one of their top assassins, the man called Nile, when he fell out of the balloon. How did that happen, by the way?"

"He slipped," Alex said shortly. He didn't want to go over it again.

"I see. Well, you might like to know that Julia Rothman also died."

That was news to Alex. He had assumed she must have escaped.

Mrs Jones took up the story. "The platform underneath the balloon fell on her as she was trying to escape," she explained. "She was crushed."

"I'd have been disappointed too," Alex muttered.

Blunt sniffed. "The most important thing of all is that London's children are going to be safe. As that scientist – Dr Stephenson – explained, the nanoshells will slowly pass out of their bodies. I have to tell you, Alex, that the terahertz dishes were transmitting for at least a minute. God knows how close we came to a major disaster."

"I'll try to move a little faster next time," Alex said.

"Yes. Well. One other thing. You might be amused to hear that Mark Kellner resigned this morning. The prime minister's director of communications – remember him? He's telling the press that he wants to spend more time with his family. The funny thing is, his family can't stand him. Nobody can. Mr Kellner made one mistake too many. Nobody could have foreseen that stunt with the hot-air balloon.

But someone has to carry the can, and I'm glad to say it's going to be him."

"Well, if that's all you called me in for, I'd better get home," Alex said. "I've missed more school and I've got a lot to catch up on."

"No, Alex. I'm afraid you can't leave quite yet." Mrs Jones sounded more serious than Alex had ever heard her and he wondered if she was going to make him pay for his attempt on her life.

"I'm sorry about what I nearly did, Mrs Jones," he said. "But I think I've more or less made up for it..."

"That's not what I want to speak to you about. As far as I'm concerned, your visit to my flat never happened. But there's something more important. You and I have never spoken about Albert Bridge."

Alex felt cold inside. "I don't want to talk about it."

"Why not?"

"Because I know what you did was right. I've seen Scorpia for myself now; I know what they are capable of. If my father was one of them, then you were right. He deserved to die."

The words hurt Alex even as he spoke them. They caught in his throat.

"There's somebody I want you to meet, Alex. He's come into the office today and he's standing outside. I know you don't want to spend any more time here than you have to, but will you let him talk to you? It will only take a few minutes."

"All right." Alex shrugged. He didn't know what Mrs Jones wanted to prove. He had no wish to return to the circumstances of his father's death.

The door opened and a tall man walked in, bearded, with brown curly hair that was beginning to grey. He was casually dressed in a beaten-up leather jacket and jeans. He looked in his early thirties and although Alex was sure he had never met him, his face seemed vaguely familiar.

"Alex Rider?" he asked. He had a soft, pleasant voice.

"Yes."

"How do you do?" He held out a hand. Alex stood up and felt his hand taken in a grasp that was warm and friendly. "My name is James Adair," he said. "I think you've met my father, Sir Graham Adair."

Alex was hardly likely to forget. Sir Graham Adair was the permanent secretary to the Cabinet Office. He could see the similarity in the faces of the two men. But he knew James Adair from somewhere else too. Of course. He was a lot older now. The hair colour was different and he was more thickset. But the face was the same. He had seen it on a computer screen. On Albert Bridge.

"James Adair is a senior lecturer at Imperial College here in London," Mrs Jones explained. "But fourteen years ago he was a student. His father was already an extremely senior civil servant—"

"You were kidnapped," Alex interrupted. "You

were the one Scorpia kidnapped."

"That's right. Look, do you mind if we sit down? I feel very formal standing up like this."

James Adair took a seat. Alex waited for him to speak. He was puzzled and a little apprehensive. This man had been there when his father was killed. In a way, it was because of this man that John Rider had died. Why had Mrs Jones brought him here now?

"I'll tell you my story and then get out of here," James Adair said. "When I was eighteen years old, I was the victim of an attempt to blackmail my father. I was snatched by an organization called Scorpia, and they were going to torture me and kill me unless my dad did exactly what they said. But Scorpia made a mistake. My father could influence government policy but he couldn't actually change it. There was nothing he could do. I was told I was going to die.

"But then, at the last minute, there was a change of plan. I met a woman called Julia Rothman. She was very beautiful but a complete bitch. I think she couldn't wait to get out the red-hot pokers or whatever. Anyway, she told me that I was going to be exchanged for one of her people. He'd been captured by MI6. And they were going to swap us. On Albert Bridge.

"They drove me there very early one morning. I have to admit that I was terrified. I was certain there was going to be a double-cross. I thought they might shoot me and dump me in the Thames. But everything seemed to be very straightforward. It was just like in a spy film. There were three men and me on one side of the bridge. They all had guns. And on the other side of the bridge I could see a figure. That was your dad. He was with some people from MI6." The lecturer glanced at Mrs Jones. "She was one of them."

"It was my first major field operation," Mrs Jones murmured.

"Go on," Alex said. He had been drawn in. He couldn't help himself.

"Well, somebody gave a signal and we both began to walk – almost as if we were going to fight a duel, except that our hands were tied. I have to tell you, Alex, the bridge felt a mile long. It seemed to take for ever to get across. But at last we met in the middle, your father and I; and I was sort of grateful to him, because it was thanks to him that I wasn't going to be killed, and yet at the same time I knew he worked for Scorpia; so I thought he must be one of the bad guys.

"And then he spoke to me."

Alex held his breath. He remembered the film Mrs Rothman had shown him. It was true. His father and the teenager had spoken. He had been unable to hear the words and had wondered what they had said.

"He was very calm," James Adair went on. "I hope you won't mind me saying this, Alex, but, looking at you now, I can see him as he was then. He was totally in command. And this is what he said to me.

"There's going to be shooting. You have to move fast.

"What? What do you mean?

"When the shooting starts, don't look round. Just run as fast as you can. You'll be safe."

There was a long silence.

"My dad knew he was going to be shot?" Alex asked.

"Yes."

"But how?"

"Let me finish." James Adair ran a hand across his beard. "I took about another ten steps and suddenly there was a shot. I know I wasn't meant to look round, but I did. Just for a second. Your father had been shot in the back. There was blood on his padded jacket; I could see a gash in the material. And then I remembered what he'd told me and I began to run ... hell for leather. I just had to get out of there."

That was another thing Alex had noticed when he'd watched the film. James Adair had reacted with amazing speed. Anyone else would surely have frozen. But he'd clearly known what he was doing.

Because he had been warned.

By John Rider.

"I tore up the bridge," he went on. "Then all hell broke loose. The Scorpia people opened fire.

They wanted to kill me, of course. But the MI6 lot had machine guns and they fired back. All in all, it was a miracle I wasn't hit. I managed to get to the north side of the bridge and a big car appeared out of nowhere. A door opened and I dived in. And that was just about the end of it, as far as I was concerned. I was whisked away and my father met me a couple of minutes later, hugely relieved. He'd thought he'd never see me again."

And that made sense. When Alex had met Sir Graham Adair, the civil servant had been surprisingly friendly. He had made it clear that he was in some way in Alex's debt.

"So my father ... sacrificed himself for you," Alex said. He didn't understand. His father had worked for Scorpia. Why should he have been prepared to die for someone he had never met?

"There is one other thing I have to tell you," the lecturer said. "It'll probably come as a shock to you. It certainly came as a shock to me. About a month later I went down to my father's home in Wiltshire. By then I'd been debriefed and there were a whole lot of security things I had to know about just in case Scorpia tried to have another crack at me. And" – he swallowed – "your father was there."

"What?" Alex stared.

"I arrived early. And as I came in, your father was leaving. He'd been in a meeting with my dad."

"But that's..."

"I know. It's impossible. But it was definitely him. He recognized me at once.

"How are you?

"I'm fine, thanks very much.

"I'm glad I was able to help. Look after yourself.

"That was what he said to me. I remember the words exactly. Then he got in his car and drove off."

"So my father..."

James Adair stood up. "I'm sure Mrs Jones can explain it all to you," he said. "But my dad wanted me to tell you how very grateful we are to you. He asked me to pass that on to you. Your father saved my life. There's no doubt about it. I'm married now; I have two children. Funnily enough, I named the eldest John after him. There would be no children if it hadn't been for him. My father would have no son and no grandsons. Whatever you may think of him, whatever you've been told about him, John Rider was a very brave man."

James Adair nodded at Mrs Jones and left the room. The door closed. There was a second, long silence.

"I don't understand," Alex said.

"Your father wasn't an assassin," Mrs Jones said. "He wasn't working for Scorpia. He was working for us."

"He was a spy?"

"A very brilliant spy," Alan Blunt muttered. "We recruited the two brothers – Ian and John – in the same year. Ian was a good agent. But John was the better man by far."

"He worked for you?"

"Yes."

"But he killed people. Mrs Rothman showed me. He was in prison..."

"Everything Julia Rothman thought she knew about your father was a lie." Mrs Jones sighed. "It's true that he had been in the army, that he had a distinguished career with the Parachute Regiment and that he was decorated for his part in the Falklands War. But the rest of it – the fight with the taxi driver, the prison sentence and all that – we made up. It's called deep cover, Alex. We wanted John Rider to be recruited by Scorpia. He was the bait and they took him."

"Why?"

"Because Scorpia was expanding all over the world. We needed to know what it was doing, the names of the people it was employing, the size and structure of its organization. John Rider was a weapons expert; he was a brilliant fighter. And Scorpia thought he was washed up. He was welcomed with open arms."

"And all the time he was reporting to you?"

"His information saved more lives than you can imagine."

"But that's not true!" Alex's head swam. "Mrs Rothman told me that he killed five or six people. And Yassen Gregorovich worshipped him! He showed me the scar. He said my dad saved his life."

"Your father was pretending to be a dangerous killer," Mrs Jones said. "And so – yes, Alex – he had to kill. One of his victims was a drug dealer in the Amazon jungle. That was when he saved Yassen's life. Another was an American double agent; a third was a corrupt policeman. I'm not saying that these people deserved to die. But certainly the world was able to get along very well without them and I'm afraid your father had no choice."

"What about the others you told me about?" Alex had to know.

"There were two more," Blunt cut in. "One was a priest, working on the streets of Rio de Janeiro. The other was a woman in Sydney. They were more difficult. We couldn't let them die. And so we faked their deaths ... in much the same way that we faked your father's."

"Albert Bridge..."

"It was faked." Mrs Jones took up the narrative again. "Your father had told us as much as we needed to know about Scorpia and we had to get him out. There were two reasons for this. The first was that your mother had just given birth to a baby boy. That was you, Alex. Your father wanted to come home; he wanted to be with you and your mother. But also it was becoming too dangerous. You see, Mrs Rothman had fallen in love with him."

It was almost too much to take on board at once. But Alex remembered Julia Rothman talking to him in the hotel in Positano.

I was very attracted to him. He was an extremely good-looking man.

Alex tried to grasp at the truth through the swirling quicksand of lies and counter-lies. "She told me he was captured. In Malta..."

"That was faked too," Mrs Jones revealed. "John Rider couldn't just walk out of Scorpia; they'd never have let him. So we had to arrange things for him. And that's what we did. He had been sent to Malta, supposedly to kill his sixth victim. He tipped us off and we were waiting for him. We staged a ferocious gun battle. You know what we're capable of, Alex. We did more or less the same thing for you with that multiple pile-up on the Westway. Yassen was there, in Malta, but we let him escape. We needed him to tell Julia Rothman what had happened. Then we 'captured' John Rider. As far as Scorpia were concerned, he would be interrogated and then either thrown back into prison or executed. They would never see him again."

"So why...?" Alex still couldn't make complete sense of it. "Why Albert Bridge?"

"Albert Bridge was a bloody mess," Alan Blunt said. It was the first time Alex had ever heard him swear. "You've met Sir Graham Adair. He's a very powerful man. He also happens to be an old friend of mine. And when Scorpia took his son, I didn't think there would be anything I could do."

"It was your father's idea," Mrs Jones went on.

"He also knew Sir Graham. He wanted to help. You have to understand, Alex, that's the sort of man he was. One day I want to tell you all about him – not just this. He believed passionately in what he was doing. Serving his country. I know that sounds naive and old-fashioned. But he was a soldier through and through. And he believed in good and evil. I don't know how else to put it. He wanted to make the world a better place."

She took a deep breath.

"Your father suggested that we send him back to Scorpia as an exchange. He knew how Mrs Rothman felt about him; he knew she would agree to anything to get him back. But at the same time, he planned to double-cross her. There was a gunman in place, but the gun was loaded with blanks. John had a squib in the back of his jacket – a little firework – and a phial of blood. When the shot was fired, he activated it himself. It blew a little hole in the back of his jacket. He went sprawling and pretended to be dead. It looked as if MI6 had killed him in cold blood. But we never hurt him, Alex. That's why I wanted you to meet James Adair. The idea was that now he would be safe again and he could simply disappear."

Alex buried his head in his hands. There were a hundred questions he wanted to ask. His mother, his father, Julia Rothman, the bridge... He was shaking and he had to force himself back under control. At last he was ready.

"I have just two questions," he said.

"Go on, Alex. We'll tell you anything you want to know."

"What was my mother's part in all this? Did she know what he was?"

"Of course she knew he was a spy. He would never have lied to her. They were very close, Alex. I never met her, I'm afraid. We don't tend to socialize much in this business. She was a nurse before she married him. Did you know that?"

Ian Rider had told Alex that his mother had been a nurse, but he didn't want to talk about that now. He was simply building himself up, finding the strength to ask the worst question of all.

"So how did my father die?" he asked. "And my mother? Is she still alive? What happened to her?"

Mrs Jones glanced at Alan Blunt and it was he who answered.

"After the affair on Albert Bridge, it was decided that it would be best if your father took a long holiday," he said. "Your mother went with him. We arranged for a private plane to take them to the South of France. You were meant to go with them, Alex, but at the last minute you developed an ear infection and they had to leave you behind with a nanny. The two of you were going to follow them out when you were better."

He paused. His eyes, as ever, showed nothing. But there was a little pain in his voice.

"Somehow Julia Rothman discovered that she

had been tricked. We don't know how; we'll never know. But Scorpia's a powerful organization: that much should be obvious to you by now. She found out that your father was still alive and that he was flying to France, and arranged for a bomb to be placed in the luggage hold. Your parents died together, Alex. I suppose that's something of a mercy. And it was all so quick. They wouldn't have had any idea..."

A plane accident.

That was what Alex had been told all his life.

Another lie.

Alex stood up. He wasn't sure what he was feeling. On the one hand he was grateful. His father hadn't been an evil man. He had been the exact opposite. Everything Julia Rothman had told him and everything he had thought about himself had been wrong. But at the same time, there was an overwhelming sadness, as if he was mourning his parents for the very first time.

"Alex, we'll get a driver to take you home," Mrs Jones said. "And we can talk more whenever you're ready."

"Why didn't you tell me?" Alex cried, and his voice cracked. "That's what I don't understand. I nearly killed you, but you didn't tell me the truth! You sent me back to Scorpia – just like my dad – but you never told me that it was Julia Rothman who killed him. Why not?"

Mrs Jones had also got to her feet. "We needed

your help to find the dishes. There was no question about it. Everything depended on you. But I didn't want to manipulate you. I know you think that's what we always do, but if I'd told you the truth about Julia Rothman and then given you a homing device and sent you in after her, I'd have been using you in the worst possible way. You went in there, Alex, for exactly the same reason that your father went to Albert Bridge, and I wanted you to have that choice. That's what makes you such a great spy. It isn't that you were made one or trained to be one. It's just that in your heart you are one. I suppose it runs in the family."

"But I had a gun! I was in your flat..."

"I was never in any danger. Quite apart from the glass, you couldn't even bring yourself to aim at me, Alex. I knew you couldn't. There was no need to tell you then. And I didn't want to. The way Mrs Rothman had deceived you was so horrible." She shrugged. "I wanted to give you the chance to work things out for yourself."

For a long moment nobody said anything.

Alex turned away. "I need to be on my own," he mumbled.

"Of course." Mrs Jones went over to him and touched him lightly on the arm. It was the arm that was the least burnt. "Come back when you're ready, Alex."

"Yes – I will."

Alex moved to the door. He opened it but then

seemed to have second thoughts. "Can I ask one final question, Mrs Jones?"

"Yes. Go ahead."

"It's just something I've always wondered and I might as well ask you now." He paused. "What's your first name?"

Mrs Jones stiffened. Sitting behind his desk, Alan Blunt looked up. Then she relaxed. "It's Tulip," she told him. "My parents were keen gardeners."

Alex nodded. It made sense. He wouldn't have used that name either.

He walked out, closing the door behind him.

A MOTHER'S TOUCH

Scorpia never forgot.

Scorpia never forgave.

The sniper had been paid to take revenge and that was what he would do. His own life would be forfeit if he failed.

He knew that in a few minutes, a fourteen-year-old boy would walk out of the building which pretended to be an international bank but was really nothing of the sort. Did it matter to him that his target was a child? He had persuaded himself that it didn't. It was a terrible thing to kill a human being. But was it so much worse to kill a twenty-seven-year-old man who would never be twenty-eight than a fourteen-year-old boy who would never be fifteen? The sniper had decided that death was death. That didn't change. Nor did the fifty thousand pounds he would be paid for this hit.

As usual he would aim for the heart. The target area would be a fraction smaller this time but he would not miss. He never missed. It was time to prepare himself, to bring his breathing under control, to enter that state of calm before the kill.

He focused his attention on the gun that he was holding, the self-loading Ruger .22 model K10/22-T. It was a low velocity weapon, less deadly than some he might have chosen. But the gun had two huge advantages. It was light. And it was very compact. By removing just two screws he had been able to separate the barrel and the trigger mechanism from the stock. The stock itself folded in two. He had been able to carry the whole thing across London in an ordinary sports bag without drawing attention to himself. In his line of work, that was the critical thing.

He squared his eye against the Leupold 14x50mm Side Focus scope, adjusting the cross hairs against the door through which the boy would pass. He loved the feel of the gun in his hands, the snug fit, the perfect balance. He had had it customized to suit his needs. The stock was laminated wood with water-resistant adhesive, making it stronger and less likely to warp. The trigger mechanism had been taken apart and polished for a smoother release. The rifle would reload itself as fast as he could fire it – but he would only need a single shot.

The sniper was content. When he fired, for the

blink of an eye, as the bullet began its journey down the barrel, travelling at three hundred and thirty-one metres per second, he and the rifle would be one. The target didn't matter. Even the payment was almost irrelevant. The act of killing was enough in itself. It was better than anything in the world. In that moment, the sniper was God.

He waited. He was lying on his stomach on the roof of an office block on the other side of the road. He was a little surprised that he had been able to get access. He knew that the building opposite him housed the Special Operations division of MI6 and he had supposed that they would keep a careful watch on all the other offices around. On the other hand, he had picked two locks and dismantled a complicated security system to get here. It hadn't been easy.

The door opened and the target appeared. If he had wanted to, the sniper could have seen a handsome fourteen-year-old boy with fair hair, one strand hanging down over his eyes. A boy wearing a grey hooded sweatshirt and baggy jeans, and a wooden bead necklace (he could see every bead through the scope). Brown eyes and a slightly hard, narrow mouth. The sort of face that would have attracted plenty of girls if the boy had only lived a little longer.

The boy had a name: Alex Rider. But the sniper didn't think of that. He didn't even think of Alex as a boy. He was a heart, a pair of lungs, a convoluted system of veins and arteries. But very soon he would be nothing at all. That was why the sniper was here. To perform a little act of surgery – not with a scalpel but a bullet.

He licked his lips and focused all his attention on his target. He wasn't holding the gun. The gun was part of him. His finger curled against the trigger. He relaxed, enjoying the moment, preparing to fire.

Alex Rider stepped out onto the street. It was about five o'clock and there were quite a few people around. He was thinking about all the things he had been told in Alan Blunt's office. They still wouldn't quite register. It was just too much to take in. His father hadn't been an assassin; he had been a spy, working for MI6. John Rider and Ian Rider. Both spies. And now Alex Rider. At last they were a family.

And yet...

Mrs Jones had told him that she wanted him to make a choice, but he wasn't sure that the choice had ever been his. Yes, he had chosen not to belong to Scorpia. But that didn't mean he had to be a lifelong member of MI6. Alan Blunt would want to use him again: that much was certain. But maybe he would find the strength to refuse. Maybe knowing the truth at last would be enough.

All sorts of confusing thoughts were racing through his mind. But he had already made one decision. He wanted to be with Jack. He wanted to forget his homework and go out for a film and a blow-out dinner. Nothing healthy. He had said he would be home by six, but perhaps he would call and meet her at the multiplex on the Fulham Road. It was Saturday. He deserved a night out.

He took a step and stopped. Something had hit him in the chest. It was as if he had been punched. He looked left and right but there was nobody close to him. How very strange.

And here was something else. Liverpool Street seemed to be running uphill. He knew it was flat, but now it was definitely slanting. Even the buildings were leaning to one side. He didn't understand what was happening. The colour was rapidly draining out of the air. As he looked, the world went from colour to black and white, apart from a few splashes here and there: the bright yellow of a café sign, the blue of a car...

...and the red of blood. He looked down and was surprised to see that his whole front was turning crimson. There was an irregular shape spreading rapidly across his sweatshirt. At the same time, he became aware that the sound of the traffic had faded. It was as if something had pulled him out of the world and he was only seeing it from a very long way away. A few pedestrians had stopped and turned to look at him. They were shocked. There was a woman screaming. But she was making no sound at all.

Then the street played a trick on him, tilting so suddenly that it seemed to turn upside down. A crowd had gathered. It was closing in on him and Alex wished it would go away. There must have been thirty or forty people, pointing and gesticulating. Why were they so interested in him? And why couldn't he move any more? He opened his mouth to ask for help but no words, not even a breath, came out.

Alex was starting to feel scared. There was no pain at all, but something told him that he must have been hurt. He was lying on the pavement, although he didn't know how he had got there. There was a red circle around him, widening with every second that passed. He tried to call for Mrs Jones. He opened his mouth again and did hear a voice calling, but it was very far away.

And then he saw two people and knew that everything was going to be all right after all. They were watching him with a mixture of sadness and understanding, as if they had always expected this to happen but were still sorry that it had. There was a little colour left in the crowd, but the two people were entirely black and white. The man was very handsome, dressed in military uniform with close-cut hair and a solid, serious face. He looked very much like Alex, although he seemed to be in his early thirties. The woman, standing next to him, was smaller and seemed much more vulnerable. She had long, fair hair and eyes that were filled with sorrow. He had seen photographs of this woman and he was astonished to find her here. He knew that he was looking at his mother.

He tried to get up, but he couldn't. He wanted to hold her hand, but his arms would no longer obey him. He wasn't breathing any more, but he hadn't noticed.

The man and the woman stepped forward out of the crowd. The man said nothing; he was trying to hide his emotions. But the woman leant down and reached out a hand. Only now did Alex realize that he had been looking for her all his life. She reached out and touched him, her finger finding the exact spot where there was a small hole in his shirt.

No pain. Just a sense of tiredness and resignation.

Alex Rider smiled and closed his eyes.

READ OTHER GREAT BOOKS BY

ANTHONY HOROWITZ...

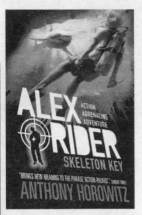

Alex Rider – you're never
too young to die...

Sharks. Assassins. Nuclear
bombs. Alex Rider's in
deep water.

High in the Alps, death
waits for Alex Rider...

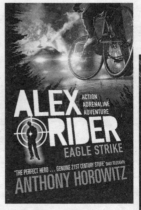

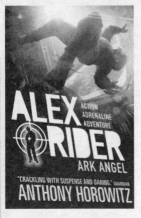

Alex Rider has 90 minutes
to save the world.

He's back – and this time
there are no limits.

Once stung, twice as
deadly. Alex Rider wants
revenge.

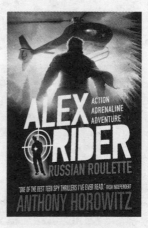

WELCOME TO THE DARK SIDE OF ANTHONY HOROWITZ

THE POWER OF FIVE

BOOK ONE
He always knew he was different.
First there were the dreams.
Then the deaths began.

BOOK TWO
It began with Raven's Gate.
But it's not over yet. Once
again the enemy is stirring.

BOOK THREE
Darkness covers the earth.
The Old Ones have returned.
The battle must begin.

BOOK FOUR
An ancient evil is unleashed.
Five have the power to defeat it.
But one of them has been taken.

BOOK FIVE
Five Gatekeepers.
One chance to save mankind.
Chaos beckons. Oblivion awaits.

Photograph © Jon Cartwright

Anthony Horowitz is the author of the number one bestselling Alex Rider books and The Power of Five series. He has enjoyed huge success as a writer for both children and adults, most recently with the latest adventure in the Alex Rider series, *Russian Roulette*, and the highly acclaimed Sherlock Holmes novel, *The House of Silk*. His latest novel, *Moriarty*, is also set in the world of Sherlock Holmes and was published in October 2014. Anthony was also chosen by the Ian Fleming estate to write the new James Bond novel which will be published this year. Anthony has won numerous awards, including the Bookseller Association/Nielsen Author of the Year Award, the Children's Book of the Year Award at the British Book Awards, and the Red House Children's Book Award. In 2014 Anthony was awarded an OBE for Services to Literature. He has also created and written many major television series, including *Injustice*, *Collision* and the award-winning *Foyle's War*.

You can find out more about Anthony and his work at:
www.alexrider.com
@AnthonyHorowitz